INNISFREE

D.M. Herrmann

Advance Praise on *Innisfree*

"*Innisfree* is an interesting read, and a fairly accurate portrayal of human nature in extreme circumstances. Set in current times, with much of the unrest of the world today, D.M. Herman captures a possible future for us."

—Brian Oppermann, US Marine Corps Combat Veteran of Desert Storm/Desert Shield

"*Innisfree* confronts the terrifying reality of a world without the conveniences we've so heavily relied upon and just how far you would go to protect your family. This novel will keep you reading until the very end, securing its place among the top necessities you would grab if the world were to crumble.

—Callie Trautmiller, Author of *Becoming American*

INNISFREE

Book One of the
John Henry Chronicles

D.M. Herrmann

Green Bay, WI 54311

Publishing Editor: Brittiany Koren
Editor: Larry Segriff
Copy-editor: Dale Shepherd
Cover Art Designer: Sunny Fassbender
Interior Layout Designer: Katy Brunette

Category: Post-apocalyptic Military fiction
Description: *Following a devastating event that destroyed the North American power grid, a US Army veteran strives to help protect his family in a post-apocalyptic reality as the world crumbles around him.*
Hardcover ISBN: 978-1-7335034-4-0
Paperback ISBN: 978-1-951375-00-3
Ebook ISBN: 978-1-7335034-6-4
LOC Catalogue Data: Applied for.

First Edition published by Written Dreams Publishing in August, 2019.

Green Bay, WI 54311

Books by Don Herrmann

Innisfree, Book One of the
John Henry Chronicles

The Clio Boru Series written as
Evan Michael Martin

Sorceress Rising, Book 1

Sorceress Revealed, Book 2

Sorceress Resurrected, Book 3

For our families.

Author's Note

While this is a work of fiction, it contains elements of fact. The story involves an EMP or Electro Magnetic Pulse impacting the US.

In 2001, the US Congress established the EMP Commission. Its purpose was to assess the likelihood of a nuclear weapon being used to create an EMP and its impact on the civilian infrastructure of the United States. In 2005, they reported that our civilian infrastructure was completely unprepared for such an event.

This story contains information that anyone wanting to be prepared could use. But that isn't really the purpose of this story. The story is about people. People who call themselves *family*. More than a biological family, it is about how people come together and *become* family. Through deed and circumstance, they form a bond.

This is the story of one such man, divorced and living apart from his family, he struggles during a time of enormous crisis to bring them together, keep them together, and protect them. He longs for peace, and he dreams of a forest glade, where he is safe and they are, too. Yet, he faces the reality of a great evil and the natural tendencies of man. This is the struggle of all who cherish their families. This is the struggle of John Henry.

This book is dedicated to families, families together, families apart, families created by circumstance. Families drawn together for good and bad, families driven apart because of words. Families reunited because of hurt. Cherish your families, regardless of where you are. Family is the very root of our existence.

Some may find parts of the story disturbing. They should. However, all of the so-called experts agree that our civilization on any given day is about three days away from completely breaking down, if the right circumstances occur. This is the nature of the human animal. The inability to provide the basic necessities of life will quickly degenerate, and as the animals that humans are, the violent tendencies we naturally have will return, if for no other reason than to survive.

Unlike some books in this genre, this story contains profanity. I felt it was a more accurate portrayal of life in stressful times and did not want to paint an inaccurate picture of the environment or characters. I hope you enjoy the story of John Henry.

—D.M. Herrmann

The Lake Isle of Innisfree

William Butler Yeats, 1888

I will arise and go now, and go to Innisfree,
And a small cabin build there, of clay and
wattles made;
Nine bean-rows will I have there, a hive for
the honey-bee,
And live alone in the bee-loud glade.

And I shall have some peace there, for peace
comes dropping slow,
Dropping from the veils of the morning to
where the cricket sings;
There midnight's all a glimmer, and noon a
purple glow,
And evening full of the linnet's wings.

I will arise and go now, for always night and
day
I hear lake water lapping with low sounds by
the shore;
While I stand on the roadway, or on the
pavements grey,
I hear it in the deep heart's core.

Prologue

"This ain't no shit…"

Asoft, warm breeze drifted across the darkness. Crickets and other sounds echoed in the night as the two men sat by the glowing embers of the fire pit. The occasional cherry red glow of a burning cigar shone brightly as they puffed. The two men sat silently, staring at the fire pit, sipping beer and smoking their cigars.

"Hard to believe it would be this way," the first man said.

"Yeah, who knew we'd do this again."

Returning to their silence, the two men sat there. The only sounds being of nature and the soft breeze through the trees, moving the leaves on the many hardwoods surrounding them.

A crunching on the grass declared the footfalls of another person. Sidling up to the men, a younger voice announced her presence. "You guys doin' okay?"

"Yeah, we're fine," one of the men replied.

"What ya' thinkin' about?" she asked.

Silence answered her, the dark night wrapping it like a blanket, or a shroud. A shifting in a chair, the nylon seat squeaking as one of the men moved. "We're just rememberin', sweetie," he replied.

"Anything you want to share?" she asked.

"You sure you're ready to hear this?" he said, making eye contact.

"Yes, I'm sure." A slight hint of uncertainty was in her voice.

"Well, then," the first man said, "it all started…"

"Hold on," the second man interrupted, "you know you can't tell it that way. What would *he* say?"

"You're right, he wouldn't start the story that way. You can't tell a true story with anything that sounds like a fairy tale. 'Once upon a time' isn't real. Neither is 'It all started…'"

Pausing, he took a breath, exhaled, sipped his beer, and then started again with a big grin. "Okay, sweetie, this ain't no shit…"

***

Hyun Gwang, II took in the view before him. The launch facility at Soha was remote, surrounded by thick, dark forests that had grown in the area since 1952. The heavily modified Unha missile stood tall, almost 98 feet, in the steel and concrete gantry before him. Cloudlike wisps of white emanated from it as the liquid oxygen and liquid nitrogen flowed from the bleeder valves to keep the fuel tanks from becoming over pressurized. Its four clustered Nodong rockets would power its first stage.

In all, the rocket had three stages, each driving its payload further into the atmosphere. To his front was the gantry that held the rocket, its payload, attached to the very tip, was all that he cared about. The dark grey gantry structure, open on all sides, had an elevator shaft going almost to the top of the rocket. Carrying the technicians who prepared the rocket for launch, it provided the only shelter for them.

Behind him, the white brick preparation building blocked what little breeze there was. The cold February day would have been even colder with a wind. He was grateful for the protection the building gave him.

Teams of men scurried about the area. Even in their heavily quilted winter parkas, the men moved as if their lives depended upon it. They were right—as failure would be their death.

Hyun did not want to die. All he hoped for was to make the Supreme Leader, Kim Jong-un, proud.

As the men finished, they began to move away from the long concrete launch pad, leaving the rocket with the gantry as its only companion. Hyun watched the last of the men depart the area and then, getting into a waiting staff car, he drove the short distance to the launch control center.

A few minutes after arriving, Hyun stopped and stood next to General Kim Kyok Sik, Vice Chairman of the Korean People's Army General staff.

"Everything is prepared, Comrade General," Hyun said softly. He bowed at the waist, his eyes cast downward, in a show of respect.

The general remained silent, a stony expression on his face. He was nervous. Nervous in anticipation, nervous from fear. Fear that the rocket may not launch. Stealing himself silently, so as not to let the others see his fear and shame at being afraid, he placed his hands behind his back, and clasping them together, he said, "Give the order to launch."

"Commence the launch sequence," Hyun ordered. He, too, stood nervously, lost in a thousand thoughts about the next few moments. The dream of success for the Dear Leader, and the terror of failure.

Technicians began pushing buttons, flicking

switches, and talking through microphones attached to headsets as they communicated each step. The large monitors in front of the room portrayed the rocket as it began to emit even more wispy white clouds. A roar soon sounded from the base of the rocket as white clouds, and then yellow flames, grew from its base. The boosters of the first stage ignited, and as the missile slowly rose, the support cables fell away.

Rising higher, the Unha lifted completely free of the gantry and moved upward into the air. For the next two minutes, the Nodong rockets pushed her skyward. They stopped as suddenly as they had started as the red fuming nitric acid fuel in the second stage ignited.

The rocket continued to climb for almost another two minutes before the third stage ignited, pushing itself away from the second stage and thrusting itself and the payload into orbit. Now, some 482 kilometers—more than 300 miles—above the earth's surface, the third stage released its payload. The KMS-4 satellite was now in orbit joining its brother KMS-3 that had been launched three years earlier. Its path would take it over the central part of the United States several times each day.

"Now, we wait for our Supreme Leader's instructions," General Kim said quietly.

"The American dogs will soon be no more," Hyun replied. A demonic grin crossed his face as he watched the monitor before him.

The Washington Post, February 6, 2016
By Anna Fifield

TOKYO — North Korea on
Sunday declared that it had
successfully put an "earth

observation satellite" into orbit under the direct orders of leader Kim Jong-un, and said it planned to launch "many more."

Both the South Korean defense ministry and the Pentagon said that the rocket, launched at 9 AM North Korean time from a launch pad near the Chinese border, appeared to have successfully reached space.

The United States, Japan, and South Korea immediately condemned the launch, a move widely seen as another step toward North Korea mastering the technology for making a missile capable of striking the mainland United States. The UN Security Council called an emergency meeting for later Sunday to discuss how to respond to the country's latest provocation.

But North Korea gloated about its most recent advance into space. It said that it had fired a Kwangmyongsong-4 (the name translates as "lode star"), a newer-model satellite than the one launched three years ago, and one that is said to be equipped with devices for Earth measurement and communication.

*"Today's success is a proud result
of scientific achievement and an
exercise of our legitimate right
to space," Ri Chun Hee, North
Korea's most famous newsreader,
who was brought out of retirement
to announce last month's nuclear
test, declared in a special broadcast
from Pyongyang following the
launch.*

Chapter 1

"Everybody has to be somewhere!"

—Spike Milligan

I'd settled in Lake View, Wisconsin, which disappointedly, wasn't on a lake. In fact, the closest lake was over 20 miles away. It was, however, near the Wolf River, making it quite the destination for spring and fall walleye fishing. Locals joked they'd named it Lake View for the lake they couldn't see.

The town wasn't a big place. A short strip of shops, a gas station convenience store that doubled as a local grocer, Carol's Diner, and of course a tavern. You can't throw a rock in Wisconsin without hitting a tavern. There were probably all of 200 people that lived here in Lake View. Most, like me, lived outside of town on farms, hobby farms, or farmettes. I still don't know what a farmette is.

I'd invested in land here shortly before I retired from the US Army at the ripe old age of thirty-eight. Originally, it was to be a retirement home, so when I got older I could hunt, fish, and enjoy the twilight years.

Wisconsin is home, and as I traveled the world, I compared everywhere to here. It's the home of my ancestors, having immigrated to Wisconsin almost 175 years ago. I spent a lifetime traveling and never having roots. Dad always spoke of Wisconsin as if it were the only place any sane person would live. He had more stories about growing up in Appleton than anyone I knew. Most of his childhood antics would land you in jail today, but back then, it was merely mischief.

I didn't grow up in Lake View, but I'd spent my summers here. My home—well, my *home* is America. I grew up everywhere. So before I retired, I took a personal getaway to make certain leaving the army was what I wanted.

I went camping here in the Nicolet Forest where my dad and I spent a lot of time following his retirement from the US Air Force. It was on that trip that I found my land. Over 180 acres on the Wolf River with my northern border being the National Forest. I bought it for a song and about two weeks later asked myself, "What in the hell did you do that for, John Henry?"

I remembered, almost as if it was yesterday, what brought me up here to Lake View. I was facing a major life-changing event. I had to decide if I was going to retire from the army or go back overseas again. My soldier wife and our young son would of course come with me. It was the challenges of having two pre-teen boys from a previous marriage and flying them overseas for visits that troubled me. So, I went where my dad always went to clear his head and think.

Lake View, Wisconsin, is "up nort" as they say around here. It's the local dialect for up north. *It's a small town, a stop on the road. No one famous is from Lake View. It doesn't have any festivals, unique geographic features, or much at all that sets it apart as anything special. Home to about two hundred people, they're scattered all over the National Forest and adjoining land. Not far away is the "rez," more specifically known as the Menominee Reservation. They have something special. Low cost cigarettes, low cost gasoline, at least compared to outside the reservation, and, of course, a casino.*

I found Lake View by chance on a drive. Leaving my hometown of Appleton, I headed north. North to where Dad used to take me fishing when we were both younger and where we "hunted musky." The area, dotted with small lakes, some without names, had always attracted me. Small towns like up here Hiles, I was familiar with.

When I saw Lake View, it appeared to be a hidden gem, situated on a county road, its few town buildings lining either side. I instantly noticed the small gas station and convenience store, the hardware and sporting goods store, the tavern, an insurance office, and Carol's Diner.

The large window in front of the diner was painted. Oversized gold letters, arched with one word over the other, said simply, Carol's Diner. I parked alongside the road across the street and stared, wondering if it was open. The lights were on, but it didn't look like anyone was inside. A gurgle in my stomach told me I was hungry.

Hopping out of my truck, I loped across the street, my heavy leather hiking boots loud on the blacktop road. I wore my usual riveted jeans and a dark blue T-shirt, the warm weather not so warm that I could have swapped the jeans for shorts. I had let my hair grow since I was on leave from the army and the soft breeze blew it around, causing it to drop in front of my eyes. I needed a shave, too, as a few days'worth of stubble had sprouted on my face.

Reaching up to brush the hair out of the way, I stepped up onto the sidewalk, took a few steps up the wooden steps into a slightly covered doorway, and pushed open the door. Walking into the diner, I glanced around. No one here. Are they open?

"Hello, are you open?" I called. Like any good army sergeant, I could make my voice heard without shouting.

"Be with you in a second," a voice answered from the back of the diner.

I stood there waiting. As I surveyed the room, I saw pictures of deer, fish, and airplanes.

A movement in the shadows caught my eyes. Glancing in that direction, I saw a woman, probably my age or a bit younger, come into the room. She wore a plaid short-sleeved shirt, with red and white squares on it. Her jeans were cuffed at the bottom and I noticed her hiking boots. They were like mine, heavy duty but hers had bright red laces.

Her brown eyes welcomed me. The scraggly look of her shoulder length brown hair suggested she had been working in the back. She was tall for a woman, probably 5'8" or so.

"Are you open?" I asked.

"Of course. Booth, table, or the counter?" she said.

"I'll sit at the counter." I strode over and sat on one of the stools in front of the counter. Red with chrome trim, just like the old days.

"So, what can I get ya'?"

"How about a diet soda?"

"Cola or White?" she asked.

I smiled. Only in the Midwest is a non-colored soda called white soda. A unique quirk in the culture here that sometimes confused outsiders. I was surprised she didn't correct me and call it "pop," which was common in most parts of Wisconsin.

"Cola."

She brought the soda to the counter and placed it in front of me. "Hi, I'm Carol, I own the place."

"Pleased to meet you, Carol. I'm John, John Henry."

"So, what brings you to Lake View, John Henry?"

"Nostalgia. My dad and I used to fish and camp not far from here."

"Ah," she said. "You've been to Lake View before?"

"No. Truth be told, I didn't know it existed. I was just driving around with no destination in mind, and here you were." I reached over and took a straw out of the dispenser on the counter. Sticking it into my cola, I took a sip. "Are you from here, Carol?"

"Kinda. Grew up over in Antigo. Left the air force a few years ago and decided to move back home. Ended up divorced and needed to get out of town. I learned this place was for sale, so I bought it, changed the name, and here I am."

"I'm on leave from the army."

Carol laughed, a soft tinkling sound. "Is this where we start teasing each other about our respective branches?"

"No, not necessary. I already know who'd win." I smirked.

We shared a chuckle and then, standing back, Carol asked, "So what can I fix you to eat?"

"How about something simple, like a burger and fries."

"Coming right up."

I sat back on the stool and took in the diner. Looks like an old store. *The wooden floors, worn through the varnish, showed the place was well-used. The tin ceiling spoke of another time, and the large, long mirror behind the counter allowed me to smile back at myself, the wall behind me a backdrop to another time. It was a friendly, homey place.*

Carol brought my food in what seemed like an instant. "Here you go," she said.

"Smells good."

"It is good. I was a cook in the air force."

"Oh, gawd. Really?"

Before Carol could reply, someone came in and she went to wait on them. With nothing else to do, and getting the reason I came in here to begin with, I ate my burger and fries.

She came back and refilled my soda. "How was the burger?"

"Very good," I said as I munched on the last fry.

"So where to next, John Henry?"

"I'm going to find a real estate agent and buy some land. I like it up here, and I think my wife and youngest son will, too. Maybe one day we'll eventually move here."

"What's so special about here that you want to stay?"

"It reminds me of a poem. I need some solitude."

She gave me a funny look, confused. "A poem?"

"Yep. 'I will arise and go now... And a small cabin build there...'"

"So you're a poet?" Carol said, "Interesting profession for a soldier."

"No, not a poet, just one I remember by William Butler Yeats. It's called the Lake Isle of Innisfree. *"*

"You're an interesting man, John Henry. I don't know too many soldiers, or airmen for that matter, that like poetry."

"Nah, I just like poetry. Know any good real estate agents?"

"I can send you to one. He doesn't live here, but he knows the area. Looking for anything special?"

"Just someplace where I can build a small cabin."

"I should have known. Let me get his info for you."

Carol went into the kitchen and returned a few minutes later. "Here you go," she said. "I don't know him well but tell him I sent you. Maybe he'll stop by." Waving her arm in a small circle, she added, "I can use the business."

Regardless, the land served its purpose. It was mine, and it couldn't be taken away. It gave me somewhere to go to start new traditions. Traditions are important.

My second wife and I had settled in Appleton, and over time, built a cabin here in Lake View. Winning a small "chunk of change" in the lottery helped make it a reality. Several years later, when things stopped working between us, Donna and I divorced. The cabin became mine while she got the house in Appleton.

I thought living here would bring all of my children up for frequent visits. As it turned out, the family didn't come to visit as often as I thought they would. So I got a dog, a nice male German shepherd I named Max. A year later, I got another shepherd and named him King.

A year after that, here I was sitting in Carol's Diner in the booming metropolis of Lake View—I jest—on a warm summer morning, sipping coffee, waiting for my standard bacon, eggs over easy, and hash browns with wheat toast breakfast. The TV was on behind the counter.

I watched the never-ending riots that had been occurring since before the election. It seemed like the entire country was filled with anger and divided more than we had ever been, including the Civil War. This riot was close, in Milwaukee. Cars were on fire, people chanted and threw things. They blocked traffic, burned stores, and the day before, several people had exchanged gunfire with police. The governor called out for the National Guard to calm things down, but it only seemed to make things worse.

Similar riots were going on across the country. I was glad I lived in what my army son Brian called Podunk; actually, he called it BFE. If anything rioted here in Lake View, it'd be deer, turkey, or bears. We'd suppress the rioters, and then we'd eat them.

Nevertheless, thanks to 24/7 news channels, there in all their high rating glory were the riots. Anti-government, pro-government, anti-everything groups, my rights are more important than your rights groups all marching and shouting. I shook my head at the sadness of it all.

Sometimes, like today, the rioters erupted into violence. Burning the cities, destroying property. I didn't think we'd have riots like this again, but agitators are agitators, and they come in all flavors.

"Here you go, John." The movement next to me and Carol's voice as she set my platter in front of me took my eyes away from the TV to the pile of goodness waiting invitingly on the white Buffalo China plate. Carol didn't scrimp on her portions, which might explain the ten pounds I'd gained since I'd moved to Lake View.

I picked up my fork, slid it into the hash browns, and moved it toward my mouth after I set my coffee down. Then, I reached for a slice of bacon. I hate a cold breakfast. She stood there watching me.

Realizing she was waiting to hear how I liked it, I said, "It's good, Carol. It's always good." My mouth was full, and a couple of pieces of potato almost dropped out.

Carol laughed, and as she walked away, said over her shoulder, "I know you didn't learn those manners in the army." Carol had been a cook in the air force, and I made a point to tease her about it constantly.

The sounds of the theme music from ESPN's Sports Center played in my ear. Reaching up to my Bluetooth, I pushed the button, answering the call.

"Hi, Brian, what's up?" I asked. He and his wife, Nancy, and their five-year-old son Mike were stationed at a base in Texas.

"Hey, Dad, what ya' doin?"

"I'm at the diner having breakfast. It is Saturday, you know," I said.

His laugh at the other end of the call told me he had forgotten my normal routine.

"So, what's up with you?" I asked again.

"I've got some time-off coming, and we thought we'd come up to visit you for a week or so."

"Absolutely," I said. "When are you gonna get here?"

"We're leaving tomorrow and should be there by Tuesday."

His words concerned me. "Something wrong?"

"No, we've decided to take some time and come see you, that's all. You're up there all alone, and we thought we'd bring you some company."

I didn't believe him, but I took the bait. "You know you're welcome anytime. Can you find the cabin okay?"

He laughed. "I'll use GPS. I just need your address again."

I rolled my eyes. "It's not on the GPS, son. Use Carol's Diner as an address, then call me before you get here. I'll drive out and meet you, then you can follow me to the cabin."

"Who's Carol? You got a girlfriend or something?" Brian asked.

Laughing, I replied, "Or something. You really don't get up here much. Carol is a friend who owns the diner here in town. It's where I am now." I gave him the address and told him to write it down.

"Yeah, I want to talk to you about that. I really need to see you more. Talk more, too. I've never even seen your new place."

I gave him my full attention. "Brian, is something wrong?"

"No, Dad, I just feel guilty. It's family, and like Grampa always said, family is all that matters. I need to remember that."

Brian and my dad not only shared a birthday, but they had become close following Brian's time in Iraq; closer than me and Dad had ever been. Unfortunately, that didn't last long. Dad died suddenly of a stroke about two months after Brian returned to the States. Mom passed a few years after that.

"Okay, I'll see you Tuesday. You call me if you have any problems on the road. When you get to Wausau, you're about two hours away from here, so call me when you pass through so I can be here at the diner."

"You got a girlfriend?" he asked again.

"Kiss my ass," I said with a chuckle. "You bringing my granddog, too?"

I thought of the five-year-old Great Dane they had who loved his grandpa.

"Nancy and I want to. Is it okay?"

"You know it is."

"Okay, Dad, see you in a few days. Love you."

I smiled at his words. "Love you, too, son. Give my love to Nancy and Mike."

"I will, bye."

I pushed the button on my Bluetooth to end the call. *Something's up. He doesn't sound like himself.*

Returning to my breakfast, I finished eating. The TV was still showing special bulletins about the riots taking place all over the country. Cities on the east and west coasts had major areas with buildings on fire. Larger cities were experiencing ANTIFA, a group claiming to be anti-fascist, but in reality, they seemed to be against anything they disagreed with. They appeared to be the most violent and the best organized. The news reported casualties as well.

Interesting—and disgusting—times we live in.

"Pretty disturbing stuff isn't it, John?"

I hadn't heard Carol walk up to my booth. She'd startled me.

"Yes, it is," I said. "I just don't get it. How we've turned out generations of people like that in this country is beyond me. It isn't the country I grew up in or served; I'll tell you that."

"Me, either. Makes you glad we live here, doesn't it?"

"Well…"

"John Henry, you know damn good and well you love it here, so stop that," Carol mockingly scolded me, but then grinned with that mischievous smile of hers.

I knew she was sweet on me. Truth be told, I liked her, too, but after two failed marriages I wasn't going to get into another relationship, at least not yet. Guess you could say I had commitment issues.

I wiped my lips with my napkin, then said, "It's a great place, Carol. I worry about my boys, though."

"Heard from them lately?"

"As you know, my youngest lives down in Appleton with his mom, and that's not too bad. Brian's in the service, so he's probably closest to all of this. I just got off the phone with him. He's coming for a visit next week." The excitement of seeing my son and grandson probably showed on my face. I couldn't help but grin at the thought of seeing them soon.

Carol picked up on it and slid into the booth bench across from me, grinning herself like a Cheshire Cat. "That's wonderful. What about your oldest?"

The words no sooner left her lips before I could tell she regretted the question. My excitement over Brian's visit was jerked away.

"He, well, we don't talk much." John Jr. and I had grown apart over the last few years. It was for silly reasons, but we were now not much more than birthday and holiday text messages, or the occasional social media comment—and most of those were generated by me. He had two children, Wayne and Darla. My own grandchildren, and I doubt they'd know me if I stood next to them. I hadn't seen them since they were still in diapers.

"I'm sorry, John," Carol said. "I shouldn't have asked."

"It's okay. There's always hope that one day I'll look out my window and see him coming up the driveway, though that will probably never happen. He didn't make his grandmother's funeral, so I suspect I'll never see him again. I have to accept it."

"So, when does Brian get here?" Carol asked, changing the subject.

"Tuesday. So, I had better get home and start getting things together for them. Those extra two bedrooms I have are getting used finally."

She looked at me pointedly. "Need any help?"

"Thanks, Carol. I don't know yet. If I start acting all weird over their coming, I may." I laughed. "I'll let you know."

She laughed. "John, we live in Lake View. We're all weird here."

"You got me there." I stood up and reached for my wallet.

"Put that away, John. Your boy is coming. You bring them here for a meal, and I'll write this one off as a marketing expense."

"Thanks, you are so sentimental." I headed for the door, my faded black NRA baseball cap in hand.

Outside, I breathed in the fresh north woods air, put the hat on my head, looked both ways before crossing the street, and walked to my dirty, black 1964 Ford pickup truck. She was old, but she ran good. She handled the forest roads on my property well, and I didn't have to worry about breaking it. Max and King liked riding in her, too.

Starting the vehicle, I turned on the radio and drove home, listening to the news about how my country was tearing itself apart fast.

***

The morning was pleasantly cool, not cold but comfortable. The sun had been up for a bit, and I looked at the yard in front of the house, surveying my kingdom. Late May in Wisconsin can be nice—unless the frozen north decides to remind us of where we live.

Today, the cold had stayed away.

This Tuesday was like many as I heard the birds and the chatter of a couple of squirrels. No deer or turkeys at that time of the morning, but eventually they would show up. The dogs liked them. Sometimes, they'd lay there and watch. Other times, they acted like the kids they were and tried to chase them.

I didn't know what either of the dogs would do if they ever caught one. Reminded me of years ago, when a black lab-greyhound mix I had ran one down. The dog never did anything but knocked it over.

A fawn scared both the dog and me bad enough one day that she jumped up into my arms. Neither of us saw the deer until we almost stepped on it. It made a sound like "blaaaaah" and then it took off. My lab, up in my arms, whimpered. I wasn't about to put her down, although I knew she wouldn't harm the fawn intentionally.

The silence was broken by the ESPN theme, my ringtone for Brian. I almost spilled my coffee grabbing for the phone.

"Where are you?" I answered.

"Morning to you, too. We're at Carol's Diner waiting for you. I figured you'd need your beauty sleep."

Brian always had been something of a jokester. It was hard for him to talk about much of anything without his smile or humor coming through. I often wondered if that would cause him difficulty in his job, since he was in Military Intelligence. Some of the stories he told of his time in Iraq let me know, at least as he told them, that he was humorous and good-natured even there.

"Thought you were supposed to call me when you got to Wausau," I said.

"It was early. I thought I'd let you sleep. I was gonna call before we got into town, but before we knew it, here we are."

"I'm on my way."

"Okay. Carol is nice. She knew us right away and is making breakfast for us. Everything here is made to order, Dad. Mike is getting chocolate chip pancakes."

"Carol is going to spoil you guys," I said. That was true. Carol didn't make chocolate chip pancakes. She didn't make banana walnut pancakes, a favorite of mine, either, so she was going out of her way for my grandson. "I'll be there soon."

"See you when you get here."

Getting up, I went to the door, opened it and let the dogs inside the cabin. Then, I grabbed my keys off of the small table by the door and headed to Carol's.

Arriving in town, I saw a black Escalade parked across from Carol's with a U-Haul trailer behind it. Seemed like a lot for a short visit, but it confirmed my suspicion that something was up. Parking behind it, I almost forgot to turn off the truck before I got out. Guess I was excited.

I could see them in the front window. Brian saw me and waved; Nancy was pointing me out to Mike. He was standing on the booth bench looking, a huge smile on his face.

As I crossed the street, the front door of the restaurant opened, and Mike came running out.

"You better look before you step into the road," I hollered.

He didn't; he kept running. "Grampa!" he yelled, jumping up into my arms with a big hug.

I hadn't seen Mike but maybe once a year, and it had been over a year since I saw him last. He'd grown. Our frequent Facetime calls made sure we knew what each other looked like, but it wasn't the same as seeing each other in person.

I hugged him tightly. "How's my boy?"

"I'm good, Grampa. I missed you."

"I missed you too, son," I said.

He looked like a typical city kid. Tan pants, Air Jordan sneakers, and a shirt with a button-down collar.

We'll have to get him dressing normal. Jeans and a t-shirt will be fine. His parents will probably have a cow.

"Let's go see your mom and dad," I said.

As we started across the road, a woof behind me made me turn and look. There was Grady, their Great Dane. Trying to get out of the Escalade through a partially open window, his long tail wagged behind him. I'd wait to see him until we got to the cabin.

Inside, I walked to their table. Nancy was already standing, but Brian was still sat in the booth. He described his wife as his ABW, or Angry Black Woman jokingly, and she could be. She was nothing like that now.

"Hi, Fil," she said, her arms held out wide for a hug. She liked to call me Fil, short for father-in-law.

Hugging her, I couldn't help but notice she needed a change of clothes, too. A dress, heels, and a sweater weren't exactly normal wear here in the north woods, but she, like Brian, had always been a clothes horse and fashionista.

Brian slid off the bench and stuck out his hand.

I took it and pulled him in for a hug, too. I wasn't raised a hugger, but later in life, Dad started to and it kind of caught on. It was a tradition now. Traditions are important.

Stepping back, I looked at Brian. "They sell men's clothes where you got those?"

He laughed.

"We're going to have to outfit you guys for the wilderness while you're here," I said.

His shiny painter pants and logo sports jersey wasn't

acceptable, especially since it wasn't a Packers jersey. It might have been the patent leather athletic shoes he was wearing, though.

Everybody sat down, and Carol brought me a cup of coffee.

"Good morning, John," she said, then disappeared as quickly as she'd showed up. The smile on her face was telling, though. She liked them.

"I see Carol likes you, so I guess you can stay," I said a bit too loud. I knew she'd heard me because I heard her laugh from the kitchen.

We chatted about the trip across country as they finished their food. I wanted to get them home. The curiosity about the trailer was nagging at me.

After they'd finished, I made Brian pay for breakfast. Carol refused his money, too. He tried to tell me it was his natural charm, but I knew better.

They followed me home and I had them park in front of the cabin so they could unload it easily. The dirt drive, curving through the woods from the road, veered off toward the barn and outbuilding. I told Brian to drive on the grass, knowing it would bother him after his time in the army. "Get off my grass" was a common expression in the army.

I let Max and King out. The real moment of truth was at hand. They dashed out and ignored everyone. Running straight to the Escalade, they began to *talk* to Grady. Their barking sounded more like a fox hunt, only deeper.

Brian let Grady out, and the dogs sniffed around each other, then took off running toward the back of the cabin.

"They gonna be all right?" Brian asked.

"They'll be fine, unless they catch a skunk. Don't worry; I've got a case of stuff for that if we need it." The look of shock and displeasure on Nancy's face was priceless.

We spent a few minutes watching the dogs run in the huge field, almost fifteen acres, which surrounded the back and one side of the cabin. It was like watching three kids who'd been cooped up indoors for too long.

"Can I go, too, Grampa?" Mike asked.

"Go for it," I said.

He looked at his mom and dad, didn't even give them a chance to answer, and took off after the dogs.

"The skunk stuff works on people, too," I said with a chuckle.

"Wonderful," was Nancy's somewhat alarmed response. I think she might have been a bit taken aback by all of the rusticness of her surroundings.

"C'mon in," I said. "I'll give you the tour, show you where you can put your stuff, and then we can talk about what's in the trailer."

The tour took a good half hour. Being off the grid, everything was solar, wind, or wood in the cabin. I had satellite TV due to my History Channel, HGTV, and DIY addiction. Except in bad snowstorms, it worked great. So that added time, as I explained how everything worked.

Nancy wasn't thrilled about well water, but I showed her the reverse osmosis filter plus the large Crown Berkey Water Filter I had in the kitchen. With more people here, we'd probably have to fill it every day instead of every three or four days, but it made her smile—especially when I explained that after all the filtering, it was cleaner than any city water anywhere on the planet. I couldn't wait to see her reaction with the outhouse and the hand pump for the well. They weren't needed, but I'd put them in for emergencies. Now I could have some fun with them, too. Guess Brian got being a jokester from me.

We got all their belongings unloaded, I made lunch,

and we hollered for the dogs and Mike. I figured the dogs would hear us before Mike would.

It was a few minutes before I saw them running across the field.

Nancy had a fit; Mike was mud and sticker-covered, as were all three dogs. We made him undress on the porch and she got him cleaned up.

Lunch was simple; sandwiches, chips, and lemonade. After we finished, I showed Mike how to turn on the TV, and he asked if he could set up his Xbox. I didn't see any harm in it. While he played, us grownups went out on the porch and sat in lawn chairs. Nancy and Brian lit up cigarettes, and I had a cigar.

"This is a really nice place, Dad. Not at all like I figured," Brian said.

"It's pretty here, but it's going to take getting used to," Nancy added. "There's no noise or sounds at all."

"Wait 'til night," I said. "You won't say that then."

"Oh," she answered, an eyebrow raised in a perfect imitation of every mother I ever knew.

I shrugged. "That's when all the critters make noises."

Nancy looked out into the forest, as if searching for them. "Wonderful."

"Yup. Owls, bugs, birds, the occasional coyote. Music." Changing the subject, I said, "So, what's up with the trailer?" I couldn't hold off my curiosity one more minute.

Brian shifted in his chair, glanced at Nancy and then at me. "I was hoping Nancy and Mike could stay here for a while. Things are getting bad, and with my work…" He stared at me, as if trying to find the right words.

I knew his work made him more aware of what was really happening in the real world before almost anyone else did.

"With the North Koreans and their missiles, things are escalating," Brian said. "ISIS and their growing terrorist threats are bad enough, but all the riots and attacks seem to be growing in numbers. We've had them in town, and attacks against the private vehicles of soldiers are getting worse. Rioters have been picketing at the gate and the general has put the town off-limits, except for those who actually live there. They can go to and from home, but that's it. I need Mike and Nancy to be someplace safe."

"Of course they can stay. This is *our* home." Then it was my turn to shift as I asked, "How bad is it?"

"With all the riots and how long they've been going on, we've raised the security level to Orange, but some think it should be at Red."

"Because of riots and angry kids?" That surprised me. Orange meant the risk was high. Red was severe, and the highest level.

"No. Everybody who hates us has been chattering and we think something could happen. Nothing specific. I couldn't say anyway, but it doesn't look good, Dad."

My cigar had burnt out, and I put the butt down. "Have you let Craig or John know?"

"No." Brian shook his head. "John doesn't answer calls or texts. We haven't spoken in years. I don't even consider him my brother anymore."

"What about Craig?" I prodded.

"We chat. We've worked up a way of using email without using email."

I scrunched my face in confusion. "What's that mean?"

"We have a common email account. We write notes but don't send them. They stay in draft form so no one can read them but us."

"That's pretty slick."

"Yeah, learned about it through my work. Craig has a good idea of what's going on. He dropped out of college because of all the foolishness, as he calls it, happening on campus."

"What? He dropped out of college? I didn't know."

"Yeah, for now. Don't worry; he'll go back. He said he and his mom are trying to keep a low profile, and that he needed to be available to protect her."

I tsked. "That's Craig, always protective of her. We'll talk about that part about John not being your brother later, just you and me," I said, probably a bit too sternly. I did understand the issue. They'd had a huge blowout at his mother's second husband's funeral, and the damage was bad. "I should at least let Craig know that you're here and have concerns, though."

"I know, but not over the phone, Dad. You never know who's listening."

"Maybe I can get him to come up here while you guys are visiting. I know he would want to see you."

"I'd love to see him, too. It's been awhile." Brian's voice drifted off, his disappointment in himself for not being closer to his brother beginning to show.

"Anyway, Nancy, you, and Mike can stay here as long as you'd like. But we need to get you some clothes that are more appropriate than what you have. As it is, if you haven't noticed, you already stand out. Lake View isn't known for its diversity. It'll help you fit in better."

"She can tell everyone she's Native American, Dad," Brian said in a serious tone.

The questioning look I gave him generated his humorous answer. "Blackfoot."

"Brian," Nancy scolded.

But we all laughed. I loved my modern family.

***

The next few days were nice, spending time together. I taught Mike some basic woodcrafts, and because we made a game of it, he thought it was wonderful.

Of course, the day I let him shoot my old Savage single shot bolt action .22 was probably the best so far. I was in the dining room, with the rifle and a box of CCI Longs waiting on the table. I'd discussed it with Nancy the night before. She wasn't thrilled, but I had guns in the house and she knew it was the best way to get past his curiosity.

Mike's eyes were big as saucers when he saw the rifle on the table. Over breakfast, we talked about gun safety and how to use a rifle properly. We went out into the field behind the house and I let him shoot 'til he was tired. Of course, we ran out of bullets first. I promised him we would do it again soon.

That afternoon, Brian and I were sitting on the porch enjoying a cigar and beer. The screen door squeaked, and Mike came outside by us.

"Grampa, can you fix the TV? It doesn't work."

"Sure," I said, and followed him inside.

I went over to the TV and tried the remote. Nothing. I pushed the power button on the back of the TV. Nothing again.

"Hmm…" I walked down the hall and checked the circuit breaker box; all were in the right position.

"Can you fix it, Grampa?" he asked.

I glanced at him, then back at the box. "It doesn't seem to be working, son. I may have to call someone to come fix it."

"Okay. I'll go play with the dogs." They had become his constant companions, but I think it had more to do with the four of them discovering the joys of mud than anything else. He ran off, and I went back out on the porch.

A few minutes later, Nancy came out. "My radio doesn't work."

"It probably stopped liking rap," I replied, Brian's humor rubbing off on me.

"No, seriously," she said. "It doesn't work."

Getting up, I went back inside to see if my radio worked. Finding my way to my small office, I turned the radio on. Nothing. Not even static. Checking to see if it was plugged in, I tried it again. Nothing.

I checked the switch on the wall and noticed none of the lights in the office worked. The refrigerator in the kitchen wasn't humming like it usually did. *Hmmm… this was unusual.*

I went out on the porch and joined them. "My radio doesn't work, either. Nothing electric in the house is working."

"Was it plugged in?" Brian asked with a chuckle.

"Yeah, smart-ass, it was." I glared at him.

Brian took his smartphone out of his pocket and pushed the home button. The screen stayed black. He pushed the power button on the right side of the phone and it didn't come on. "My phone doesn't work."

I hadn't looked at mine yet. Opening the screen door, I picked up my phone off the small table inside. Like Brian's, it didn't power on. "Mine doesn't work, either," I called.

What the heck was going on?

"Now what?" I said, joining them again.

Standing, Brian walked off the porch and across the yard. Getting into his Escalade, he fiddled around. I saw him stare up at the ceiling, then he got out and came back toward the cabin.

"What's up?" I shouted as he walked.

He didn't answer, but I could tell he was thinking by the look on his face.

Back on the porch, he sat down and leaned forward,

his forearms resting across his thighs. He always furrowed his forehead when he was in deep thought or concerned. Taking a deep breath, he said, "I think we just had an EMP."

Chapter 2

"Life is a series of natural and spontaneous changes. Don't resist them—that only creates sorrow. Let reality be reality."

—Lao Tzu

"What's an EMP?" Nancy asked. We had forgotten she was on the porch with us. A quick glance between Brian and me was the only delay before he answered.

"An EMP is an Electro-Magnetic Pulse," he said.

Interrupting, she said, "Brian, in English please."

"It's a burst of energy that is transmitted through the air."

Her stare at him signaled loudly that this, in her mind, wasn't any better. "What does it do?"

"Well, if it's big enough, it kills all the electronics. Some types of equipment can survive, but modern stuff is basically fried."

"So the TV and radio won't work anymore?" she asked.

"Not only that, but apparently our vehicle, too."

"I didn't hear or see anything," she said. "I don't like this."

"I don't, either, Nancy," he said, trying to comfort her. "This is one of the things I was afraid of. As to the EMP, no one will have seen anything. It's energy—you can't see it."

She rubbed her hands over her forearms, as if suddenly cold. "At all?"

I felt the same way. An EMP attack wasn't good.

Brian shrugged. "Depends on what kind. A solar flare could be seen and so could a nuclear blast, but if it's high in the atmosphere, we won't see it. If it's a ground burst, well, if we saw it, we wouldn't be talking right now."

"So, poof, just like that, all the electricity stops working," she said.

I could tell Nancy was scared. A city girl wouldn't know how to survive without electricity. I was worried about the bigger problem, though. *What did this mean?*

"Not all. Most, especially modern things. This happened once before, a big solar flare back in 1859. A big one that impacted the world. A giant solar flare that made a light show in the sky that amazed everyone who saw it. Of course, we didn't have a lot of technology back then, but from what I read, it destroyed telegraphs and people could see colors in the sky, like the Northern Lights, all over the world."

"Damn," I said.

"No shit. I'm not exactly certain if this was one or not," Brian said. "I'm sure we would have heard something if we were expecting solar flares or storms. Sadly, the government knows that this can happen either naturally or on purpose."

"On purpose? What does that mean?" Nancy asked, her voice reaching a higher tone.

"Yup. Nuclear blast, the best scenario to create one

would be a nuclear weapon airburst a couple hundred miles above the earth. The government kinda has a plan to deal with it, but nothing has been done."

"Typical," I said. "What plan? I hadn't heard of that."

"Well, it started back in 1989, when massive solar flares were occurring and several places in Canada experienced EMP effects from it. It happened again in 2012, but the effects narrowly missed the earth. Astronomers and NASA said had it hit, it most likely would've been worse that the 1859 one."

"I had no idea," Nancy exclaimed.

Brian blew out a breath he'd been holding. "A few years before that, the EMP Commission…"

"We have an EMP Commission?" Nancy interrupted.

"Sure do, hon. Anyway, they reported that if one like the Carrington effect—that's what they called the 1859 one—were to happen again, the outcome would be catastrophic. All modern technology in the world would stop working. Most automobiles, machines, everything would stop. Old stuff, like Dad's truck, would run just fine because they don't rely on electronics or computers."

I couldn't help but smirk. "I knew my truck was special."

He smiled at me, but still with a nervous look on his face, Brian continued. "They predicted that ninety percent of the world's population would die as a result. Mostly from violence or pre-existing diseases that required medication or equipment, starvation, and so on. People with pacemakers, for example, would die almost instantly because the pacemakers would be shut off. Those people would be some of the first to go from this. So in 2016, Congress inserted a protection bill into the National Defense Authorization Act that was to start protecting our infrastructure through hardening. Unfortunately, they haven't gotten around to it."

"What's hard-en-ing?" Nancy asked, articulating the word.

"That's providing screens and other things to protect electronics," I answered. "I have some things I store in a homemade Faraday Cage in the basement."

"This is too much," Nancy said, shaking her head.

"Grampa!" Mike shouted from inside the cabin.

"Except that kind of energy. That won't be affected, but it will affect us," I said. Laughing, I stood up and walked toward the door. "Coming, Mike." The screen creaked its familiar tune as it opened and closed.

Nancy walked over to the chair I had been sitting in and sat down. "So it's bad?"

"Possibly," Brian replied. "It depends on how big and widespread it is."

Mike's needs dealt with, I had come back out and stood on the porch, a cup of coffee and a cigar in my hands.

Brian got up and walked over to his vehicle. After several tries and absolutely nothing happening, he hung his head. "Shit," he muttered.

He went over to my truck. Pulling down the sun visor, the keys dropped into his lap. Putting the key in the ignition, he started the truck right up. He turned it off, put the keys back, and got out of the truck. He stood in the yard, his hands on his hips, staring off into the distance. I knew that stance. He was frustrated, concerned, scared. Taking his usual deep breath to deal with the stress, he turned and came back to the cabin porch.

"She started right up, didn't she?" I asked.

"Sure did," Brian said.

"Then it's definitely an EMP."

He frowned. "Yup."

I took a sip of my coffee and sucked on the cigar, the blue smoke trailing slowly from my mouth as I exhaled. "I need you to keep an eye on things here for a day or two."

"Why, where are you going?" Brian asked, a somewhat accusatory tone to his voice.

"I'm going down to Appleton to get your brother before things get bad."

"But Dad, he won't come without Donna."

I half-shrugged. "Then she'll come, too."

"Okay, whatever you say."

"Fil, when are you leaving?" Nancy asked.

"In the morning, but first I have to show you some things. Follow me." I walked into the house, Brian following behind me.

"I'll be right back," he said to Nancy.

Nancy remained on the porch. The concerned look on her face had told me everything. She was scared and nervous. She'd nodded her head, too numb to move.

Brian and I trooped down into the basement and through a doorway into my store room. The lights still worked, as the cabin was on solar. The wiring, as well, as the converter were all protected by a very large and efficient Faraday system and surge suppressor. It was quite a storeroom.

"This is what I want to show you," I said.

Standing in racks along the wall were six Ruger AR-15s, two Remington 700s, two shotguns, and the old Savage .22 bolt action rifle I had used to teach Mike to shoot. That was the same gun I'd taught Brian to shoot with, too. Underneath the rifle rack were cases of ammo. "Jesus, Dad, you planning on World War III?"

Ignoring his question, I said, "Looks like I planned right. There are over 15,000 rounds of 5.56, about 1000 12 gauge shells, 1000 .308s for the Remingtons and another 10,000 .22 rounds. Over here," I said, as I turned and went to my right, "are four Glock 19s in 9mm and four in .40mm. There are 5,000 rounds each for those, too. In the back is a complete reloading set for everything except the .22 and the shotguns."

"Okay," Brian said as he reached for one of the ARs. It was familiar in his hands as it was near identical to what he regularly carried in the army, along with a Beretta M9. "Where are the magazines for these?"

Reaching under the shelf below the handguns, I pulled out an old GI OD footlocker and opened it. "There are fifty 30 round Magpuls in here. The box next to the handguns have thirty 15 round magazines. Holsters for the pistols are on the shelf over there, as are 6 tactical vests."

Turning, Brian glanced toward the shelf I was speaking of. Three floor to ceiling shelves filled with 82 quart weathertite tote boxes were shelved there.

"What's in those?" he asked.

"Food."

"Please don't tell me you have storage bins filled with MREs," he said with a grin.

"Oh, I have some, but mostly, those are freeze dried foods I got online. I have three years' worth for one person, so after I get your brother here, and assuming his mom comes, too…"

"She will," Brian assured me.

"Well, with her, plus what we can grow and can, and what I have upstairs, we'll have food for all of us for a year."

"Then what?"

"I have the garden out back, which we'll have to expand, and in those boxes over there, I have heirloom seeds."

"What the hell are heirloom seeds?"

"For all your smarts, you don't know much, son. That means the seeds aren't hybrids, which means you can grow the exact same plant from the seeds you get from it."

"So we'll become vegetarians?"

"I doubt it. I have 180 acres here. We have deer, rabbit, squirrel, and even bear."

"Don't tell Nancy about the bear."

"They keep to themselves. Mostly won't be seen, but we have them. There's the river nearby for fishing and we also have lakes. We'll be okay until…"

"Until what?"

"Hell, I don't know."

"I'm sure the National Guard will be called in to help and be around, Dad."

"Don't bet on it. They'll either try and make us share all of this, or make us move to some central location. If they show up, tell them nothing. Don't even mention you're an officer."

"You think it could be that bad?"

"Don't you? I'm not taking any chances. *Our* survival comes first. Yours, Mike's, Nancy's. That also means if somebody shows up here hungry, you run them off. We aren't sharing."

"Nancy's not gonna like that."

"I don't care. We don't have a choice. We aren't sharing." I stood firm on this point. I had to.

Taking another glance around the storeroom, Brian heaved a sigh. "Alright, we'll tell her together?"

"Yes, ya' little coward, we'll do that. Take that AR upstairs, grab a couple magazines, and that ammo can there. I'll bring some more up in a second and we'll talk to Nancy."

"Okay, Dad."

We no sooner got upstairs and back onto the porch when Nancy's questions started.

"Why do you have all of these guns, Fil?" She was no stranger to guns, as she enjoyed skeet shooting and was an accomplished hunter in her own right.

Brian answered for me. "Dad's going after Craig and

he wants us to have them handy here, just in case."

"Just in case what?"

Brian gave Nancy a *don't ask* look.

Not sure what he meant, she asked again, "Just in case what?"

"We are far enough away from civilization that we should be okay for a while. Once people start realizing that their electricity won't be coming back on, that normal conveniences aren't going to happen anymore, things will start getting ugly."

"Getting ugly?" she prodded.

"People will be scared, Nance. They'll get desperate when they realize that grocery stores won't have more food, the restaurants won't be able to feed them, that they can't get medicine, all of that shit. So they'll start taking it. That kind of situation may already be going on right now. People who know about these things will be taking what they can get from grocery stores. I wouldn't want to be near a Big Box warehouse store right now. Once the stores run out, they'll head for where they think the food is. That means farms, and farms aren't in the city. Then, we'll have to start to worry."

"But we need *stuff*," Nancy said, jumping up in a panic.

"I already took care of that," I said. "Not to worry. I wasn't expecting an EMP, but I've prepared for one. I have plenty of supplies downstairs. I showed it all to Brian. We'll be fine. We have to be prepared to protect it, though. Brian, I almost forgot. In the basement, back in the store room, is a metal trashcan with a lid. It's taped shut with aluminum tape, that's my homemade Faraday Cage. Let's go down there and I'll show you what's in there. I need something from it anyway."

"But..."

"Nancy, we'll be okay," Brian assured her.

The two of us went into the basement. I opened the container and said, "There are some hand crank radios in here. You'll need one to listen for any news broadcasts, or anything else that might be on the airwaves. Also," I reached inside and grabbed a black object, "there are six of these walkie talkies. They have a range of about twelve miles. Keep one upstairs and use the solar charger for the battery. I'm taking one with me. We can stay in touch this way."

"Okay. Good to know."

"There are sixteen channels in this thing. We'll use channel 5. If that doesn't work, go to 10 and then 15. This way we stay off of channel 9, which I'm sure most people will try to use."

"Dad, it won't reach Appleton."

"I know, but when I get close, I'll be able to call you and let you know I'm coming. I suspect Carol might show up here. Give her one and a spare solar charger. There are half a dozen on the shelf in a metal box. I've got one in my bag in the truck, too."

"When are you leaving?"

"Early tomorrow morning. It's too late to go today and I don't want to get to their place in the dark. Use the food that is upstairs before you get into anything down here. Load up another AR and the shotgun. Keep them nearby. And Brian, keep a handgun on you at all times."

"You make this sound like Iraq."

"It could be. We don't know. Stay prepared."

"You're going a bit overboard here, Dad."

"I hope I am, but better safe than sorry."

"We'll be okay here." It was Brian's turn to assure me.

"I know. If you need to go anywhere or get around the property, use the UTV. There's a 1000 gallon tank alongside the barn and it's full. Kerosene lamps and fuel are in the garage, plus Coleman lanterns and fuel."

Seeing Mike was keeping busy with a puzzle upstairs, we went outside on the porch.

"C'mon, let me show you around. I have some other things you need to know about." I stepped into the yard and went toward the barn.

Brian and I spent the rest of the afternoon touring the yard, garage, barn, and outbuildings—everything I had that would help get us through this situation, no matter how long it took. For once, I was glad I had the training of an army man.

Chapter 3

"Every day is a journey, and the journey itself is home."

—Matsuo Basho

The sun rose as it always did. I got up before it did, as usual, and made coffee on the camp stove I had brought in from the store room in the barn. The barn had been original to the property, so I left it up when I built the cabin. I had this silly dream of having horses, so I figured the barn and stalls, along with a tack room, would come in handy. The horses and tack never happened. And the tack room was now just another storage room for all my stuff.

I hooked the camp stove up to a propane container that I had for my gas barbecue grill. I had three others in the barn. I could've used the gas stove, but I felt like sparing the big propane tank until later. It was full, so with normal use we probably had a good six months with that. I knew Nancy would want to use the stove, but this way I could "train her" to be frugal with things.

As I made coffee, Brian came into the kitchen and mumbled something unintelligible. It sounded like

"Morning" but I wasn't sure.

I moved closer to him and gave him a big hug. "Morning, son."

He pulled away and gave me a serious look. "Be careful, Dad."

"I will. I'll stay in touch with you as much as possible on the radio. I wouldn't expect to be back before day after tomorrow. I'll call you when I think I'm in range."

Brian nodded, showing he understood.

"Explore what's downstairs so you know what is all there. Never be unarmed, never. You should tell Nancy that, too. Each of you take an AR or one of you the shotgun. Everybody gets a handgun. We don't know what we're dealing with here."

"Yes, sir…"

"Hey, I was a sergeant. I worked for a living. You're the officer." I smiled at him as I said it, showing Brian my joy in his accomplishments. "I'm proud of you, Brian. You done good."

I grabbed a thermos of coffee and the rest of my things, then walked through the door. I shouted, "Max, King!"

My German shepherd dogs, lying on the porch next to one another, stood up, ears perked forward, staring at me.

"You stay."

They laid back down, both sighing as they relaxed.

I climbed into the truck, turned the key, and the engine roared to life. Sticking my arm out the window and making a fist, I extended my thumb upward to Brian, who watched from the porch. Putting the truck in gear, I drove in a circle and headed down the long, curving drive. I made it to the street before radioing Brian.

"I forgot to tell you, go out by the road and take

down the mailbox. No sense in announcing that there's a house down the dirt drive."

"Roger wilco, Dad. Time for me to get to work."

I imagined Brian's ear-to-ear grin, an indicator that he was in a mischievous mood.

There was no traffic. I saw cars alongside the road, some with people sitting in them, doing nothing. A few tried to flag me down, but I kept driving. I was on a mission and that mission was my youngest son, Craig.

I turned off of the county road and headed south on Highway 55. I would take that all the way to Highway 29, through the Menominee Indian Reservation. Highway 29 would take me to Highway 47, to Appleton.

I bypassed the larger communities like Shawano and Green Bay driving this route, which would help me avoid people and whatever trouble they might cause. I had an operating vehicle, and while I was certain I was not the only one, I also knew someone might want it.

My AR and a loaded Glock were on the seat next to me. I'd packed extra ammo in my bag. The holster on my hip was empty. If I needed a gun, I'd need it quick.

There were a lot more cars on the road than I thought there would be. Most were empty and alongside the road, some were blocking the way with where they stopped. Others appeared to have coasted into odd positions or into things like other cars, trucks, road signs, the occasional tree, and unfortunately, a now spewing fire hydrant.

The occupied vehicles had bits of cloth tied to the antenna, as if the owners thought someone would see that and come rescue them. A few shouted at me as I drove by, but I avoided eye contact and kept moving. I couldn't help them. Besides, I was worried they might want me to take them somewhere, or worse, take my truck. Times had changed in a flash, and I had to put my own family first.

The farther south I drove, the closer to towns I came, the volume of abandoned, broken down, and crashed cars increased. A few people tried to chase me. I wasn't stopping.

An hour into my trip trouble found me. A small group of people, three men and two women, stood in the road waving their arms. They shouted, "Stop!"

They were young, at least younger than me, and appeared to be unarmed. A car blocked most of the road, but it was clear on either side of it. However, two people from the group stood on either side of the car, filling those gaps.

I was a bit nervous as I reached across the seat and picked up my Glock. I held it in my hand. I already had a round chambered.

Slowing down, I approached the group. I slowed the truck to a crawl as I came up on them, but I had no intention of stopping. They continued to shout and wave their arms, stepping further onto the road.

"Stop, god dammit," one of the men yelled. Scruffy-looking with a ragged beard, the man wore jeans and a long sleeve t-shirt with some kind of symbol on it. His eyes showed anger.

I instantly tensed and chose not to stop.

One of the other men stepped in front of my truck, banging on the hood with his fists as I continued to creep forward. I should've floored the gas pedal and drove through them, but I didn't. Instead, I raised my hand showing I was armed.

"Fuck you, asshole," the woman yelled.

The guy in front of the truck, seeing the Glock, backed up and out of the way.

BAM!

Something large hit the windshield, startling me. Fortunately, it didn't break.

I pointed my Glock at big mouth with the angry eyes.

He looked shocked for a second, then shouted at me, "You don't have the balls. Go ahead. Shoot me, fuck stick!"

Putting my arm out the half open window, I pulled the trigger, aiming in his general direction, though making sure I didn't hit him.

He jumped, and I shot again.

He fell to the ground, crab crawling away as he tried to get back on his feet.

Something hit the back window.

The man who had been in front of my truck was now out of the way so I floored it, leaving them behind. I could hear their shouted obscenities as I pulled away.

I was glad the group was behind me, but I'd probably see them again on my way back through and most likely many others like them.

I saw a few trucks, pickups like mine, some older Suburbans, and even a Harley motorcycle driving on the highway as I continued my journey. A few drivers waved at me, and being neighborly, I waved back. Most didn't look my way as we passed each other, suspicion and fear of strangers already taking a firm hold.

As I made my way into the small town of Bonduel, a few people watched me as I drove by, as did others in Black Creek. The abandoned cars, and the cases where people had chosen to stay with them, continued to grow in number. I didn't see anyone else doing anything I would've called unusual, under the circumstances, until I came to Appleton.

Crossing Interstate 41 and entering town, my only reaction was shock. The interstate was littered with cars, obviously stopped when the EMP hit. Even here, people were still sitting in their vehicles as if somehow everything was going to return to normal. The late spring weather was decent enough to not cause any discomfort. Had this happened during a Wisconsin winter, they'd all be frozen solid.

People walked up and down Highway 47 as it went over Interstate 41. Many seemed to be heading for a couple of fast food restaurants at the end of the overpass. No one seemed to care if they were in the road or not.

A fight had started over what looked like grocery bags of food. In another day or two, that would be routine and bloodier. With nothing moving, people were going to get hungry. That hunger would make them desperate, and desperate people do bad things. Most of them would be early casualties of this mess. I shook my head in sadness. I had to get to Craig's house and soon.

I had to drive slowly, about 15 MPH. Cars and people continued to block the roads. Some people stared at me. The shouts for help continued, as did getting objects thrown at my truck. I was surprised no one tried to jump into the back of the truck, as I wasn't driving that fast. I did what everyone else was doing. I went wherever I could to get through—over the curbs, on the sidewalks, around cars, and through the yards of properties alongside the road. I stopped for no one.

It took me better than thirty minutes to reach the street Craig and his mom lived on. Normally, it would've been about a five-minute trip after I crossed the I-41 bridge.

Turning onto the street, the state of it immediately got my attention. It was quiet. Too quiet. There were no people outside, no animals, nothing. A few cars were parked on the side of the road. I could see one in the middle of the road a few blocks up, but otherwise it was so quiet.

I turned into their driveway and parked in front of the

detached garage. As I got out of the truck, Craig came out the front door of the house.

***

Brian wanted to spend the morning getting acquainted with his dad's property, or so he told himself. He had been sitting on the porch for about thirty minutes when he saw Carol driving up the driveway on an ATV. He stood up as she pulled in front of the porch and came to a stop.

"Hi, Carol," Brian said. "Good to see you."

"Hi, Brian, is John here?" She glanced around the property.

"No, he went to Appleton."

"Appleton, after this?"

Brian nodded. "Yeah, he went to get Craig."

"Oh, that's right. I forgot, with the power outage. It's been a bit stressful. Do you think Craig'll come? I've heard he's close to his mom."

Brian shrugged. "Not sure. I hope so. If Dad can get Craig to come here, I can guarantee Donna is coming, too. Craig and Dad won't leave her alone."

"I remember when your brother visited; he didn't like leaving his mom alone. We talked a lot at the diner. He's a good kid."

"Yeah, he's my little brother. But I love him anyway."

"You need anything while your dad's gone, call me."

"I would, but our phones don't work."

Carol reached into her vest pocket and pulled out a radio, wiggling it back and forth. She smiled, laughed, and said, "On this. Channel 11."

Taking the device, Brian said, "Dad give you that?"

"A few of us got together and bought them. We figured you never know—storms, alien attack, EMP."

"So you think it's an EMP, too?"

"Can't be anything else. Cars don't work, TVs don't work, cell phones, nothing electronic works."

"Well, then we've screwed the pooch, cuz it will take forever and then some to fix this."

"I'm headed to Sam Karpinski's. I'm going to see what I can find out."

"What makes you think he'll know anything?" Brian asked.

"Sam's old school. He has a tube type ham radio. It will work," Carol said.

Brian glanced away toward the barn, then back at her. "I have to figure out how to contact my unit."

"The guard over in Antigo is probably your best bet. When's your leave up?"

"I have ten more days."

"Well, enjoy it. Maybe we'll know more by then. Your dad has plenty of gas for that old truck of his. He can get you to the armory. Anyway, call me if you need anything." Carol started up the ATV, then sped off across the yard and back down the drive.

It seemed like forever before the sound of the ATV faded away. *Sound sure does travel far out here.*

Brian headed toward the barn. He stopped at the doorway and peered inside. Sitting just in front of him was John's quad UTV with a bed. A smile crept across Brian's face as he eased toward the vehicle.

Dad said if I needed to go anywhere to take the UTV. Time to tour the property.

He climbed into the driver's seat and saw the key dangling from the slot just below the steering wheel. As he reached for it, he was startled by a flurry of activity—brown blurs and a thump to his right.

"Wha—?"

With one sitting on the seat and the other on the floor, Max and King had jumped in. Both German

Shepherds sat there grinning as only a dog can, pink tongues hanging out and slowly panting, their heads turning side to side staring up at Brian.

Grady had come in, too, and stood outside the UTV, not sure what he was supposed to do.

"C'mon Grady, it's okay," Brian said to the Great Dane.

Grady hopped into the back seat.

Guess we're all going for a ride.

Starting up the UTV, Brian headed through the door, across the yard, and out into the wide meadow behind the house. The tall grass had a path already blazed through it—the UTV had been this way before.

Uncertain what the grass hid, Brian stayed on the path and drove toward a tree line a couple hundred yards away. The entire meadow was fenced in by trees and thick woods.

Wow, 180 acres is a lot of land.

Max and King sat there, bouncing along like UTV experts, as Brian drove. Grady had laid down on the back seat, his head hanging over the edge as if he could care less.

Stopping in front of the trees, Brian looked left and right, marveling at how expansive and clean the property was. Looking back and over his shoulder, he could see the house, surprised that Nancy and Mike weren't out and about yet.

Sleeping in, maybe.

He turned off the vehicle and stepped out, heading into the tall grass, up to his knees in some places. Hands on his hips, he took in the land in front of him. *Dad has his own kingdom here.*

Interrupted by a commotion behind him, Brian quickly turned.

Max and King were both standing. Max, his front paws on the back of the passenger seat, King trying to get next to him, had alerted toward where they had come from.

Grady, true to form, was asleep.

Brian reached for his waist. No weapon. Remembering his dad had told him to never be without one, he felt foolish.

I spent twenty-two months in Iraq. I should know better.

He stood there watching, observing, trying to see what had alerted the dogs.

A tan mass jumped up and took off across the field. *Deer.*

Chuckling to himself, he got back into the vehicle, turned it around, and went toward the house.

That's enough of a tour today.

***

"Dad," Craig shouted as he came out of the house.

We rushed to each other and shared a back-slapping hug.

"How are you, Craig?" I asked.

"Good. I guess you're here because of this," he said as he waved his arm across the air.

Stepping away from him, I took in the sight of my son. He looked fine. "Yeah, I came to get you to take you back to my place. It'll be safer there."

"You need to talk to Mom. Our car doesn't work."

"I figured," I said. "Is there room in the garage for my truck?"

"Yeah, Mom's car is at work. She walked home," Craig said.

"Okay. Let's get the truck in there so no one is tempted to borrow it, then we'll talk with your mom."

Craig went to open the garage door, an old-fashioned wooden one, while I drove the truck inside. Leaving the bag but taking my weapons, Craig rolled the garage door down. We went inside to the house through the back door.

"Mom's in the living room."

"Let me guess, she's sitting in her chair, reading, with a bag of peanut M&M's."

"I heard that," a female voice shouted from the living room.

I stepped into the room and there she was, Donna, my ex-wife. We had divorced after realizing we were better friends than husband and wife. Friends we had stayed. She sat in her chair, a recliner. A lap throw was across her legs and a book in her hands. Underneath the book was an ever-present bag of peanut M&M's. She had on an orange, short-sleeved shirt. She would have said it was some other color I'm sure, but I didn't see colors the same way she did. I'm a guy. I only recognized nine colors: red, green, white, black, yellow, brown, blue, orange, and camouflage.

"Hi, Donna," I said, sitting in the other recliner in the room, probably Craig's usual seat.

"Why are you here?" Donna asked.

"I've come to get you and Craig, and bring you both back to my cabin." I'd decided on the route there that it made no sense in trying to talk Craig into coming alone. I had no problem with Donna. So, there was no reason to outcast her. Besides, she was a hunter and a veteran. We'd met in the army. I knew she could shoot.

"You think it's that bad, John?"

I'd gotten her full attention. "Yeah, it's an EMP outage, and while I have no idea how much of the country has been affected, it's going to be a long time before anything returns to normal around here. It's not safe to stay here."

"My car is downtown at work. It wouldn't start when I left work the other day. When I saw no one else had a car that worked, plus with the cell phones, TVs, and radios not working, I figured it might be an EMP. No traffic lights, either. If it's reached all the way up there to Lake View, it's probably bad. So, when do we go?"

"I figure we can leave in the morning. You wouldn't believe the fights I saw, people trying to make me stop, and you know damn good and well, they'd have stolen the truck if I would've. If we leave in the morning, I figure most of them will be sleeping a drunk off and we should at least get safely out of town."

I had expected an argument, either from Donna or from Craig. I was pleasantly surprised at how this had turned out.

"We should load everything in my truck tonight," I said. "It's secured in the garage, so it'll be safe. Craig and I can take turns sitting up and keeping an eye on things, just in case."

"Where's the truck now?" she asked.

"In the garage."

"Sounds like a plan, Dad," Craig said from the doorway.

"Can I finish my book first? I only have about twenty pages to go and you know how I am when I get this close to the end," Donna interjected.

I laughed. Same old Donna. "Yes, you can finish your book. Craig and I will get started."

"I'm kidding, John. Jeez. I'll finish it later. Besides, you don't know where everything is. Let me show you."

For the next half hour, Craig and I trudged up and down the stairs to the second floor, or down to the basement. We grabbed boxes of canned goods, tools, clothes, Craig's duffle full of his collection of knives, swords, battle axes, throwing stars, and all the other paraphernalia he'd bought, a fireproof box full of important papers, two ARs, two Springfield XDs, and ammunition for both.

Meanwhile, Donna sorted through cupboards, putting things on the table in the dining room that she wanted to bring along.

Just about the time Craig and I had everything stacked up in the dining room for transport to the truck, Donna announced, "Finished."

I looked at her.

She grinned an exaggerated smile of innocence. She had a large pile of canned goods, first aid items, and spices for cooking. "It's all important stuff, John," she said.

I shook my head. "Okay. Let's start taking it to the truck."

It took us another hour to get everything loaded, adding some things from the garage. Shovels, rakes, a hoe, a chain saw, pruning shears, and a couple of hand tools. I'd left the weapons and some ammo in the house. We'd need it handy for the ride back.

Craig and I covered their belongings in the truck bed with a tarp from the garage. We put most of the ammo in the truck cab behind the seat except for what I kept inside.

Trooping back indoors, Craig asked, "So, what's for supper?"

There was still a fair bit of food thawing in the freezer, mostly items we felt wouldn't make the trip. Among those were some semi-frozen hamburger patties.

I sent Craig to the garage to grab a bag of charcoal out of the truck—after all, he was the hungry one. We grilled three pounds of hamburger patties and ate those for dinner.

About the time we'd finished, there was a knock at the door.

Shit, we should've been keeping an eye out.

Taking my Glock out of its holster, I went to the door. I asked, "Who's there?"

A man's voice responded. "I couldn't help but smell your grill. Do you have any extra food you could share?"

"I'm sorry, but we don't. We have just enough for ourselves," I said without opening the door.

"I haven't eaten all day, and I have a family." His voice had raised. His anger and frustration over the situation was clear.

"We can't help you," I said firmly. "I'm sorry. Now please leave."

He pounded on the door, shouting, "It's not fair. You *have* to help us. You have food, give us some. We'll starve!"

Craig had come up behind me and whispered, "Just give him something, Dad. We have plenty."

"No, he'll come back. We'll need everything we have. We can't help everyone, and we can't do this. Besides, if we give it to him, others will follow. They'll find out, and the next thing you know we'll have people from all over the neighborhood here asking for help. Then, trying to take from us what we won't give them."

"Okay," he said, "I get it."

I could hear the sadness in my son's tone.

"Get your AR and come over here with it," I said.

The man continued to pound on the door. He wasn't giving up.

When Craig returned, I said, "Stand here. I'm going to open the door and make him leave. You put that gun at the ready and back me up. Under no circumstances is he to get into this house."

"Yes, sir," Craig said, but the look in his eyes showed he was terrified.

"You'll do fine, son. Just don't let him inside.

I'm going to count to three and then I'll open the door. When I get on the porch, you stand here in the doorway. Nobody but me gets inside. Understand?"

"What are you going to do?" Craig asked.

"Make him leave."

"John, shouldn't we give him something?" Donna said from the table.

"No, that's a mistake. We'll end up giving away more all night long and we'll have nothing." I glanced at her and saw her frown. "It has to be this way, Donna. You ready, Craig?"

"Ready," he said, without a lot of conviction.

Our eyes met and I nodded.

Craig held the AR up in a firing position. His cheek was against the extended stock, and like I had taught him, his finger near but not on the trigger. I did a quick press check of my Glock, verifying I had a round in the chamber. I put my left hand on the door knob, my right held the Glock, and I began to count.

"One, two…three," I said, and pulled open the door, pushing myself into the man. I drove my left hand into his chest while sticking the Glock into his face with my right.

He backed up onto the porch and stumbled down the stairs, falling as he went.

"I said leave, asshole. Do you not understand?" I kept my voice firm with the Glock pointed at him.

He sat on the sidewalk, his arms and hands supporting him from behind.

"Leave, and don't come back," I said. "We can't help you."

"Don't shoot me, Mister. I just want to feed my family."

"I understand. I want to feed mine, too, but we can't help you," I explained.

He repositioned himself, moved his arms and

wrapped them around his knees, sitting there, accepting his fate. "But I…"

"I said we can't help you. Now leave." I waved the Glock to shoo him away.

He slowly stood and walked away. With his head hung down and his arms limp at his sides, he went down the sidewalk and up the street. As he walked away, I remembered the most basic rule I had just broken. Never, ever wave your weapon like a pointer. Keep it on target and stay focused on the target the entire time.

The street was again empty, so I turned to go back inside and saw Craig standing there, the AR held in his hands across his chest. "Your weapon isn't loaded, son."

"What?" he said, turning the weapon sideways in his hands. He glanced down and saw the empty magazine port.

"Unless you were going to hit him with the rifle, it wouldn't have done any good," I said with a grin.

Craig might be in his twenties, but he was still a kid to me. This was all new to him and I didn't want to break his spirit. That would be challenged enough in the coming days, weeks, and months ahead.

"Wow." Letting loose a chuckle, he stood there and shook his head. "That was really dumb."

I chose to ignore his comment. He knew he was right and didn't need me reminding him about it again.

"In the future, we'll need to keep these locked and loaded. We never go anywhere without them, and, son, you need to be able to use it."

"I can shoot," he said defensively.

"I understand that, but shooting another human being may be necessary. You need to accept that circumstance as a possibility right now. You've never done that, and video games don't count."

He stared at me for a moment as the reality sunk in. We went inside and I locked the door.

Craig walked toward the dining room, setting the weapon against his chair. Going over to the box along the wall where we had placed all of the ammo, he grabbed an empty magazine and a box of 5.56 NATO. Sitting back down, he opened the box and began to put rounds into the magazine. He didn't say anything as he pushed and pressed, pushed and pressed.

As I sat in a kitchen chair at the table, I set my Glock on top of it. On a placemat, of course.

Donna asked, "I still don't understand why we couldn't have given the man something? We have more than enough."

"We can't. This kind of thing will happen more and more often, especially on our way back to the cabin and after we get there. We can't give things away. We'll run out, or worse, be overrun by hungry people. They'll eventually overwhelm us, and we'll have nothing for ourselves. We could die."

"It's that bad?"

"Not yet, but it will be. Most people haven't prepared at all. Look at how little you and Craig had, and you always hoarded."

She glared at me, disliking the term and how I used it on her.

"Most people have maybe two to three days' worth of food at home, and many more have almost none. The grocery stores have already been looted and soon will run out. No one is delivering anything. Appleton isn't big enough for the military to show up anytime soon, if it even does, they'll provide refugee centers and help. This will make Hurricane Katrina that hit the south look like a minor incident. A lot of people are going to die…of starvation, disease, running out of meds, and they will kill each other over stale moldy bread slices.”

“I didn’t know,” she whispered. “You didn’t have to be so blunt.”

“It’ll be okay, Mom,” Craig said as he got up and wrapped his arms around her. His eyes were tear-filled. He grabbed a napkin from the table to wipe them. “We’ll be okay, you’ll see.”

Donna sat there and said nothing as she took in what was about to become our new reality.

I hoped Craig was right.

Chapter 4

"We hope all danger may be overcome; but to conclude that no danger may ever arise would itself be extremely dangerous."

—Abraham Lincoln

Brian arrived back at the barn, parked the UTV, and went into the cabin. Nancy was in the kitchen. She'd made fresh coffee using the multi-fuel Coleman stove top and seemed to be enjoying the quiet.

"Mike still sleeping?" Brian asked.

"Yes, this fresh air and all outdoor play has been good for him," she said. "Where were you off to?"

"Surveying the kingdom. We have wild animals."

"Oh," she gasped.

"Nothing to worry about. A deer jumped out of the grass near the tree line."

She looked relieved. "That's good. Don't need any dangerous ones around."

"Dad said we have bear and coyotes here. Said wolves and coyotes don't mix well, so we shouldn't have to worry too much about those."

"I get a gun, right?" Nancy quipped. Her eyes

sparkled in mischievous anticipation over her coffee mug.

"Of course, you can use the shotgun and everybody gets a hand gun."

"Good."

"Should we spend some time teaching Mike how to use a gun and shoot?" Brian asked.

"I'm not really comfortable with that, Brian, but I suppose it's a good idea. What about the .22? He could use that."

"That's probably the best option. I'll start today. I don't think Dad will object. They've already been shooting together, and I know Mike liked it."

"Mike liked it a lot," she replied.

They finished their coffee in silence. Before long, the pitter-patter of six feet caught their attention as Mike and Grady came into the kitchen. Grady must have gone upstairs and woke him up.

"I'm hungry," Mike announced as he rubbed the sleep from his eyes.

"I'll fix you some oatmeal," Nancy said.

"I want pancakes, like Grampa makes."

"Grampa can make you pancakes when he comes home. I'll make you oatmeal," she said sternly.

Nancy went about relighting the stove and made oatmeal for Mike. Brian went out onto the porch, calling Grady to follow. Max and King were already there. The dogs spent a few seconds getting reacquainted and then all three sat in a row, staring at Brian.

"I guess you guys want to eat, too."

The three dogs stood up with their tails wagging rapidly.

Brian went inside, got a bag of dog food from the kitchen pantry, and then went back onto the porch to feed them. Finishing, he put the food away and then walked out to the barn.

Finding the resaw on the bench, he made sure it had a blade on it that would cut metal. Attaching a battery to it, he checked to see if it worked. It whirred to life, as Brian, seeing the hand hacksaw on the bench, let out a sigh of relief.

Getting into the UTV, he drove down the drive and out to the road. Seeing the mailbox on top of the post, he took the saw and quickly cut it off the post. Then, he wrestled the post free from the ground, toeing in the dirt to cover the hole.

Tossing both in the bed of the UTV, he drove the couple of hundred yards down the winding drive back to the barn.

***

We settled down for the night. I told Craig I would take the first watch and settled myself in the recliner that Donna had been sitting in. The front door was to my left and the TV almost directly across for me. I reached for the TV remote and caught myself.

That isn't going to work anymore.

Cradling my AR in my lap, I leaned back in the recliner and relaxed. I could hear shouting and high-pitched screaming coming from down the street. A couple of shots rang out in the early evening. Glancing at my watch—at least, that still worked—I saw it was 9 PM. It was getting dark and I hoped the night would be quiet.

Boom! Boom!

I awoke with a start as two shotgun blasts broke the silence. I was instantly mad at myself for falling asleep. The front door swung open, swinging toward the recliner.

Boom!

Another shot sounded as someone rushed into the living room and got past me.

Instinct took over, and I didn't even hesitate. Pulling up my AR to aim, I squeezed the trigger and put two quick shots into the back of the intruder. He took another step and fell to the floor, sliding forward and into the chair legs around the dining room table.

I heard more footsteps rushing down the steps and rolled out of the recliner, putting it between me and the front door.

"Dad!" It was Craig coming down the stairs.

"Stay there," I shouted.

I heard him as he went back up the stairs, then heard footsteps above me on the ceiling. He was in his room, safe.

I crawled around the chair toward the front door.

Bam! Bam! Bam!

Three more shots rang out, this time it came from a rifle. Rolling toward the door, I fired back with three shots of my own.

"We know you have food in there, now give it to us!" a voice rang out from the front yard. I heard others, too, how many I wasn't sure.

"Fuck you," a male voice rang out from upstairs, followed by a flurry of shots that could only have been from Craig and Donna. The firing was so fast it had to be two weapons.

I rolled further across the room and placed myself by the front window on the opposite side of the door. Peeking over the windowsill, I saw a body sprawled on the porch and two more in the yard, a man and a woman. The clear sky and full moon made it easy to see details.

They both laid on their backs, arms and legs splayed out. Neat holes in the center of their chests showed the aim of Craig and Donna had been true. Several other holes in the bodies suggested it was more a case of fire supremacy.

Easing myself up, I slowly made my way to the door, my weapon leading me in a ready to fire position. As I walked out on the porch, the body in front of me twitched. Shooting once more, I made sure they were dead. I didn't want to be a casualty in this.

Stepping around, I glanced down at the now motionless body. It was the man who had visited earlier.

I walked out into the yard, my AR held at the ready, extended stock on my cheek, the muzzle pointing where I was looking, and this time, my finger on the trigger. Nudging each of the bodies with my foot, I confirmed they were dead. Letting my eyes move across the neighborhood, I saw a few people standing on a porch several houses down. A woman had her hand over her mouth, obviously in shock. No one else was visible.

As I reached down to pick up the weapons the two had dropped, a .308 Winchester and a .22 that looked similar to mine, I heard a noise behind me.

Spinning around, I saw Craig standing on the porch, his AR held low across his body. Donna was behind him, trying to push him behind her.

He was having none of that.

"Stop, Mom," he said. "Get behind me. We've got this."

"Are you two all right?" I asked.

Craig just stood there, staring at the bodies. I could see the shock starting to show on his face as I walked toward him and Donna.

Setting the two rifles down, I got closer to him, putting my hand on his shoulder. "Are you all right?" I asked again softly.

"I shot them," he said.

"Yes, you did. You done good, son."

"Are they dead?"

"Yes," I confirmed.

"Is everything okay down there?" Donna said, motioning with her head toward the neighbors from behind him.

"Yeah, looks like it," I said.

Craig slowly sunk down on his knees and let out a sob.

I sat down next to him, saying nothing but keeping my eyes on the neighborhood. Donna came out on the porch and sat down beside him, putting her arm across his shoulder.

"I had to do it, Dad," he said. "I had to."

"Yes, you did, Craig. I fear it won't be the last time, either."

"Is it always going to be like this? Will we have to do this again?"

"Most likely," I said. "Things will be bad for a while."

"Craig, are you all right?" Donna asked.

Being her only son, I could tell she wanted to protect and comfort him. Her AR leaned against her. Donna might be a Southern California girl by birth, but her life and her time in the army gave her the cojones needed to get through times like this. She was a strong woman.

Craig stood up without saying a word and went back inside the house.

Donna and I followed him in. She reached out to him, but he brushed her hand aside as he slung his rifle over his shoulder, went over to the body laying by the dining room table, and dragged it outside by the man's foot.

I went over and grabbed his other foot. Together, we hauled him out, past Donna and down the steps, putting him next to the man and woman lying in the yard.

As Craig stood there looking down, I went and grabbed the man by the steps. Donna came out and helped me drag him toward the others.

"We'll leave them here," I said.

Craig took in a deep breath accented by a sob.

Donna looked at him, her concern evident on her face, but she knew he needed to process this on his own.

"Okay," he replied.

We all walked back into the house, closing the door behind us. With the lock gone off the door, I wrestled a chair in front of it.

"Why don't you get some sleep, Dad? I'll stay up."

"You sure? I can do it."

Craig shook his head. "I won't be able to sleep. I'll be okay. Besides, you're driving in the morning."

"Well, then," I grinned. "I'm sleeping in your bed."

"G'nite, Dad."

"Nite, son."

Donna went to him and hugged him. She whispered something to him, and I heard him say, "I'm okay, Mom."

"I'm here if you want to talk," she said.

"I had to do it. I'll be okay," he repeated.

"I love you, Craig."

"I love you, too, Mom. Go you two, get some sleep."

I went over and hugged him. "You did the right thing, son. I know it was hard, but you did the right thing."

He said nothing. What he'd just done was tough, and I knew he'd most likely have to do it again. I let him go and trudged up the stairs with Donna.

"He'll be okay," I said.

She stopped at the top of the stairs. "This is gonna be so hard on him when it all sinks in."

"I know. We'll have to help him where we can."

"He isn't a soldier, John, not like we are. He's still a kid with a big heart."

"He'll be fine. I know he will."

"Oh, I hope so," she said, and went into her room, closing the door behind her.

I found Craig's room. Leaving the door open, I set my rifle next to the bed. Lying down fully clothed, I put my head on the pillow.

He needs to be all right.

***

Outside, two pairs of eyes watched the house from beneath the large Norwegian spruce across the street from Donna's house. Silently, they backed into the darkness, and then, in a quick burst, they ran behind the house.

***

I woke with a start. Sitting up, I heard nothing. No birds, no crickets… It was still dark.

Getting out of bed, I grabbed my AR and took the stairs. They creaked, as old stairs do, as I made my way down. In the dining room, I could see Craig, asleep in the chair.

Some guard.

I sat in the other chair as I finished waking up. Watching Craig sleep, I couldn't help but think about him being my youngest, and until yesterday, perhaps my most innocent son in the ways of the world. Last night he did something no one should have to do, but he rose to the occasion and did what was necessary. I was proud of him for protecting his family, but also proud that he hadn't reveled in it.

As I watched him, Craig started to stir. He opened his eyes, blinked, and sat upright quickly.

"Good morning, Sunshine. Sleep well?" I asked.

"I fell asleep," he answered.

"No shit. They shoot you in the army for doing that." I quickly realized that my joke might not have been the best one this morning.

"Sorry," he muttered and stood. "What time we leaving?"

"Shortly, I hope. The sun will be coming up in about an hour, and we need to get a move on while the troublemakers are still sleeping off last night's revelries."

"Is Mom up?"

"No, not yet. Why don't you wake her?"

"Okay, I will," he said and headed for the stairs.

"Craig," I said, stopping him.

He turned and looked at me, his eyes questioning.

"You did the right thing last night."

"I know," he replied. He had no emotion in his voice, just a matter-of-fact statement acknowledging what he'd done.

"I just wanted you to know that."

He turned back and continued up the stairs.

And in that moment, I knew he'd never be the same again.

***

Brian went out on the porch, a steaming cup of coffee in one hand and one of his dad's cigars in the other.

He'll probably kick my ass for taking one of his cigars, but I don't care.

A smile crossed his face as he took in the morning air. The sun was just beginning to rise and the cool air, crisp and smelling of pine, helped wake him further.

The click, click, click of Grady's nails on the hardwood floor announced he was up early. Max and King continued to snore on the porch, where they'd been since Dad had left yesterday.

Sitting down in one of the chairs, Brian took a sip of the hot coffee. It warmed him as it made its way down. Setting it on the floor, he put the cigar in his mouth and used the matches in his shirt pocket to light it. He sat back in the chair, stuck his legs out, and enjoyed the world as it awakened.

Peering down the road that led to the cabin, he saw a doe and two fawns emerge from the woods. He quickly glanced at the dogs to make sure they stayed. The dogs were oblivious.

Some watchdogs.

A few minutes later, the deer wandered into the woods.

Breakfast, hmm, I'm hungry.

Getting up from the chair, Brian went back inside, leaving his cigar to burn out in the ashtray he placed it in. He figured his banging in the kitchen would wake Nancy, and then she'd make him breakfast. Otherwise, he'd be on his own.

Chapter 5

*"There is no mile as long the final one that leads
back home."*

—Katherine Marsh

It didn't take us long to get on the road. Having
packed up almost everything last night, all we had
to load was a few personal effects, our weapons, and
ammo.

We had left out a box of granola bars for breakfast.
Donna ate them like candy bars and washed them
down with water from an old, cleaned out milk jug.
The water pressure was already low when I filled it. I'd
tried the tap to see if we could get more, but no luck.
Whatever had been in the pipes was gone.

Once we finished, we headed to the back steps and
into the garage, then down the driveway in the truck. I
had my AR at the ready, just in case.

I had to laugh when Donna insisted on locking the
doors before we left. Old habits die hard.

In the semi-dark, cool morning, I saw the bodies still
lying in the front yard as I backed the truck onto the
street. We didn't see anyone else outside, so my guess

78

about no one being up was a good one. The three of us
jammed to our own tune in the front bench seat of my
truck with the hope it would help us stay warm, as the
heater didn't work all that well.

I wanted a cigar, but I had left them at home. I knew
Donna and Craig would've raised hell about the smoke
and smell anyway. I smoked premium cigars, so as far
as I was concerned they didn't smell. Not everyone
agreed, but what did they know?

Donna and Craig both had an AR by their legs,
magazines in, and rounds chambered. That was a bit
of an argument with Craig telling me it was against the
law. I guess the look I gave him clearly explained there
was no real law anymore.

The look he gave me back suggested he might've
been kidding. Always a rules stickler that son, I'm not
so sure, but every now and then he surprised me.

I had my Glock on the dashboard in a leather inside-
the-waistband holster. Having it on my hip or small of
the back would have jammed both Craig and me, so as
long as we didn't bounce around or slide off the road, it
was where I would need it if something happened.

I retraced the route I took coming in. I figured it was
still early enough in all of this that we wouldn't have
to worry too much about trouble using the same route.
I made a mental note to explain some of these tricks
of the trade to everyone at the cabin once we returned.
School was about to be in session and I'd forgotten a
lot myself. My waving the pistol around yesterday to
point was a good example.

Things would be quiet for a while, and we would use
that time to make sure everyone knew what to do and
how to do it if something should happen. Donna was
a nurse, so our medical needs had a good resource.
That was probably my most immediate concern.
Because she tended to bring home samples and other

castoffs, we had a small drug and medical supply in the truck bed. We'd be fine for now. She was also into herbal remedies, and part of what we took out of the house was a collection of seeds for a variety of uses.

I weaved between the stalled cars on I-41, saw that some of the people were still there with their cars, as if waiting for them to magically start or a tow truck to come get them.

After that, Highway 41 was pretty clear, except for the clusters of stopped vehicles. Clear, that is, until we passed the high school, a gas station, and ran into a roadblock.

Two men, both with shotguns, sat in collapsible camp chairs. A car was blocking most of the road. They had on orange hunting jackets and ball caps. They were rather healthy-sized men, both looked to be close to 300 pounds apiece.

I reached for my Glock and set it in my lap as we got closer. I told Craig and Donna to grab their XDs and hold them low and out of sight.

As we approached, one of the men held his hand up to stop us while the other stood there, the shotgun held high and across his body. I coasted up and stopped, rolling down my window.

"Can I help you?" I asked.

"You can't go through here," the man said.

Before he could say anymore, Craig said, "Why not?"

"I was about to say, there's a toll, boy," said the man.

"This is a state highway," I said to him. "There are no toll roads in Wisconsin."

"Well," he laughed. "There are now, so you gotta pay."

I held my ground. "I'm not paying anything."

"You have no choice, dipwad," the man said angrily.

I raised my Glock and rested it on the windowsill of

the door, pointing it directly at him. "I'm not paying shit, 'dip wad,'" I said, throwing the name back at him.

As soon as I said it, Donna rolled down her window and reached out it, positioning her pistol on the other guy. "Drop it, buddy," she commanded.

Like me, Donna had been a soldier. She knew how to give strong voice commands. For a woman with a feminine voice, she could get threatening with it real easy. I had been on the receiving end of it myself a time or two.

The man dropped his shotgun with a clatter. I ordered the other to do the same. Donna and I got out of the truck, our weapons trained on the two men. I slowly bent down, keeping my eyes on my new friend as I grabbed his weapon by the barrel and tossed it into the back of the truck on top of the tarp.

Craig had gotten out, too. Holding his weapon in front of him, he walked over by his mother. Imitating me, he reached down and picked up the shotgun, stepping back with it.

"Start walking," Donna commanded her guy.

He stood there, not moving.

"I said, start walking," she yelled.

I knew that when she used that tone, people listened to her.

I looked at the man standing in front of me and said, "Follow your friend." I briefly moved my weapon back and forth before I stopped the action. *Don't do that, bonehead.*

The man moved off toward the other guy, who was now walking away.

"Move!" I shouted, and he picked up his pace, catching up to his friend.

I fired a shot into the air and the two took off. Running would be kind as they both waddled and jiggled as they moved quickly.

I met up with Craig and Donna, watching the two men jog away. Once they were farther along, I said, "Let's get back in the truck. They might have friends."

We went back to the truck. I turned the key, it roared to life, and I drove up on the median as I headed north.

We continued our drive through the town of Black Creek and on to Highway 29, turning toward Shawano. We passed small groups of people, what seemed to be mostly families, walking along the road. Some were pulling wagons, others had grocery carts full of a variety of clothes, food, and other necessities. A few people were armed, but none of them tried to stop us. Several waved, but we didn't wave back. After the roadblock, we weren't in a neighborly mood.

When we got to Highway 47, just outside of Shawano, I headed toward where I had my run in with the neighborhood welcome wagon the day before.

We were making good time. We'd made it to the Menominee Reservation and hadn't seen anyone for a while. The few houses we could see from the road were quiet. A couple had smoke coming from chimneys, used now, I suspected, as a way to cook.

As we neared the northern boundary of the reservation close to Markton, I started to tense up. This was where I had my conversation with the gang of five. Donna had dozed off, so I said softly to Craig, "I had some trouble near here on my way down. Keep an eye out. We don't need any more."

"Okay, Dad. What kind of trouble?"

"Some kids tried to make me stop the truck. I don't think they wanted directions, either."

"So what happened?"

I explained my run-in with them to Craig and how I had to fire a warning shot at one of them.

He chuckled and said, "I bet they won't try that again."

"Probably not, but they might try something else, so we need to keep watch. I'm not really warm to the idea of using warning shots with anyone anymore, especially after last night."

I must have jinxed us, because there they were, standing alongside the road. Only this time, one of them had a gun.

"That's them," I said.

Donna had awakened. "Trouble?"

"Yeah," I said.

Taking her AR, she pointed it out the window at them. The only noise was the truck as we slowly cruised past them. I was in no mood to play games. My hand held my Glock, ready to use it as necessary, or maybe even use it and save others the trouble these punks would bring.

Donna kept the muzzle of her weapon trained on the group as we went by. Her eyes were like steel as she stayed focused on them.

"Tough man," the one with the gun said as we passed.

Donna pulled the trigger on her AR, sending a round into the ground next to him.

One of the women screamed, and they backed off.

"Fuck you, bitch, you'll get yours," one of the men shouted.

Donna leaned out the window and kept the rifle trained on him as we continued on. I pushed the gas pedal down to increase the speed, and we moved on.

"Nice neighbors," Donna remarked.

"I almost wish they had tried something. I think we'll see them, or others like them, again," I said.

"Should we go back?" Craig asked.

The look on my face must've been priceless.

"You know, to end it," he clarified.

"Maybe we should, son, but not yet." I wanted to be

ready, but I wasn't fully in a kill-or-be-killed mode. But I knew it was coming, so I was a little surprised by Craig's reaction.

We made it the rest of the way through Markton without any problems. I had about half a tank of gas left and maybe ten more gallons in the back of the truck, which was plenty with some to spare to make it home.

As we neared the turn off to the county road that would take us home, I asked Craig to get the radio out of the glove box.

He reached over, grabbed it, and gave it to me.

Turning it on as I drove one-handed, I pushed the button and said, "Hello, Home Base."

There was no response.

Maybe we were still out of range. I set it by my pistol on the dash and kept driving. Turning on the county road, I reached for the radio and called again.

"Hello, Home Base," I said.

There was silence and then, "This is Home Base." It sounded like Nancy.

"Home Base, we are about five miles out."

"Roger," came the reply. Brian must have taught her to be brief on the radio. Good.

***

We relaxed and enjoyed the last miles of the ride as we got closer to home.

Suddenly, a truck dashed out of a dirt road, positioning itself in front of us and stopped.

I slammed on the brakes, throwing Donna forward.

"Dammit," she shouted, stopping herself from crashing into it by putting her hand up quickly on the dashboard.

A man got out of the truck and pointed a rifle at us.

"Grab your weapon," I said. "We have trouble."

I threw the truck into reverse and backed up almost half a football field. I stopped the truck, but kept it running.

We sat there in a standoff, him with his rifle raised and us holding ours ready.

Finally, I turned off the truck, opened my door, and remaining behind it, shouted, "What do you want?"

He shouted back. "We don't want any strangers up here."

"I live up here," I called back. I gripped the Glock tightly, but I kept it out of sight behind the door.

Donna had gotten out her side of the truck and rested her AR on the open truck windowsill. Craig took up a spot behind her, aiming his AR.

"How do I know that?" the man asked.

"I live in Lake View. My home is there," I replied. Then I whispered, "Hold your fire" to Craig and Donna.

"I have him, John, center mass," Donna said softly.

"Who are you?" he shouted.

"John Henry of Lake View."

"I don't know you. I go there all the time!"

"Do you know Carol Jensen?" I asked.

Not budging, he shouted, "Never heard of her! Now git, you don't belong here."

I was starting to get pissed. Who the hell was this jackass to tell me I couldn't go home?

"I'm telling you, I live in Lake View. Carol owns Carol's Diner."

"I know the diner, but I don't know no Carol."

I took a deep breath, my patience at an end, and said, "If you've been there, you've seen her. Tall, brunette, slender."

"Oh, the good lookin' one!"

"Yeah, that's her."

He paused again. "Walk up here slowly."

"Lower your weapon first."

He stood there for a moment as if he was thinking over my request. Then he slowly lowered it, holding it in front of him in what in the army we called a high port.

I stepped away from the door and keep my pistol to my side, but in plain sight. I stepped in front of the truck and looked around, checking the edge of the woods on either side of the road.

I expected Donna and Craig would keep their weapons trained on him.

"What you waiting for?" he asked.

"I'm making sure you're alone," I answered.

"I ain't sayin if I am or ain't," he shouted back.

"Well, you better make sure that if you aren't, they don't shoot. As you can see, I have two more guns here," I said, motioning with my head toward the truck. "This won't end well."

"Ain't nobody gonna shoot unless they have to," he yelled.

Thinking neutral ground was best, I said, "Why don't we meet in the middle?"

"I'm comfortable standing here."

"It would make me more comfortable if you did."

Once again, he stood there as if mulling things over. "Okay," he finally agreed, and slowly walked toward me as I moved toward him.

We got about ten feet apart and we both stopped.

He was older than I was, probably in his late sixties. The stubble of his growing beard looked mostly gray, and his hair was almost all white. Like many locals up here, he wore a flannel shirt—green plaid, and in his case, tucked into a pair of canvas workpants with a wide leather belt. On the belt was a Buck hunting knife. He wore what looked like well-used work boots.

"You gonna let us through?" I asked.

He glared at me. "I said we don't want any strangers up here. With all the power out and things, we can't have that. We have enough of our own troubles. Don't need anybody else's."

"Can't say I completely disagree with you, but as I said, I live in Lake View. I'm taking my son and his mother there."

"So you said, but *I* don't know you."

"I live about three miles down this damn road. I'm going home."

"Kinda irritable, aren't you?" he asked, cocking his head to the side.

"You'd be irritable, too, if some old fart stood in the road and pointed a rifle at you. How the hell am I supposed to feel?"

He ignored my statement. "Where in Lake View do you live, exactly?"

"Off the county highway, about three miles from here. You turn off onto a paved logging road and my cabin is about a mile down."

"You got dogs?"

Infuriated, I said, "What the hell does my having dogs got to do with anything?"

"Just answer the question, sonny."

"Yeah, I have two German shepherds."

He slowly lowered his rifle, grinned, and said, "Yeah, I know who you are. You're that soldier."

"That would be me," I said.

He took his right hand off the rifle and extended it. "Sorry about that. My name's Quint Stepanik."

I walked over and shook his hand. "John Henry, that's my son, Craig, and his mother, Donna."

"You can come out now, Rick," Quint said.

Behind him and to my right, a boy walked out of the woods carrying a deer rifle with a scope. Seemed everyone up here had one.

"That's my grandson, Rick. He lives with me. His dad was in the army, too."

Rick wore a floppy desert boonie hat and what my son called digitals, pants and jacket. He looked all of about fourteen years old. I could tell he was scared, even from the distance we were from one another. He held the rifle like he was comfortable with it, but not comfortable enough to use it against someone.

"Oh?" I asked.

"Yeah, he didn't come home. Rick's mother dropped him off one day and that was the last we saw of her."

"I sorry to hear that. My other son Brian's in the army. He's at my place with his wife, Nancy, and their son, Mike. They have a Great Dane."

Quint shook his head. "Not sure we have much of an army anymore. Heard on the shortwave that Washington was nuked."

"What?" I said, shocked at the news. "Nuked?"

"Right about the time the power went out, it seems."

"Jesus Christ."

"Don't blaspheme, son," Quint said. "It ain't polite."

No one had ever said that to me before. I was embarrassed into silence, but also at a loss for words. That didn't happen often. I could only muster, "I'm sorry."

Quint nodded his head, saying nothing else. Rick had joined us, but he looked nervous.

I acknowledged him, waiting to see if he'd say anything. It was Quint who spoke again.

"Yep, nuked. From what the radio said, it was a bomb on the ground. Big one, too. Seems almost all of the city is gone. No word about the president or anybody else."

"Da—," I caught myself. "Um, wow." I was stunned. All the power gone. What else could happen?

"It's gonna be bad, John," Quint said, breaking into my thoughts. "The dying hasn't even started yet. Once the stores run out of food, the gangs and hungry people will begin killing each other, taking anything they want. That's why I stopped you. They'll find their way out here, looking for food, 'cuz of course farmers and country people have lots of food. I already turned back one group, pushing grocery carts and pulling wagons. I think they went over toward the State Park. I don't want them here, probably nothing but trouble."

"When I was in the army, that's what they told us. Some estimated as much as ninety percent of the population would die from starvation, disease, running out of medicine, or violence. Good thing you turned them away. I suspect we'll have more, but we aren't going to stop them all."

"Anyway, sorry to be the bearer of bad news. You should get on home to your family. I hope you're prepared."

"I am," I said. "Thanks, I guess, and good to meet you. You, too, Rick."

The boy nodded but didn't say a word.

I turned around, went back to the truck, and got in. Donna and Craig were already seated, waiting for me.

"What was that all about?" Donna asked.

"Nothing good. When we get to the cabin, I'll tell everyone." I was lost in my thoughts and at a loss for words. How do you tell your family that their world has ended? That our enemies, whoever they were, had finally pulled it off and stuck a fatal knife into us? The United States of America, a world power, was no more.

The rest of the drive was in silence.

Chapter 6

"The future belongs to those who prepare for it."

—Ralph Waldo Emerson

I saw the entrance to the drive a few hundred yards ahead. I couldn't miss it, as the mailbox post was gone but the post displaying the big red fire marker was still there.

I thought I told him to cut that down.

I turned into the dirt and gravel drive, honked the horn a couple of times, then drove to the cabin.

It looked different as we broke into the clearing. For once, I felt as if I was coming home. More than that, coming to a restful, peace-filled home. The trees were full of leaves this late spring day. Birds flew above us, and all three dogs stood on the porch, tails wagging. All it needed was some deer grazing nearby, rabbits hopping in the yard, and a "V" of Canadian geese flying overhead. It also needed John, Jr. and his kids, my other two grandchildren—Will and Darla.

Brian came out of the house, a cup in his hand. I saw him reach over to *my chair* and pick something up, putting it in his mouth.

Dammit, that's one of my cigars.

He lit it, and then waved at us as we pulled up to the side of the house.

"Hey, Bro," Brian yelled to Craig.

"Hey, Brian," Craig said, getting out of the truck after Donna.

"Hello, Donna," Brian said. "Haven't seen you in a while."

"Hi, Brian, you've grown so big," she said.

Brian was a weight lifter—the formerly chubby but healthy guy had become a "you need custom-made military uniforms because you bulked up" guy.

"Yeah, I work out," he replied, imitating the melody of a song with those words as a refrain. It sounded funny coming from him.

I stood there as all three dogs ran to Craig, jumping around and barking at him. He scruffed their heads, Grady standing in front, so tall that he could almost look Craig directly in the eye. King and Max sat dutifully by, waiting their turn.

"Hey, what the hell am I?" I said, grinning sheepishly. "Nobody is gonna welcome me home? And what the hell are you doing smoking my cigars?"

"Oh, hi, Dad," Brian said in a monotone voice, a big ear-to-ear grin on his face. Such a comedian, that kid.

The front door burst open in a flurry of energy, and out flew a short bolt of motion.

"Grampa!" Mike shouted. He ran into my arms as I squatted down with a few creaks and hugged him.

"Who's this?" he asked, pointing at Craig.

"That's your Uncle Craig," I answered.

Mike stood there, eyeballing Craig. Craig is about six feet tall, large and a bit portly. He had a thick bushy head of brown hair and a rather innocent-looking face. I knew that part of him was becoming deceptive, but he was still rather innocent and naïve. Besides, he was my baby, and as I told him many times, he would suffer that label for as long as I lived.

As I watched Craig and Mike get acquainted, I felt something cold and wet on my hand. Looking down, I saw Max sitting there nudging my hand with his nose, his tail sweeping the grass behind him.

"Oh, so now I get greeted. What do you want?" I said as I stared Max in the eye. I guess King felt like he was going to miss out on some attention because he came over, nudged Max out of the way, and started licking my hand. Grady forgot I existed.

"All right, everyone," I said, taking control of the situation, "let's get to work here. Craig, you get yours and your mom's stuff upstairs into your bedroom. Brian, let's start taking the other stuff to the basement storage room."

"Okay, Dad," both boys answered at once.

"When we get done, we can all sit on the porch and talk. We have a lot to talk about." I guess my tone sent a message to Brian.

He looked at me with curiosity. "Something wrong, Dad?"

"Nothing except the end of the world as we know it," I said. "Let's get this done and we'll talk."

We spent the next hour unloading the truck, putting things away, and then, after Nancy made iced tea and coffee, we all gathered on the porch. As I sat in my chair, I glared at Brian and asked, "Do I have any cigars left?"

"I left you one."

I shook my head in dismay. "There better be more than one, son. I had almost two hundred in that humidor."

"Just kidding, Pops," he said. "They're all there."

"Good." I gave him a not-too-pleasant glare. I went back inside to my office, took one out of the humidor, clipped its end, and went back to the porch. Sitting down, I felt everyone's eyes on me as I lit the cigar.

I leaned forward and began. "We all know about the EMP and what it did. That alone is bad enough. On the drive back, we kinda met a guy."

"Met, hell Dad, he tried to *shoot us*," Craig interrupted.

"Yeah, he did. That's taken care of…"

"Did you shoot him?" Brian asked.

"No," I shook my head. "It was a case of mistaken identity. He thought we weren't from here."

"What does that have to do with anything?" Nancy asked. "You can't be from this area?"

"Just hold on, everyone, and let me finish. His concern was that with the EMP, people not from around here would start finding ways to get into this area. That will bring all kinds of things we don't want, mostly trouble. So, he's taken it upon himself to be his own version of immigration enforcement." I paused as I drew on the cigar, waiting for a question. I was surprised that they kept silent. "Anyway, I'll get back to that. What he told me was that he heard on the shortwave radio that DC had been nuked."

"You gotta be shittin' me," Brian said. "A nuke, how?"

"From what he gathered from the broadcast, it was land-based. He doesn't know who or why or anything like that. But the concern is obvious. We most likely have no working federal government. Even if we do, it'll be a long time before any help comes this way, such help as the government can bring, anyway."

"But…" Brian started.

"Hush, and let me finish. Anyway, the issue is this. Cars aren't working, electricity is out, and that means food is in short supply except for those who are prepared or grow their own. The grocery stores, if they haven't been looted already, will run out of food in a few days. Most people have no more than a week's worth of food available, and many don't even have that. People will get hungry and desperate, and they'll try and take it."

"Tell them what happened back home, Dad," Craig interjected.

All eyes were on me. "We had an incident," I said.

"Incident, my ass," Donna said. "They tried to storm my home and shoot us."

"What?" Brian and Nancy both said at the same time.

"A man came to the house and wanted food," I explained. "I told him no. A while later, he came back with friends and they tried to take it by force, using guns." Looking at Brian, I said, "We stopped them. They won't ever be doing that again."

"Wow," Brian said softly.

Not one to dwell, I said, "So, the situation is this. Hungry people will look for food and they will do anything to get it. The strong will prey on the weak. People with guns will take it from those without. Groups will form, more like gangs, and they will take more. They will do other things, too, mostly because they can."

"The police, the army, they'll stop them," Brian said.

"No, I don't think they will. They won't be any different than the rest of us. They have families to protect, food for them will be limited, and they'll not want to help others. This is our new existence, kids."

"Jesus," Brian said.

"Don't blaspheme," I said, remembering Quint's words to me.

The look Brian gave me told me a lot. I was probably the least likely to say that, and it surprised him.

"So, in time, a lot of people will start dying," I

said. "From hunger, disease, no medicine, or through violence. I read somewhere that as much as ninety percent of the population will die in the first year after something like this happens."

"We're doomed," Nancy said, looking down at the floor planks.

"Dad's prepared," Brian offered, touching her knee.

"How?" she asked, glancing over at me.

"Well, that's the good news, Nancy. I have about a year's worth of food stored downstairs. Some stuff will last even longer. We'll increase the size of the garden and we can grow and can even more. We have 180 acres here with plenty of deer, turkey, rabbits, squirrels, and even bear."

"Squirrels," she said, incredulous.

I smiled just a little. "Yup, squirrels."

"Tastes like chicken," Brian interjected.

Nancy glared at him.

I continued, "I also have plenty of weapons and ammunition, although you never have enough ammunition. Thanks to Donna, we have a large inventory of first aid supplies and other things we may need. The solar panels can power the lights and the pump for the well. We're better off than most. The people around Lake View will help each other out. A few are ex-military and all of us are outdoor types. We'll be able to weather the storm."

"If nothing works, how come we have the two-way radios? They work fine," Nancy said, curious.

"Good question. I made a Faraday cage out of a metal trashcan. It's lined with Styrofoam. Inside it, I put the radios and other electronic stuff. I sealed it shut with aluminum tape so it was shielded from the EMP. So everything that was in it works. We have solar chargers so we can keep them charged. I've got two 500-gallon tanks of gas by the barn, and several bottles of Sta-bil to help preserve it. That will keep the UTV and some of the other tools going until we can find a way to get more from the gas stations or syphon it from the abandoned cars that aren't working anymore."

"So we'll scavenge for more stuff?" Craig asked.

"Yes, we'll scavenge," I confirmed. "Others will, too. It won't last forever, and in time, we probably won't have any left."

"What about other stuff—medicine, those kinds of things?" Nancy asked.

"I know a lot about herbal remedies," Donna answered. "There are a lot of natural things we can use. They may not work as fast or as well, but they'll work."

"I have a small library of books in my office that will help us with finding herbs, edible plants, mushrooms, stuff like that," I said. "I also have a book on making medicine from tree bark and other things, too. We brought Donna's herb seeds along."

"So, we're living in pioneer days again," Nancy said.

I gave her a half-shrug. "Pretty much. We stepped back in time to at least the nineteenth century, maybe earlier. I have an old wood cook stove in the barn. We can move it into the cabin once the propane runs out for the main stove and the camping stove. It'll take getting used to, and I'm sure somebody will burn something."

"Are we gonna die, Grampa?" Mike asked, his eyes showing his worry.

I had forgotten that Mike was there. Nancy grabbed him and held him close until he struggled out of her grasp.

"No, Mike, we aren't gonna die," I said. "I have everything we'll need to survive. It will be hard, but everything will be okay. You just can't play video games anymore."

96

"Can I watch TV?"

I held back a laugh. "No, but I have a laptop and about five hundred DVDs with movies. You can watch those at night, okay?"

"At night?" he asked.

"Yup," I nodded, "'cuz during the day you'll have to help the rest of us around here. We'll even go hunting."

Nancy didn't seem to enjoy the sound of that.

"Sweet," Mike said.

"Fortunately for us, it's May. We can till out the garden, if the tiller works, and I have those heirloom seeds stored downstairs. Those are important, because we can reuse the seeds from them and grow more vegetables. We should be able to plant in another week or so, and in about sixty days we'll start harvesting. Donna, I know you can veggies. I have the canning supplies from before… Um, maybe, you can show Nancy how to do that, and Mike can help when the time comes."

"No problem," Donna said as she looked at Nancy. They shared a smile.

"I have about five cords of wood, but we'll need a lot more. Brian and Craig, you'll have that task. It will be a good workout. If the chain saw and splitter work, so much the better. If not, you'll have to use the saws, axes, and the splitting maul. We'll need to start now so it's good and cured before winter comes."

"But it's May…" Nancy said.

Craig and I laughed, which got us both a dirty look. "You're right. Could be by September we'll have frost, and snow could easily come before Halloween. We need to be ready. Plus, eventually we'll be cooking with the wood and heating the cabin, so we'll need a lot. The less heavy work we have to do come winter, the better."

"Lovely," she groaned.

"We should probably start guard shifts, too, and that won't be easy. We'll need someone by the road and someone behind the cabin all the time. None of the adults should go anywhere without a loaded gun. Speaking of the road, I thought I told you to cut the mailbox down, Brian."

"I did," said Brian.

I cocked my head to the side. "Yeah, but you left the post up with the fire marker on it. I don't want anyone travelling by to know the cabin is here. They can't see us from the road, and the drive will look like any other dirt road going into the woods. With the fire marker, it'll draw attention. So, when we're done, your first job is to cut the post down."

"Yes, sir," he said sheepishly.

"Don't call me sir. I work for a living." That old saying got a grin out of him.

"Okay, any questions?" I asked my family.

Most shook their heads. It'd be a new way of living for Nancy and Mike, but Donna and my boys had roughed it before. We'd be okay.

"Brian, go cut down the post. Craig, let's go see what works in the barn. Brian can join us when he's done."

"Nancy and I can get acquainted," Donna said.

"Sounds like a good plan," I said.

Chapter 7

"The danger we face can only be subdued by preparation and perspiration. We cannot do just one or the other."

—John Henry

Craig and I were in the barn, going through all that we'd need for making firewood. I had the Husqvarna 18" on the floor, along with the chain oil and a gas can waiting for gas and oil. I also had chain saw safety pants. A chain saw injury could be fatal, so safety was a must.

We pulled the tarp off the Craftsman wood splitter. Alongside it was a manual hydraulic splitter that didn't need any gas. I figured we'd all get used to using it, as well as my splitting maul and wedge. Both would give us a good workout. We had to not only get proficient at it, but develop our bodies to the labor they would experience once we ran out of gas. We were pulling the Craftsman out when the radio squawked.

"Hello, Henry Base."

I went over to the bench and picked it up. "This is Henry Base," I replied.

"So, you're back." It was Carol.

"Yup, and back to work."

"I'm coming to you," she said. "We need to talk."

"See you soon," I said, and set the device down.

"Who's that?" Craig asked.

"Carol."

"It will be good to see her again."

"Yeah, she likes you. I don't know why, though," I quipped.

"Dad!"

"Craig!" I mocked.

We laughed and went back to work.

***

Brian had taken the UTV down the road and was cutting down the fire marker post when he heard something.

He looked up and saw an ATV cruising his way. The woman riding it had blonde hair that was blowing in the breeze. *Carol?*

She pulled up next to him. "Brian, what are you doing?"

"Cutting down the post," he said. "Dad doesn't want anyone thinking people live down this road." Disappointed he had forgotten to take it down earlier, he tossed the post into the weed-filled ditch nearby.

"You might want to take that back to the house. People might see it, and the post could be used for something else."

"Good idea. Hadn't thought of that."

"We're all gonna have to change how we think," she said.

"True story. Dad's back. You here to see him?"

"Yeah, I called him on the radio." She took off down

the drive and Brian went to retrieve the pole.

Carol arrived at the barn to find Craig and me mixing the gas and oil.

"Hello, you two," she called.

"Hi, Carol," Craig said.

"So, what brings you out this way?" I asked.

"I got some news about what's going on. Talked to Gary Jones." She walked towards us.

I stopped, brushed my hands together to get the excess dirt off. "You going to tell us about the EMP or the nuke?"

"You heard about the nuke?" she asked, surprised.

"Well, I guess that makes it true, but a guy down the road—Quint Stepanik—told me."

Carol put her hands on her hips. "Older guy, has his grandson living with him?"

"He's the one," I said. "Kinda an odd duck, if you ask me, but a good sort."

"He is eccentric, that's for sure. He forgets a lot of things, too. Came by the diner at least once a week."

I smirked. "Said he didn't know you."

"Oh, he knows me," Carol said, a snicker in her voice. "He just forgets. Usually when it's convenient."

"They nuked DC, huh?"

"So it seems. I can't emotionally get my head around it. Who would do that, John?"

"Russians?" Craig asked.

"Funny, kid," I said. "But possible, I suppose."

"It wasn't a missile," Carol interjected. "From what Sam Karpinski said, it appears to have been a ground-based bomb."

"Yeah, that's what Quint said," I confirmed.

Carol gave me a look. "How does he know?"

I shrugged. "He said he heard it on the shortwave— the BBC, I think."

"I guess it *was* terrorists, then, but who? How in

the hell did they get a nuke big enough to take out Washington without it being detected?" Carol asked.

"Beats me, but it scares the hell out of me. What else is out there that we don't know about?"

"Sam will find out. He has connections all over the world. His ham set is old, all tubes, so it survived the EMP. I'm sure he's reaching out and touching someone right now."

Carol and I laughed at the old reference to a phone system commercial. Ham and our walkie talkies were going to be the only way of communication for some time. We'd probably have to either adapt the old jingle or make up a new one.

"I need to go see Sam, see what all he knows and can find out," I said.

"Yeah, you do. He wondered why you hadn't come seen him sooner," Carol said.

Brian finally showed up. Guess it was a major undertaking to cut that post down. He took it out of the bed of the UTV, brought it into the garage, and set it by the rolls of chicken wire, barbed wire, and scrap wood I had.

"Well, boys, guess it's time to cut some logs and drag them back here," I said. "There are some standing dead trees way in the back, off the trail. Let's start there."

"Now?" Craig asked.

"Yeah, now," I said. "When else? Put the saw and axes into the bed, and let's go."

"I'm driving," Brian said.

"Nope, it's mine," I told him.

"Shit."

"Nope, my rules."

"I'm gonna go up to the cabin and say hi," Carol said.

"Donna is inside. You're not gonna help us cut

wood?" I asked.

She laughed. "Hardly."

She walked toward the cabin and we headed out to do what our ancestors before us had done—make wood.

***

We managed to haul an even dozen oak logs, each almost 15 feet in length. Dragging them back to the barn behind the UTV in a chain of three logs at a time, it was all I could do to not turn it into some kind of amusement ride. The boys would collect the larger branches to add to the firewood pile. The smaller ones were left in a pile off the trail to encourage deer and other animals to have a place to hide out. After dealing with the big logs, we were tired.

As I parked the UTV in the barn and put away the tools, Brian and Craig went to the pump, filled a bucket full of water, and poured it over themselves. They seemed to enjoy the old-fashioned hand pump. I know I had as a kid. The dirt and sweat washed to the ground, but the mud the water created splashed up on their legs. As I went to the barn, I watched them horsing around. "Don't bring those muddy feet in my house."

"Yes, Mother," they both chimed.

"I'll mother you, and I mean it. No mud in the cabin," I shouted.

I stepped into the barn, put the tools away, then walked to the cabin. Donna and Nancy sat on the porch. Mike was somewhere, and the dogs were probably with him, as none of them were on the porch. I slowly made my way up the steps, plopped down in my chair, and let out a *woosh* of air.

"You look tired," Donna said.

"Let me get you some iced tea, FIL," Nancy offered,

and before I could answer she was up and going inside the cabin.

"We cut a lot of wood today, but we'll need a lot more before it gets cold."

"How much?" Donna asked.

"A lot. I figure we probably have two or three full cords from what we cut today."

"How much more do you think we'll need?" she asked.

"I think at least ten. If we have too much, that's okay. Except during the peak of the winter, making wood is going to be a constant."

Nancy came out with the tea as Brian and Craig made their way to the porch.

"Where's ours?" Brian asked.

"Inside, staying fresh for you," Nancy answered.

"Bring me some, too," Craig said, and sat down on the steps.

Brian stared at him for a few seconds, then went inside.

"I'm gonna sleep like a rock. Dad worked us to death," Craig gasped.

"Today is just the beginning, son. We still have to cut it, split, and stack it. Then get more. Plus, the garden needs work, as well as several other things that need doing."

"What other things?" Nancy asked. "Anything I can do to help."

"We can talk about it at dinner. I'm making a list. I'm sure everyone can find things to add to it. Speaking of, what's for dinner?" I asked Nancy.

"We're using all the meat from the freezer upstairs, and because of that, we're having venison meatloaf."

I nodded. "Sounds good."

"I never had it before," Nancy said. "Donna told me how to make it."

"I believe, before all of this is over, we'll be eating a lot of things you've never had before."

"Like squirrels," Craig piped.

Nancy gave him the look.

"We should think about a smokehouse, too," I suggested. "We can't freeze everything, and if the solar panels go down, there's no replacements."

"Lovely, more work," Craig said as he fell onto his back, spreading his arms across the porch.

Brian came out and handed him a glass of iced tea. "What's more work?"

"We'll talk about it at dinner," everyone answered.

"Dad, Carol said there was a National Guard unit not far from here. I should at least check in," Brian said.

"It's in Antigo, about a half hour away or so in the olden days."

"Can you take me there?"

"Yeah, we'll go tomorrow," I said. "What are you going to do if they keep you there?"

"I have nine more days, we can wait a few more."

"They wouldn't dare," Nancy said, but her tone was none too friendly.

"We'll worry about that if and when it happens," Brian said. "I doubt they will, but…"

***

For the next few days, we spent our time chopping wood, increasing the size of the garden, and preparing the cabin. The boys and I started on a smokehouse. It wasn't too hard to built it together. We had everything but the roof shingles done, so pulling an old wood stove I had in the barn and figuring out how to direct the smoke from it into the smoker was all we had left to do. I had shingles somewhere in the barn, and plenty of nails as I kept extras for repair of the cabin roof. Storms could be brutal up in the north woods, and I never knew when I'd have to replace shingles.

The ladies were getting along like old friends. Any difficulties anyone thought might've happened between Donna and Nancy hadn't. It was never an issue. Occasionally, there was a debate over who was going to do what in the kitchen, but that worked itself out as Nancy and Donna had different skills and strengths. And the boys found out they were good at doing dishes, whether Craig and Brian agreed or not.

About a week after we had returned home I found Craig out by the barn, sitting on a hunk of wood we hadn't split yet. His AR was leaning against him and his XD was on his hip. I was glad he took it everywhere with him, though I still wished he didn't have to.

Walking over to him, I said, "Quiet night."

"I'm starting to like the quiet," he answered.

"How are you doing?"

"I'm okay. Something up?"

"No. I was just thinking about you and the fight back at the house in Appleton."

"Sometimes I do, too," he said, looking down, not meeting my eyes.

"You did good, son."

"Oh, I know that, Dad. It's just…"

"Just what?"

He looked up at me. "It's just that…it doesn't bother me. I mean, I'm sorry I had to shoot them and all, but what I did doesn't seem to matter to me. That's what's bothering me."

"I'm confused." I understood what he meant, but I wanted my son to elaborate, to work out his own feelings over taking someone's life.

"It's just that, shouldn't I be more upset than what

I am? I broke through the window screen and started shooting. Then Mom did. I was mad, angry at the thought of them hurting you or her. I shot to kill them. I wasn't trying to scare them. I shot to kill."

"Well, son, I was taught that if you're going to shoot someone you had better shoot to kill. Shooting to wound people only happens in the movies."

"Well," he chuckled dryly, "it felt like a movie, or one of the video games I play—I mean, *used* to play—that you're always ragging on me over. It was so surreal."

I didn't know what to say, so I kept silent.

"So, anyways, it worries me that it doesn't bother me. Sometimes I sit out here wondering if I'm okay or if something is wrong with me."

"People have been defending themselves against evil forever. Sadly, mankind is inherently evil, or at least violent. Deep down inside all of us is that vicious gene that makes us that way. It's how mankind has survived. Over time, we became civilized and stopped because we got better at killing. So good that we learned how to destroy all of civilization with a single weapon."

"Kinda like now."

I nodded. "Yeah, kinda like now. I think we've stepped into more violent days and some of us will be up to the challenge. Some of us won't. Those who won't are already dead or will be. They'll be the victims. Those that are ready, well, some will die, but many more will survive. Eventually, civilization will return, and we'll have to be tame again."

"Tame. I guess we have gone wild."

"Some will be more wild than others. Those are the dangerous ones. That's why we have to be vigilant and keep an eye open for anything that doesn't seem right. We can't trust anyone, and sometimes, that even means people we know."

"I'm up to it," Craig said, "but it isn't going to be easy."

"I know you are, son."

Craig stood up, and taking a few steps, walked toward me. He gave me a hug and I hugged him back tight.

Picking up his AR, he turned and said, "I'm ready to go in now."

"I think I'll join you."

Together we walked as father and son to the cabin, carrying our guns to protect our family.

***

I drove over to see Sam the next day. I walked up to the kitchen door—nobody uses front doors up north—and banged on it. No one answered, but I could hear a man's voice talking inside. Sam must be on the radio.

I let myself in, went through the kitchen and headed for the bedrooms in the back where I knew Sam had his ham set up. I guess he saw or heard me come in, because he held his hand up in a stop motion as he signed off.

"K9SK out," I heard him say in the microphone. He swiveled the chair he was sitting in and faced me.

"So, what do we know, Sam?" I asked.

"Hi Sam, how are you?" he said. "I'm fine, John, and how are you doing?"

"Sorry, that was rude of me," I said. "I know you navy guys are sensitive about manners and stuff."

"You should be," he said, "and the news isn't good. DC was nuked, ground-based, so that means it was terrorists."

"I knew that already," I said.

His look was a cross between *let me finish* and *don't interrupt me.*

"When we retaliated against North Korea—that's who apparently sent the EMP—the Chinese started getting itchy feet. Russia decided that with the Chinese focusing on us and the Norks, that they'd sneak in the back door. So, they're now shooting at each other."

I whistled in exasperation.

Sam continued, "The Middle East blew up. I guess with us out of the picture, they all decided it was a good time to attack Israel. Not sure what's going on there, but the Israelis seem to be holding their own. Europe is already feeling the effects economically and have, for the most part, closed their borders, the European Union be damned. The Brits seem to be the only ones not overly affected, but it doesn't seem like they can do much more than take care of themselves. They said they'd help us, and they'll have to if for no other reason than to send food, but I don't know how much we can help them. In short, the world's gone to shit, and for now anyway, we're on our own."

"Well, you're just a fountain of good news," I said. "Heard anything from around the country?"

"Not much. Bits and pieces here and there. People are still pretty shook up, and as always, fingers are being pointed in both directions."

"Jesus," I said.

There was an old straight back chair against the wall to my left and I stepped over to it and sat down. Sam and I sat in silence for a moment, nothing much to be said and everything needing to be asked.

"So now what?" I asked. I meant it rhetorically, but he answered me anyway.

"As long as I can get power and I have the right tubes for the radio, I'll keep talking and see what I can find out. So far, I haven't had to use code," he gestured to the antique Morse code key sitting on the table next to his radio, "but I may have to. I'm not as good as I used to be at it."

"You need anything, Sam?"

"I'm good for now. I'll come out if I do."

"Get a gun, Sam. Trouble is already starting," I said.

"Oh, I've got that covered." He reached under the table and came up with an old GI webbed belt. Attached to it was a leather holster with a flap. I could see the handle of what looked like a 1911 model .45 in the holster. "I have this. It will stop a truck."

"You may need to, although not many of those are working right now." I stood up and took the few steps over to him, extending my hand.

We shook, and as I turned to leave, he said, "Take care of yourself, John."

"You too, Sam."

I left through the door I had come in and headed home.

***

The next morning, I was in my usual spot on the porch, Max and King slept on the floor alongside me. I held my morning coffee and took in the sounds of nature. That was the reason why I loved it here so much. The cool morning, the only sounds from nature. And even though I'd most likely never hear road sounds from the highway or an occasional passing plane, I enjoyed the solitude. With the increase in population here at the cabin, morning would become my rejuvenation time.

Brian and I had a lot to do today. But until he woke up, wandered outside, and said he was ready, I was going to sit and enjoy my solitude. Our family meeting last night had been emotional, and I was still drained from it. I didn't really know if they all still thought I was paranoid or if they were processing the truth of the reality of all of this. It was the trip to the basement that

110

I think sunk home with them and tipped their opinion.

"Come with me, all of you," I said.

Standing up from the table, I headed out of the kitchen and into the hall, then down the stairs to the basement. I heard chairs scraping on the floor and the shuffling of feet as they moved to join me.

I had grabbed my multi-fuel lantern from the table at the top of the stairs. It did a great job lighting up any room. Hearing them step down the stairs, I saw beams from the flashlights. We would have plenty of light to see what I needed to show them.

Everyone assembled in front of me as I opened the double doors leading into the separate storage area. I set my lantern on a small table and turned to face them.

"This is what I have stored for us. There's enough food here for a year. I have a wide variety of freeze-dried meals and other stuff like meat, butter, milk, coffee, vegetables, potatoes, fruit, and so on. There are quite a few pounds of a variety of beans and rice. I have oatmeal, grits, cornmeal, and flour, all sealed in Mylar bags."

"That's a lot, Dad," Craig remarked.

"I know some of you thought I was nuts for mentioning this in my emails to you. There are also solar powered battery chargers, rechargeable batteries, paracord, knives, salt, pepper, and other spices, several bags of dryer lint…"

"Dryer lint?" Nancy asked.

"Yes, it's great to use for starting fires. I have several magnesium fire starters for starting fires, too."

"I would've never thought of that," she said.

"There are several first aid kits, along with suture kits, lots of sutures, bandages, antibiotics, anti-diarrheal pills, pain killers, dental hygiene stuff, dish soap, bar soap, and so on. I have several cases of toilet paper."

"Figures," Brian said.

"Yeah, be sarcastic, Mister. Wait til you have to use leaves or a bucket of water with a rag."

"Never mind," he said.

"Thought so," I replied. "Over here, we have weapons, ammunition, cleaning kits, lubricants, and reloading equipment for 9mm and .223."

"This is impressive, John. Is there anything you didn't think of?" Donna asked.

"Yeah, tons of stuff, actually. I haven't mentioned everything because there's a lot here. I tried to think of what I would miss the most, and then wrote it down. Eventually, I bought it or made it. I used the basic rule of one is none, two is one, and three is two. That way, if something breaks or wears out, we have a spare. There are two hand crank AM/FM/shortwave radios here, six walkie talkies, a laptop, and a few other things I kept in the Faraday cage."

"What's a Faraday cage again?" Nancy asked.

I explained it to her.

"I don't think anyone is getting on the internet, Dad, so why the laptop?" Craig asked.

"Good question. I have several USB memory sticks with manuals and instruction books. I also downloaded and saved a lot of videos that show how to do things."

"What kind of things?" Craig asked.

"Everything from building a smokehouse,

which I looked at before we built ours, to instructions on fixing the solar panels, snares, traps, and so on. I also have a small library upstairs with all kinds of information, from cooking on a wood stove to recipes, wood crafts, and so on."

"So, we have everything then," Donna interjected.

"Not really, Donna. I guarantee we'll need something I don't have here. We'll either have to do without it, make it, or scavenge it."

The time spent in the basement was well worth it. Everyone knew what we had or where to get information to do something that needed to bc done. It was still awkward having to carry a weapon around, and that created quite a discussion.

"As I've said several times, we all need to have a weapon with us every time we leave the cabin, and always within arm's reach. I have enough for all of us, and with the weapons Craig and Donna brought, we're well set."

"I don't understand why we have to have a gun," Nancy said.

"Well, the situation is bad and is going to get worse. Right now, the grocery stores are probably empty and nothing new is being delivered. We ran into an issue over food in Appleton, and four people ended up getting killed when they demanded we give them food at gun point. As people get hungrier, they'll get desperate. They will steal from others any way they possibly can, even kill for it."

"I can't imagine that," she said. "I'm sure help will arrive from somewhere, the

government maybe."

"Let me make it real simple for you, Nancy. If Mike was starving, would you do anything necessary to get food for him? Would you steal it, take it by force, even kill to take care of him, if eating meant life or death for him?"

"Well of course, but..."

"But nothing. We all know you would, and anyone else would, too. We can't give away what we have or we'll run out fast as more and more people demand food. We have to defend what we have."

"It can't get that bad out here, can it? It hasn't been that long," she said.

"Consider this: as food runs out in the cities and bigger towns, people are going to start migrating to where they think food is. They will head out to the country where the farms are because, after all, farmers grow food. They will ask for, steal, and kill for it as they get more and more desperate. Then you have the bands and gangs that will form up for the same purpose."

"I hadn't thought of it that way. I understand; it's just hard to fathom. But I get it, Fil."

"I remember from the training I had in the army that as many as ninety percent of the population could die from an event like we are experiencing. They will die from hunger, disease, lack of medicine, and violence. Add to that, we no longer have a government because DC was nuked. While that ninety percent is dying, they will do whatever they have to in order to survive. That means we need guns and we need to be prepared to use them.

After that, the mood in the room became somber.

Everyone knew it. I had made the statement before. With everything sinking in, so had reality. In this case, reality was scary.

Brian and Craig interrupted my quiet time as they stumbled out onto the porch. Brian was wearing regular jeans for a change, not those designer ones he usually had on. A long sleeve black t-shirt with ARMY across the chest in yellow letters made his loyalty clear.

Craig was barefoot, wearing gym shorts and a baggy t-shirt with some game character on it. Added to both of their ensembles was a holstered 9mm and an AR in their hand.

"Morning," they both mumbled.

Not wanting to waste an opportunity to tease them, I said overly cheerful, "Good morning, you two, and what a fine day it is."

My words were followed by Max and King rising up, tails wagging, and nuzzling at the boys.

They sat down quietly and greeted the persistent dogs. Neither of the dogs seemed to care that the boys were silent. I watched them, wishing reality was different.

"So when do we leave?" Brian asked.

"As soon as you're fully awake. No sleeping on the trip. We have no idea what, if anything, we will run into on the drive over."

"Okay," Brian said, his voice still tired.

I had told them to get up early, and while they didn't like it, they knew sleeping in was no longer a luxury.

"Craig, you get to work here today. I need you to start building a listening post near the front drive."

Nodding his head, he asked, "Why there?"

"I want to know what's coming down the road. Build it far enough back so it can't be seen easily, but also close enough so you can see the road fairly well."

"You want a hole in the ground?" he asked.

"No, make a bunker of some kind. Take the chain saw and cut some pines to use like a cabin structure. Open in the front but the top and sides, including the back, closed in. Obviously, put a doorway in the back, too."

"Okay."

"Make it big enough for two people," I added.

"What's for breakfast?" he asked, changing the subject.

I cocked my head to the side. "What did you make?"

"I get it. I'm making pancakes. Mike will like that."

"Use the mix. It only needs water. Brian and I will take some apples with us. I want to get an early start and don't feel like waiting around. So, get your stuff together, Brian. We're leaving."

I stood up, grabbed my AR, and headed toward the truck.

I could hear the two of them whispering about something, but I figured they were bitching and I didn't need to stop that.

I heard Brian get up and troop down the stairs behind me. We both got in the truck without speaking, and I headed toward Antigo. Today would prove interesting.

Chapter 8

"If you are afraid of the wolves, stay out of the forest."

—Russian Proverb

We were completely unbothered all the way to Antigo. I was concerned because Highway 64, the quickest way to get there, is a major east-west route. We saw people, many in their yards. Most waved. That is how it is up here. A few cars were stopped alongside the road. They grew in numbers the closer we got to Antigo.

We arrived in Antigo, turned north on 45, and went the short distance to the armory. Between our turn and the armory were a few fast food places and a convenience store. I noticed the windows were broken and the insides of the buildings looked like they'd been hit by a storm. I realized people had decided to loot anywhere they could.

Trash was everywhere, as were vehicles, stopped when the EMP hit. Many cars had their hoods open, clearly the owners had tried to figure out what was wrong.

Nine days had passed since the EMP hit and already I could see evidence of society breaking down. Store windows broken, doors hanging on hinges, and people staring at us from the shadows, no longer trusting anyone. It was a sad state for a once-friendly community.

The armory was easy to find. The one-story light red building had a tank sitting in front of it.

I pulled into the parking lot. About half of it was blocked off with uncoiled rows of concertina wire, behind which were two armored up HMMWVs, each with an M2 .50 caliber machine gun mounted on top. The Ma Deuce. A couple of guard soldiers stood nearby. They watched us closely as I stopped the truck, turned it off, and opened my door.

Brian opened his door, and we sat there for a minute.

"Should we get out with our weapons, Dad?" he asked.

"I'm wondering the same thing." I was wearing a tactical vest, my Glock in the holster in the front, ammo pouches filled with magazines, my Ka-bar knife in a scabbard on my belt.

Brian was dressed the same way. It was the closest thing to a uniform either of us had.

As I exited my truck, one of the soldiers mounted the HMMWV and stepped up into the cupola by the M2. He rested his arms on it and stared intensely at us. The other man, his M4 in a sling across his body, put his hands on the weapon and watched as Brian and I made our way toward them.

"Stop right there, sir, and state your business," the soldier on the ground said.

"I'm John Henry from Lake View and this is my son, Chief Warrant Officer 2, Brian Henry," I answered.

"Please keep your hands where we can see them, sir," the man said. He walked slowly toward us, watching us both closely.

As he approached, I noticed his rank on the front of his ACUs.

"We're here to see your Commander Specialist," I said.

He stopped, eyeing us up and down. He was young, but they were all young to me now.

"I'm CW2 Henry," Brian said, breaking the silence. "I'm regular army and was home on leave when all of this started. I'd like to see your CO before my leave ends."

"You have any identification, sir?" the soldier asked.

"In my wallet," Brian said. He slowly moved his hand toward his back pocket and grabbed his wallet. Opening it, he took out his ID card and started to hand it to the soldier.

"Just set it on the ground in front of you and step away slowly," the soldier ordered.

I smiled. Some things never changed in the army, and this guy was going by the book.

Brian did as he was instructed.

The soldier came forward, stooped down, and without taking his eyes off of us, picked up the card.

I wouldn't try anything with a .50 caliber machine gun pointing at me.

Glancing at it, and seeing Brian was the person on the card, he noticeably relaxed. Handing the card to Brian, he said, "Here you are, Mr. Henry. If you'll follow me, I'll take you to see Captain Wolfe."

***

Craig finished breakfast with Mike, and typical of young men, put the dirty dishes in the sink, leaving them there to wash themselves.

"What're you gonna do, Uncle Craig?" Mike asked.

"I have to start building something out by the road. You want to help me?" Craig said.

"I should ask Mom first, but she's sleeping."

"Okay. If she says it's okay, come on out and help me."

Craig left the cabin, went into the barn, grabbed the tools he thought he'd need and put them in the UTV. Then, started out toward the road. Stopping the UTV suddenly, he ran into the house, grabbed his AR and XD.

Dad would kick my ass if he knew I hadn't taken these with me.

He headed out again.

***

Mike stood in the kitchen, looking out the window toward the meadow behind the cabin. He liked it here. He and the dogs could run and get dirty.

Mom doesn't like that too much, but it's fun.

Grampa and Dad had taught him to shoot. As he was thinking of target practice, it was then that he saw *his* rifle leaning against the wall by the back kitchen door.

On the floor next to the butt of the rifle was a box of .22 ammo. Mike sat there staring at the gun, looking out the window, and then staring at the gun again.

His curiosity got the best of him and he went over and picked it up, feeling the weight of it in his hands. He was already used to it as he, Dad, and Grampa had shot it many times. The smell of the gun oil was as familiar to him as everything else in the cabin was becoming.

Finally, he gave in and grabbed the box of ammo. A minute later, Mike was running across the field, heading toward the tree line.

***

Craig stopped the UTV near the end of the drive. It was hidden from the road, but he had a reasonable view of anything approaching from either direction. Getting the chainsaw and shovel out of the back of the UTV, he went to work clearing an area for the observation post and bunker.

Scraping an area about six feet long and four feet deep with the shovel, Craig envisioned the shape he wanted to have. The trees were a mix of pines, oak, maple, and birch. Putting the shovel down, he went to the road to see how it might look from there.

Bang!

Craig looked toward the cabin where the sound had come from.

Bang!

Oh, shit.

Jumping into the UTV, he raced toward the cabin.

Over the whine of the engine he heard it again.

Bang!

Pushing the accelerator harder, Craig sped across the yard toward the field behind the cabin. In front of him, he saw Nancy running into the tall grass. He skidded

to a stop next to her and shouted, "Get in!"

Nancy hopped in and almost dropped the shotgun she was carrying.

"It's Mike," she yelled.

Craig slammed his foot down on the accelerator and took off across the field.

Bang! Another shot sounded.

Craig saw Mike ahead about five yards and pointed toward him. "There he is," he shouted.

As they got closer, Craig slowed down.

Mike stood still there, his face a mask of fear, three

dogs sitting around him as they watched the UTV approach.

"I was just shooting," Mike hollered, a quaking in his voice as he seemed on the verge of tears.

"Dammit, Mike," Nancy yelled. "You know you aren't supposed to have that gun without an adult with you."

"I'm sorry," he muttered, his lip quivering.

"Give me that gun and get in this vehicle," Nancy said. "You scared the hell out of us."

"I'm sorry," Mike said and began to cry. He climbed into the back seat.

Craig took the .22 from Nancy and laid it in the bed of the UTV. He faced the dogs. "Nice work, you were supposed to tell us he left."

Grady began to wag his tail. Max and King moved their heads from side to side, showing the curious sides of German shepherds.

"Isn't gonna work, guys, now *go home,*" Craig said.

The dogs hopped into the bed of the UTV.

"Down, *out,*" Craig said, pointing to the ground.

The three dogs hopped out and looked at him with anticipation.

Craig pointed toward the cabin and commanded, "Go home!"

The dogs glanced at one another and sat down.

Pointing again, he shouted, *"Go home!"*

All three dogs got up and ran toward the cabin.

Craig got into the UTV, started it up, and making a wide U-turn, headed to the cabin.

***

We followed the specialist across the parking lot and into the front door of the armory. A field table was set up in the hall, a soldier sat by it talking with a tall, Native American man in uniform.

I smiled when I saw a TA-312 field phone on the tabletop, a memory surfaced using one during my time in the service.

Glad to see they still use those.

The standing soldier turned to face us as we walked inside.

I immediately checked his rank—it's what soldiers do—and noticed the three stripes over three rockers with a diamond in the middle. He was the first sergeant.

"Who are these civilians?" the first sergeant asked firmly.

"They are Mr. and Mr. Henry, Top," the soldier escorting us replied.

"Specialist Johnson, don't call me Top. Why are you bringing civilians in here?"

"Excuse me, First Sergeant," Brian interrupted. "I'm CW2 Henry, Regular Army from Fort Carson. This is my dad. He drove me here."

"Forgive the question, sir, but why is the Regular Army here? And why aren't you in uniform?"

"Fair enough, First Sergeant," Brian said. "I was home on leave and the *situation* stranded me. I'd like to see the CO if they are available."

"Chief, you look familiar. Do I know you from somewhere?"

I saw Brian's gaze wander around the first sergeant's uniform, noticing his name tape and then the combat patch on his right shoulder. "I see you were 10th Mountain, First Sergeant Rahn. When were you there?"

Understanding Brian meant Iraq, the first sergeant replied, "In 2006 and 2007. Stayed longer because of the surge."

"I was there then, too," Brian said, "but I was a specialist myself then. I was with the 2nd of the 14th."

"I'll be damned," Rahn replied. "So was I. A Company."

Brian smiled. "I was in Battalion S2."

"I remember you," said Rahn. "You were the weight lifter, the guy who always volunteered to go outside the wire. Got blown up by an IED twice, right?"

He laughed. "That would be me," Brian said, grinning ear-to-ear. "Right of the Line and Climb to Glory."

"Jeezus, small world." Rahn extended his hand.

Brian took it and the two men shook for a moment, shared a knowing look, then stepped back.

"Let me see if Captain Wolfe is in," said Rahn.

He turned and walked down the hall, the squeak of his boots echoing as he turned down another hall and out of sight.

I looked at Brian. "Blown up twice? We need to talk."

"Later, Dad," he answered, his mischievous grin prominent on his face.

A squeak of boots on tile announced the return of Rahn before we saw him. "He'll see you two. Johnson, don't you have guard duty…outside?"

"Yes, First Sergeant," Johnson said. He turned, making a hasty exit from the building.

"Follow me," Rahn said.

Brian and I trooped behind him. As we turned the corner, I let out a slight chuckle.

"Why are you laughing?" Brian whispered from the corner of his mouth.

"We're in step," I replied.

Brian glanced down at our feet, seeing that we were indeed in perfect step—left-right-left—as we moved down the hall. "Soldiers," he whispered.

"Hooah," I said under my breath.

Brian's guffaw got an over the shoulder raised

eyebrow look from Rahn.

Stopping in front of the commander's office, First Sergeant Rahn knocked on the door jam. "Captain Wolfe, I have Mr. Henry and CW2 Henry here."

"Come in, gentlemen," Captain Wolfe said.

Captain Elias Wolfe was a young-looking infantry officer. He stood about six feet tall. He had tight curly brown hair and an infectious smile. His ACUs, or army combat uniform, looked pressed, almost starched.

Brian, ever the soldier, marched into the office, stood in front of Wolfe's desk and saluted. "Sir, CW2 Henry reporting."

Wolfe returned his salute as I walked into the room. "I'm John Henry, Captain. Sorry if I don't salute, but I retired as an E8 and gave it up."

"No problem, Mr. Henry. The way things are, I hope to live long enough to retire." Then, putting his attention on Brian, he said, "Welcome, too, Mr. Henry. How can I be of assistance?"

"Well, sir," Brian began, "I was home on leave from Fort Carson when all of this happened. I can't get back to my unit and my leave ends next week. I thought I would report here and you could decide what to do."

"Well, Chief, I have no operational or even legal control of any regular army personnel. I can't bring you onto my roles; I can barely care for the few I have left."

"Few left, sir?" Brian asked.

"Most of my unit disappeared after we got word about DC, and then the looting and shit here began. I suspect they're caring for their families, and in that we haven't been called up, they really have no obligation to be here. I doubt they'd come in anyway. All I have are my unmarried soldiers and a few others that are duty bound, like First Sergeant Rahn here."

"Any suggestions on what I could do, sir?" Brian asked.

"Well, not much I'm afraid."

"I have an idea," Brian said, "if you're open to it."

"What's that?"

"Could you write a memo saying I reported here, and that under the circumstances, you could not provide me a billet? That way, when things get back to normal and I rejoin my unit, I won't be AWOL."

"I'll have the clerk write that up, sir," First Sergeant Rahn said. "I'll have it for you directly, and the chief and his father can go back home." Without waiting for a reply, Rahn turned to walk out.

"First Sergeant," Brian said.

Rahn turned around.

Brian handed him a piece of paper and his ID card. "Here's my ID and leave form. The clerk can get everything he needs."

"Thank you, Chief," Rahn said, then quickly exited the room.

"Where is home, Mr. Henry?" Wolfe asked.

"It's back in…" Brian and I had both spoke at the same time.

"It's over in Lake View, Captain," I continued. "My truck is old and wasn't affected by the EMP, so we were able to drive here."

"Fortunately, most of our vehicles were hardened and aren't affected, either," Captain Wolfe said. "We were starting to stock up for a deployment in the fall, so I have about six years' worth of MREs for the soldiers I do have. I also have enough ammo for a small army."

"We're pretty well set up, too. However, I'm always looking for more. Can you spare anything?" I asked.

"At present, I can't do that. Perhaps in the future, but right now, no. I'm sorry."

"Not a problem, Captain."

First Sergeant Rahn came back into the office holding the memo in his hand. "All ready for your signature, sir," he said, handing the paper to Captain Wolfe.

Wolfe glanced at it, signed the memo, and handed it to Brian. "Hopefully this works."

"Thank you, sir," Brian replied.

"By the way, how did you hear about DC?" Wolfe asked.

"A friend of mine is a ham operator. He picked it up from other operators that are still operating. Where exactly, I couldn't say," I said.

"His radio wasn't fried by the EMP?" Wolfe asked.

"He's old school, Captain. His set up is all tubes."

"Interesting," Wolfe answered. "Anything else I can do for you?"

"No, sir, that about covers it," Brian answered.

"If you would, leave an address with the first sergeant in case I need you for anything. Unless your ham friend can contact us and we can set up radio coms. The first sergeant will give you the frequency and call sign. I'm expecting the State Adjutant General or FEMA to eventually show up and help us out. Not much I can do now without orders."

"I understand, sir," Brian said.

"I'll talk to my friend, Captain," I added.

Realizing he was done with us, Brian saluted.

Wolfe returned his salute, and we left.

Walking down the hall, Rahn got close to us and said softly, "Wolfe can be a bit of a dick. I can give you some stuff, maybe some toys that will come in handy, if you'd like."

"That would be great, First Sergeant," I said.

"You can call me Chris."

I nodded. "Ok, Chris, I'm John."

He returned my nod and we continued down the hall, past the front desk, and outside. As we walked toward the parking lot and the cantonment area behind the armory, Rahn said, "Sometimes the captain has an inflated view of himself. I think right now he sees himself as saving everyone around here from this mess we have."

"I know the type," I replied.

"How are you set for ammo and weapons?" Rahn asked.

"I can always use more. No such thing as enough," I said before Brian could say anything I didn't want him to.

"How about a couple cases of 5.56 and a SAW?" he asked, with a grin one could only describe as wicked. "I can throw in a linker set, too."

"Hell yeah," I replied.

A SAW, or Squad Automatic Weapon, was a 5.56 caliber light machine gun. It was belt fed with linked ammo, typically from a bag or box hanging underneath it. The linker set allowed us to create linked ammo that the SAW could fire.

"You can do that without getting yourself into trouble?" I asked.

"Wolfe only knows what I tell him as far as ammo or equipment is concerned. If he figures it out, I can tell him one of our missing 100 plus troops probably took it. Or make it a combat loss."

"You have that many missing?" Brian asked.

"We had 174 on the rolls when this hit. Only 43 have shown up, and I suspect half of them will grow feet and leave. We have no way of reaching the rest of them."

"Jesus," I whistled.

"Well, it is the National Guard. We don't have the same control over them as a regular unit would. At least, not until we're called up or deployed."

"Damn," was all I said.

We entered the back lot and Rahn said, "Bring your truck in through the gate. Meet me at that Conex over there." He pointed at a group of long OD colored shipping containers surrounded by uncoiled barbed wire.

"Will do," I said.

I drove up and stopped next to where Rahn was standing. I got out of the truck and joined him.

"I sent the guards away. No sense in letting them in on this," he said.

He opened the door of the Conex, and I saw stacks of crated ammunition alongside each of the outside walls, with a path made down the middle. "You can have four full cases, plus a case of linked ammo."

I was stunned. There were six cans of ammo in a case, and each can had 420 rounds. He had just given us over 12,000 rounds of ammo. "Thank you," I said. It was all I could manage.

Being the greedy type, I collected myself and asked, "Anything else you can spare?"

"How about a couple boxes of loose links for the 5.56 and a box of M67s?" he asked.

"Sweet Jesus, are you serious?" I replied. The M67 was a hand grenade. They come thirty to a box.

"Yeah. Out there in the bush, you might need them. You know, for fishing or something," he said, laughing out loud. He walked toward the back of the Conex and grabbed a box from a stack of what looked like twenty or more similar boxes.

"Yeah, we could use them for fishing," I answered with a laugh.

We added those to the pile he'd already given us and then he said, "Wait here."

He walked toward the armory and went in through a metal door in the back. A few minutes later, he came back out with a bundle in his arms. As he got closer, I saw it was an OD army blanket wrapped around something. He went to the truck, opened the driver's door, and slid the bundle behind the seat.

"What's that?" I asked.

"Your SAW," he said stoically, and then went around to the other side of the truck.

We loaded everything up into the bed of the truck. I wanted to leave before Rahn changed his mind, or worse, Wolfe showed up.

"Why are you doing this, First Sergeant?" Brian asked, his curiosity getting the better of him.

"Well, Chief, it's like this," Rahn said. "As I said, the captain's a bit of a dick. He can't make a decision. He seems to be waiting for the cavalry to show up and rescue us. On the other hand, he's chomping at the bit to save the world and be a hero. Without orders from, as he puts it, higher headquarters, we're just sitting here guarding what we have. Half, if not most, of these kids who are here now will go home soon—wherever home is. Back to parents, most likely. I don't see any of this," he paused and waved his arms around, "getting better. If anything, it's going to get worse, worse than we can imagine."

"How so?" I asked.

"The looting we've seen is just the tip of the iceberg. They'll start killing for food soon, and some probably already have. Then other things, bad things, are going to happen because no one is there to stop them, except people like us—people with guns who have the will to use them."

"Hmm," Brian said.

Rahn shrugged. "Besides, I see it as an investment."

"An investment?" Brian asked.

"Yes, sir. An investment. I may need to bug out myself, and I have no real family nearby. So, I'm gonna need a place to go if that happens. You seem like good people, and you and I are Mountaineers. That means something."

"I understand, First Sergeant," Brian said.

"I think you do, but I don't think any of us really understands how bad this is going to get."

"Thank you again, Chris," I said and got into the truck.

"Yes, thank you, First Sergeant," Brian added.

"Stay in touch. We may need each other. Climb to Glory, Chief."

"Climb to Glory, First Sergeant."

I started up the truck and drove out of the cantonment area and back on the road. We needed to get out of there pronto.

***

Craig sat on the front porch listening to Nancy yell at Mike. Yell was a bit of an understatement. She was mad, or as Brian would say, she was ABW mad. The shouting was loud. Craig cringed at the strength of Nancy's voice and the anger she directed at Mike. Donna wisely stayed in her room, most likely reading or pretending to read. He tried not to listen, but it was impossible. Suddenly, the was silence.

The front screen door of the cabin flew outward on its hinges, smacking into the wall as it opened fully, then bounced back. Max, King, and Grady jumped up and ran into the yard. They knew it wasn't safe. Nancy came out on the porch and she was huffing mad.

"Dammit," she shouted. "Dammit, dammit, *dammit!*"

Craig started to get up to leave. He, too, knew it wasn't safe. "I should get back to work," he said.

"Dammit, dammit, dammit," Nancy said again, only this time she wasn't shouting.

"You know any other cuss words, Nancy?" Craig asked. The grin on his face was an attempt to make her feel better.

"Not now, Craig. I'm pissed."

"I sometimes find that shit, son of a bitch, or the always popular fuck works pretty good."

Nancy giggled. "I always did like your humor, Craig. You can sometimes be a pain in the ass, but I like your humor."

"I'm trying. I should've took him with me. He wanted to go."

"It's not your fault. He knows better."

"He's five, Nancy. He wants to be twenty-five."

She gave Craig a look. "You sound like your dad."

"Well, I am his son. I've learned a lot from him."

"This isn't anybody's fault. Mike just has to learn," Nancy said.

"We *all* have to learn. Ain't none of us ever seen anything like this before."

"Mom," a small voice said through the screen.

"Mike, I told you to go to your room. Now go!" Nancy yelled.

"Mom, there are men in the field, on horses," Mike said.

Craig stood up quickly. He grabbed his AR that had been laying on the porch floor next to his chair. "How many?"

"Two," Mike answered.

Nancy rushed inside, grabbing Mike as she passed him.

Craig ran off the porch and around the side of the cabin. He headed for the field, with Max, King, and Grady hot on his heels."

***

Driving out of Antigo wasn't any different than driving into it, although we did see a few more people, mostly scavengers running in and out of the ransacked stores and businesses. I saw some curtains move in houses as we drove by, and a few people sat on porches. Some waved, while others got up and went inside. Suspicion had replaced the natural friendliness that I had long seen as part of who we were up here.

The truck rumbled along the road. The broken down cars and trucks, some with rags tied to the antennas as if somehow they thought someone would come rescue them, made driving straight a challenging act.

We had left the cavalry behind us at the armory, and if First Sergeant Rahn was correct, no help was going to come from them. No one would be dashing in on a blazing Hummer and save the day.

Craig broke the silence on our drive. "Do you ever miss it, Dad?"

"Miss what?"

"The army."

"Yeah, sometimes. Usually at night, when I'm sitting alone on the porch. You can hear the crickets and night birds, sometimes a breeze rustling through the trees. It's easy to think and let your mind wander then. Yeah, I miss it. My mind goes to a different time. The faces, I don't always remember names, but I remember the close friends from back then. I can hear them then, our muted conversations sitting in foxholes, tents, or in vehicles, or around the barracks. Yeah, I miss it."

"Sounds like you miss it a lot."

"Sometimes. Part of it is just getting old, Brian. You start thinking about what you have left, and what you left behind."

"In a way, you kinda have it all back."

"What do you mean?" I asked, glancing at him.

"Now that the world's gone to shit, we're all carrying guns, building bunkers."

"True, but this is different. The rules have changed."

"What do you mean?"

"We had rules before. You don't shoot indiscriminately. You take care of prisoners. Protect other people who can't protect themselves."

"Yes, but…"

"It's simple, son. Now it's all about survival. No rule except one…we survive."

Brian had nothing to say after that.

We continued our drive and then I popped the question. "So, you want to tell me about getting blown up in Iraq?"

"It was nothing, really," Brian said.

I looked at him briefly. "What do you mean, it was nothing? How is getting blown up, twice, from what I just heard, nothing?"

"We hit an IED. The first time it rolled us over. The second time, it flipped us upside down in the air."

"Upside down in the air," I said rather sarcastically. "And you weren't hurt?"

"They medevac'd me. Flew me back to the CASH."

"CASH?"

"Combat support hospital. They didn't think I was gonna make it. That's why I was medevac'd instead of being transported to the FST."

My look asked the question. "Oh, Forward Surgical Team."

"I don't recall seeing a Purple Heart on your uniform when I last saw it," I noted.

"I told them I didn't want one. Most of the awards over there are bull shit. It's bad enough I have a Combat Action Badge—a CAB."

"How so?" I asked.

"I know guys who got those for walking outside the wire. I earned mine, but still…"

I decided to drop it. Brian was obviously uncomfortable talking about it. So, I let it go.

He changed the subject. "So, what do you think the

reaction will be to the SAW and grenades?"

"I think people are gonna shit."

We let our laughter lighten the mood as we drove home.

***

Craig got to the edge of the yard behind the cabin and looked across the field. Two people were riding toward the cabin on horseback. Both were carrying rifles, the buttstocks resting on their legs as they rode. Craig had his AR at high port, the rifle angled across his chest with the muzzle pointing up and to his left side. He put his hand on the forward receiver, the other wrapped around the pistol grip, finger by but not on the trigger. He only needed to bend it to put it in position to shoot.

As the riders got closer, he could see it was an older man and a young boy. These people were their neighbors, Quint Stepanik and his grandson, Rick. Both were dressed the same as when he saw them last.

As they got closer, Craig held up his hand in a sign of greeting, a signal to stop, and to let them know he wasn't going to shoot.

They rode up close, and the old man leaned over and extended his right hand toward Craig. They shook hands.

"I remember you from the road. I'm Craig Henry," Craig said.

"I remember you," Quint Stepanik replied. "We were in the barn and heard shooting. Thought there might be some trouble, so we took the trail through the woods to check it out. Saw we were close to your place and came on over."

"Thank you," Craig said, "but we have it under control. We were doing some target practice, but we're done for now."

"Good to know."

"Would you like to come into the cabin for coffee? We have some on, and you can meet everybody."

"That would be nice, indeed," the old man said. "Your dad around?"

"He and my brother rode over to the armory in Antigo. My brother is in the army and he figured he should see someone, being as he can't get back to his base. They left a few hours ago. I expect them back soon."

Nancy and Donna were on the back porch, weapons ready when Craig and his guests arrived.

Donna seemed to recognize them. "Mr. Stepanik, right?" she asked.

"Yes, ma'am, that's me," he replied. "We heard shooting and came over, using the woods trail."

"We appreciate that," she said.

"You might want to let everyone know when you're gonna be shooting. Gunfire means trouble now, and none of us need to be dashing around, trying to help each other," he scolded.

Craig knew that his mom, being a nurse, was accustomed to cranky, elderly people.

"We will do our best, Mr. Stepanik," she said, grinning. "C'mon up on the porch and have some coffee."

"The boy there had already invited us, but I thank you, too." Quint and Rick walked their horses up to the cabin and around the front, dismounting and letting the reigns hang loose.

Nancy had gone into the house ahead of them and returned a moment later, several empty coffee cups in her hand and a full pot of coffee in the other. "Sorry we don't have any cream or sugar," she said.

Craig saw in her eyes the small lie she was hiding. Not knowing how long the imitation cream and sugar would last, he guessed she wasn't about to share it with everyone.

"That's no problem, ma'am. I drink it black, just like…" Stopping himself, Quint gave a sheepish look before he continued. "Sorry, ma'am. I got carried away."

Nancy tried not to laugh at the older man's discomfort. "No problem, Mr. Stepanik, I've heard it before. My husband has quite the sense of humor."

"How about you, young man?" she asked Rick.

Rick put his .308 Winchester down on the steps, removed his floppy hat, and replied, "No, thank you. I don't like coffee."

"How about some iced tea, then? We have ice, even."

Smiling, Rick said, "Yes, ma'am, that would be great."

Craig grinned. At least, some things hadn't changed.

Chapter 9

"Distressed and hungry, they will roam through the land; when they are famished, they will become enraged and, looking upward, will curse their king..."

—Isaiah 6:21

Carol walked out onto the front porch and looked down the road toward Lake View. Since the EMP, everything was quiet now all the time, but she still enjoyed her alone time.

She saw a dark cloud on the horizon. It drifted slowly and continued to grow in size.

"Shit," she said aloud as she dashed into the house.

Putting on her hiking boots, she pulled the bright red laces tight before tying them, then cuffed her pants and ran out the back door towards her garage.

Inside, in its own makeshift stall, was the mare Gary Jones, a retired Marine living in the area, had given her. She saddled her quickly, put the bridle on, and then opened the garage door. It was heavy, and Carol had to remember to unlatch the door from the opener by pulling on the red cord.

138

Leading the horse out of the barn, she hopped into the saddle and took off at a gallop down the road toward town.

That's not a cloud, that's smoke from a fire.

A few minutes later, she arrived to see her diner engulfed in flames. Boxes of debris scattered out front told her what had happened.

Looters.

She walked the mare across the street and stopped near a highway sign post, where she dismounted and tied the horse up. She took a few steps into the middle of the road, then stopped.

Her stomach hurt, the pressure in her chest increased as she watched her livelihood and dream burn before her. She put her hand to her mouth and tears ran down her face as the emotion grew in her.

"Damn them, damn them," she shouted.

Other people had gathered from the few houses around the diner and were outside. Many had kept to themselves.

"Carol, are you all right?"

Carol recognized the voice, but still jumped.

"I'm sorry. I didn't mean to scare you."

"Well, dammit, Gary, you did," Carol said.

Gary Jones was a county volunteer EMT. He had learned those skills after getting out of the service. He said he wanted to save lives instead of taking them.

"They burned my diner, Gary. Those sons a bitches burned my diner." Carol shook her head back and forth.

"They got the Quik Mart, too," Gary said. "Took anything of value, then trashed it."

"Did they burn it, too?"

"No, I guess they were scared of all the gas in the storage tanks."

"That's probably the only good news."

"They took anything edible, pedaled away on

bicycles pulling carts behind them. I saw a few others pulling wagons filled with shit."

"Who were they?" Carol asked.

"I don't know. Never saw them before. I walked over here, but several of them were armed and they pointed guns at me. All I had was my Kimber 1911, and while it has a lot of horsepower, it wasn't enough. I'm sorry, Carol."

Carol looked at him, met his eyes. "Sorry for what? You didn't burn my diner down."

"I'm sorry I couldn't stop them," Gary said.

"It's not your fault." She put her arm around him. The irony of the situation was not lost on her. Her business was burning down and she was hugging a man who felt guilty for not stopping them.

"I don't know what I'm going to do now." Realizing the silliness of her words, she smirked and said, "Of course, I don't really know what I was going to do before. No one was coming to eat here, under the circumstances."

Releasing her hug on Gary, Carol went to her horse. She untied it, then mounted into the saddle.

"Now what?" he asked.

Carol shrugged. "I'll think about that tomorrow. You know, tomorrow's another day." Laughing sarcastically, she said, "I always wanted to say that. Just didn't think it would be at a time like this."

"You gonna be all right?"

"Yeah, I'll be okay. I'm going home. I think I'll get into my scotch."

"Kinda early for that, isn't it?"

"Not today, Gary. Not today."

Pulling on the reins, she rode east out of town.

***

I was enjoying the time in the truck, just Brian and me humming down the road as if nothing out of the ordinary had happened. Antigo was behind us, and the abandoned cars on the road were getting fewer.

We crested a hill, but on the other side was a jumble of cars and trucks. I slowed down, approaching the mess cautiously. As I got closer, something didn't feel right. While the cars were jammed together, they didn't seem to have crashed. I couldn't remember this being here when we came through earlier today.

"Get your weapon," I said to a dozing Brian.

With a startled jump, he grabbed his AR. "What's up?"

"I don't know," I said. "Could be nothing, but this doesn't look right." I put my Glock on my lap, my AR leaned on the seat between Brian and me. About 25 feet or so from the cars, I stopped, the engine idling. "Keep your eyes open."

I caught movement out of the corner of my eye. Turning my head in alarm, I saw two men come out of the woods. One had what looked like a baseball bat. The other was carrying a shotgun.

I didn't even hesitate, slamming the truck into reverse and stepping heavily on the gas. The truck bolted backward.

The shot gunner raised the gun and fired.

Our backward motion and what was obviously not a serious load in the shotgun made his efforts ineffective.

Brian leaned out his window and fired rapidly at the two men.

The man dropped the bat, but the other kept shooting.

All of my attention was on the shooter when the windshield cracked. A neat hole had centered in it, right between Brian and me.

"We've got another shooter," I shouted, pressing my foot harder against the gas pedal, trying to make the truck go faster.

Brian stopped shooting at the shotgun guy and spun his weapon toward where he thought the other shooter was. He fired off several rounds in the general direction of where they'd came from and we backed over the hill behind us, traveling about a quarter mile before I stopped the truck.

"Fuck," I shouted.

"Now what?" Brian asked.

"I don't know. That wasn't there when we came through earlier, and I don't know how many there are."

"Want me to get the SAW?"

"Yeah, I think so. Get it set up, and we'll try and run through their barricade."

Brian reached behind me and pulled out the blanket-wrapped SAW. Then, from the bed of the truck, he took a can of belted 5.56, bringing it with him into the truck cab.

After a moment, he had a belt of ammo set up feeding it from the can.

I had holstered my Glock and had my AR across my body, its single point strap around my neck, the muzzle aimed toward my side window.

"How are we going to do this?" Brian asked.

"I think we'll try to run through. The side where the shotgunner was should be our best bet. That will keep the other shooter away from us, with all of the wreckage between us for some cover."

"Got it."

"You see anything moving, take it out. As we get close, start some suppressive fire toward your right. That should get us through and keep them from shooting at us. I don't think they'll be expecting anything full auto."

"Roger that, Dad."

"You ready?" I asked, giving him a hard look.

"Ready as I'll ever be."

I pushed my foot on the gas pedal. The truck went as fast as it wanted to anyway, and we crested the hill. We picked up speed, roaring toward the wreckage in the road.

I saw someone kneeling by the guy Brian had shot. As soon as he saw us coming, he stood up and ran toward the woods.

"There's one now," I shouted to Brian.

"I see him," he answered, keeping his eyes focused on his side of the road.

As we got closer to the jumble of cars in the road, Brian started shooting short bursts toward the trees on his side of the road. The loud burst of fire hurt my ears, but I kept driving.

"I'm turning now," I said.

Before he could reply, I turned off the road and onto the grassy area near the side of it. I kept driving, and for a brief moment, I realized I had no idea what the condition of this side of the road was like.

Putting it out of my mind as quickly as it entered, I pushed on the gas harder, willing us to get through this and on down the road. As I cleared the wreckage, Brian shouted, "Here I go again!" He resumed firing short bursts.

Luckily, there was no return fire. I drove back onto the road and continued down Highway 64. We'd made it.

"That was too much like Iraq," Brian said, breaking the silence.

The ringing in my ears was still really strong, but I'd heard him loud and clear. "Then Iraq sucks," I said. "I hope it wasn't like that every day."

"No, somedays they tried to blow us up." His sense of humor was still present, and I joined him in the laugh.

I couldn't wait to get home.

***

The camp, if you could call it one, was spread out over the park. The picnic pavilions had blue and green colored tarps tied up like walls to give it a sense of privacy. Scattered around the park was a collection of shelters from tents to sheets of plastic using sticks as poles. Some people, having nothing to make a shelter with, plopped down where there was space—under the trees around the park or out in the open.

The pond had become a resource for everything from bathing to drinking. The outhouses in the park, porta-johns actually, were overflowing and reeked, sending their odor to mix with the wood smoke and other scents a mass of unwashed, unclean people could create.

No, it wasn't a camp. It was a pit of filth and disease put together by people who didn't know any better and who had grown too accustomed to the comforts of the modern world, a world driven by technology. That was all gone now.

Tom Harvey stood outside the picnic pavilion he was using as his home, and as something of a headquarters for the refugees. They weren't known by any particular name. They were what they were—a collection of people from the Greater Green Bay area, most of whom came from and had nothing before the power went out. Now, they had what they could find or take by force.

Tom was an imposing man. Standing six feet four inches tall, he had weighed almost 300 pounds when this situation had begun a little over two weeks ago. He knew he'd lost weight because he was on the last hole in his belt. His dirty, oily jeans were covered with as much dirt as it was with the blood of chickens, pigs, or whatever other animals they had taken and butchered, and they were feeling loose on him. His once white t-shirt, now a dingy grey, had yellow, brown, and rusty blood stains on it. It was torn around his protruding belly. He wore motorcycle boots, but he did not own a motorcycle. He liked the boots for stomping people. He had never really cared about his appearance and now it didn't matter anyway. He looked like a lot of the men in the group, only Tom was bigger and meaner. His long beard, with strands of black and grey hair protruding everywhere, and his equally shaggy long hair, completed the do-nothing, care-about-nothing appearance he wanted.

Now he found himself in charge of almost one hundred men, women, and children, most of them as lost as he was about what to do. Most, like him, were from the wrong side of town. Yet somehow, he found himself in charge. They had left Green Bay a week ago, knowing it was going to get bad. Along the way, they picked up a few stragglers and found themselves here.

Still pissed at the old man who ran them off with a gun, Tom watched a group as they came down the road into the park.

Truth be told, the old man hadn't really run them off. Tom just wasn't ready for a confrontation yet.

The group was pushing shopping carts full of food, water, beer—probably anything they had scavenged from the countryside. Some of them carried shopping bags and boxes full of stuff. Several also carried guns: guns in holsters, guns hanging from straps, and a couple of guns hung from ropes tied around their bodies to make them easier to carry.

Two of the men walked away from the line of people bringing in supplies and headed toward Tom. Each man had an AR hanging from a two-point sling and a pistol in a holster at their side.

"Looks like a decent haul," Tom said as they came closer.

"Yeah, the town had a diner and a convenience store," Kevin Schneider said. "Cleaned 'em both out. Folks got carried away and burnt the diner. Sid here managed to stop them before they burnt the convenience store-gas station. That could've been messy."

Kevin was tall and thin. He would have been called a beanpole by past generations. His beard, such as it was, presented itself more like patches of hair than anything else. The blond hair on his head was greasy and uncombed. Like many here, he wore dirty jeans, a nondescript pair of athletic shoes, and a ragged t-shirt with a heavy metal band logo on it.

"Woulda made a hell of a boom, though," Sid said. "I didn't want any of our people getting hurt."

Sid was of a different mold than the rest of them. Younger and more athletic-looking, his long hair hung below his shoulders, and unlike the others, he couldn't grow a beard if his life depended on it. His clothing was no different than anyone else's though—dirty, greasy, and torn.

"That's good, Sid," Tom said. "We may need that gas for the few operating vehicles we have. No sense wasting it by burning it. The way things are now, if someone does get hurt it's one less mouth to feed."

Kevin and Sid went back to the foot caravan bringing the new supplies into the camp. People had already started to gather around, looking at the items. Tom might be in charge, but not everyone had reached a point where they accepted his word as law. Sometimes, they had to use a little force to get people to pay attention and obey.

Tom went to his shelter and picked up his Browning

pump action 12 gauge. He had sawed the barrel off a few days ago. It now ended about two inches past the magazine cap. Heading out of the shelter, he looked at the two young women sitting inside. "Stay here if you know what's good for you," he ordered.

Pushing the tarp to his left, he headed over to where the supplies were being stored. *Need to be there to make sure none of those people steal anything.* Tom had learned quickly that food was power, and if you controlled food, you controlled people. Of course, superior firepower didn't hurt, either.

***

"Someone's coming down the road, Gramps," Rick said. He set his glass of iced tea on the steps and reached for his .308 Winchester.

"Somebody on a horse," Quint said to no one in particular.

As all the adults picked up their weapons, the rider and horse emerged from the tree-lined drive. It was Carol Jensen. She had slowed the horse to a walk just before she came into the clearing.

"Hello," she shouted as she raised her hand high. She guided her horse as it galloped toward the cabin, stopping near the other two horses that were munching on the unmowed grass in the yard.

"Hello, Carol," Nancy and Donna said together.

"Didn't recognize you on the horse. What brings you out this way?" Donna asked.

"Looters burned down the diner," she said, her voice trembling with emotion.

"Burned the diner?" Nancy cried. "No! How could they?"

Dismounting, Carol let the reins hang loose as she

walked over to the porch. "Burned it to the ground. Was nothing I could do. Almost everything I had was tied up in that diner."

"Oh, my God," Nancy choked out, her hand at her throat. "Why? How?"

Carol went to the bottom of the steps and sighed. "Like I said, looters. They got the Quik Mart, too."

"That's a gas station," Quint interjected. "Did they burn it, too?"

"Thankfully, no," Carol said. "That would've been one hell of a mess."

"Je-sus," Craig remarked.

"Don't blaspheme, son," Quint scolded.

Craig smiled, most likely remembering his dad being scolded the same way.

"What will you do?" Nancy asked.

Carol shrugged. "I guess I'll see if John will let me move in here full time."

Nancy said, "I'm sure Fil, I mean John, won't mind."

"I'll have to talk to him, I guess. You have a lot of people here and it could get kinda crowded. Plus, that's a lot to feed."

"We have plenty," Craig said.

"We'll talk to John when he gets back," Nancy quickly added.

Looking at the old man, Carol said, "Hello, Mr. Stepanik, remember me now?" She raised her eyebrows in question.

"I remember you; why wouldn't I?" Quint said gruffly.

"Well, you *did* tell John you didn't know me." Carol smiled.

Quint looked away, then met her eyes. "I said that when I didn't know who he was. You can't blame me for trying to protect the people here."

"It's okay," Carol soothed him. "Anyway, we all

need to be on alert. We have a lot of looters in the area. That isn't good."

"I'll bet it was that group I saw take the road toward the county park at Stillwell's Pond. I'll bet they're out there," Quint said.

"When John gets back, we'll need to let him know," Carol said, shaking her head. "This isn't good, and who knows where else they'll try and loot next. A lot of people out here live alone. You guys have one of the bigger groups out here."

"We don't have that many," Donna said, joining the discussion. "Two women, three men, and a little boy is all. Speaking of, where is Mike?"

"I sent him to his room," Nancy answered.

There was a movement at the door behind them.

Turning quickly, she saw Mike standing in the doorway. "Come here, young man," Nancy ordered.

Mike came out on the porch and dashed to her, grabbing her around the waist and hugging her. "I'm sorry," he said quietly. "Are the loots gonna hurt us?"

"They're called looters, Mike, people who take things that aren't theirs. We won't let them hurt us." Nancy held him tight.

***

I saw the smoke before entering Lake View, billowing over the tree tops ahead, the black clouds couldn't be missed.

"Something's burning," I said.

Brian, startled out of his daze as he stared out the window, sat up and peered through the windshield. "Wonder what it is?"

"We'll find out in a minute." The road curved ahead and brought us into what amounted to the town of Lake

View. As I turned into the curve I could see Carol's Diner, smoking heavily, as a fire continued to burn what was left of the building plus the two on either side of it.

"It's Carol's," I said.

"Geezus. Dad, you think she's in there?" Brian asked, concern showing in his tone.

"I don't know."

I slowed the truck and stopped in front of the smoky buildings. Trash was scattered all over the road. We got out of the truck, standing there, not really knowing what to do.

"Looters!" someone shouted from behind me.

Gary Jones came walking toward us. "It was a bunch of damn looters. They trashed the place and then burned it. Took everything from the Quik Mart, too."

"Is Carol all right?" I asked.

"She wasn't in there at the time, but I don't know if she's all right. She took off on her horse, headed toward your place." His tone had grown sad as he got closer to me. "There were too many of them, John. I couldn't stop them. I told her I was sorry."

"It's not your fault, Gary," I said, putting my hand on his shoulder. "If there were too many, nothing you could do. She went toward my place?"

"Yeah, took off heading on the road in that direction. I figured that's where she was going."

"Okay, if we have a gang of looters around here, we should get together and talk about what we can do. Can you get to my place?"

"Yeah, I'll take my bicycle," Gary said. "Need to save the gas I have in my Harley. Besides, the exercise will do me good."

"Stop by Sam Karpinski's, too. Have him come out. Maybe this evening?"

"Sure, I'll get him."

I patted Gary on the shoulder again, then I turned to get back in the truck. Brian climbed in on his side, and as we drove off, I yelled out the window, "We'll stop them, Gary."

Driving as fast as I could safely, it didn't take long to get to my cabin. Turning sharply onto the drive, Brian grabbed the door to keep from bouncing around. As we entered the clearing where the cabin was, I saw a small crowd gathered out front. Carol was with our family. So were the Stepaniks.

"What's up with all of you?" I asked as I stepped out of the truck.

I went to Carol and gave her a hug. "I saw the diner." I didn't think any other words were good enough to convey my emotions.

"Gary said it was a gang of looters," Carol said, returning the hug. "They burned down my diner, damn them."

"I know," I said, still holding her.

Carol pushed away, giving me a shove with both hands. "We have to find them, John. We have to find and stop them before they hurt someone."

"I'm pretty sure I saw them," Mr. Stepanik said. "I was telling these folks before you got here that I saw a group heading for the park."

"Which park?" I asked, focusing my attention on him.

"Stilwell's Pond," he replied. "Has everything they need, except maybe food. Water, shelter, the pond has fish..."

"Yeah, and access to us here," Carol added. "We have to make them leave, John."

"I told Gary to bring Sam over later today," I said. "Mr. Stepanik..."

"Call me Quint, young man," he interrupted.

Smiling briefly, I continued, "Quint, can you and

your grandson join us tonight?"

Quint bobbed his head. "We have some things to do back on the farm, but we'll be here. I don't like being out much after dark, so I might want to stay the night, if that's okay?"

My body shook as I chuckled heartily and replied, "Why not? We have plenty here now."

We watched Quint and Rick ride across the field behind the cabin and eventually enter the trail into the far tree line.

Brian had already started to share the story of our trip to Antigo and what we saw going there and back. The story of our encounter with the roadblock drew interest and a flurry of questions from everyone. He tried to answer all of them, including telling them about the SAW we got from First Sergeant Rahn.

"A SAW," Craig said, excited.

"What's that?" Nancy asked.

"A 5.56 caliber light machine gun. Uses the same ammo as our Ars do, which besides its rapid rate of fire, makes it a very useful weapon for us," Brian explained.

"Can I shoot it?" Craig asked.

"Only if you learn how to use it," Brian answered. "We have to conserve ammo, and besides, the weapon will be heard for some distance. We can't draw attention to the fact that we have it. Its existence should be a secret that will add to our defense, if its needed."

"All right," Craig said, disappointment in his voice. "I understand."

I was impressed by Brian's explanation. He was beginning to assert himself as a leader and wasn't giving in to me being in charge. I liked it, too, because I didn't want to be the only one thinking of strategies.

"John," Donna said, "Carol wants to ask you something."

"I do not. Well, not exactly." Carol groaned.

"We think she should stay with us," Nancy announced. "We have plenty of room, and plenty of other things, too."

"Is that what you want to do, Carol?" I asked. "You'd like to live out here with us and all of this madness?" I waved my arm around, indicating I was talking about my family.

Brian, ever the clown, made a face and stuck out his tongue.

"I'm scared, John," Carol said. "After the diner burned down, I saw there was nothing I could do by myself to protect my things. Gary couldn't do anything, either. So, yeah, I guess I want to move here."

"I'll clean out my office and we'll turn that into a room for you," I said, a smile on my face. "It's not like I need my computer or anything in there. Tomorrow, we'll take the truck and load your things up to bring them here. What won't fit in your room, we'll figure out a dry place to store them in the barn."

"Thanks, John," Carol said.

The cheering from everyone pretty much sealed the deal.

Of course, having another woman in the house, especially one that I liked, while also living with my ex-wife was going to be interesting.

Chapter 10

"We few, we happy few, we band of brothers."

—William Shakespeare, *Henry V*

Craig and I sat on the porch watching Mike, Brian, and the dogs run around as they played. Donna, Nancy, and Carol were inside putting together things for the meeting. Mostly, it was a variety of easy-to-make fun food that I would've never thought of. Packaged cheese on a cracker, compliments of Donna and Craig. They'd even went as far as putting a sliced olive onto each one. The women had got into my Spam supply and cut one block into cubes, then opened some canned pineapple to make mini shish kabobs.

Nancy was making biscuits to go with the sliced canned ham, and Carol was putting together chili made with venison, some canned dehydrated tomato sauce, beans, and a variety of spices. I wouldn't let them get into our onions or potatoes that were in the basement, although they had tried. Nancy also made a large batch of tea, but I'd stopped her before she put sugar in it. That was to be saved.

"What are you planning on telling everyone, Dad?"

154

Craig asked, breaking my concentration at watching the dogs and Mike tackle Brian.

I took a deep breath, then let it out. "We need to come together. Part of me wants us to force the looters to move. Though, I don't think that's a good idea. Part of me wants to fortify our defenses here and hold on, but that isn't good, either. Hell, I just want us to figure out how to survive this without anyone else getting hurt."

Craig stared straight ahead, watching. "You think that's realistic?"

"Nope, which is why we all have to agree on something. I don't think we can run off the looters. They'll just get replaced by someone else. A year from now, most of them will be dead anyway and won't be a problem. It's what we do between now and then that concerns me."

I had barely finished explaining when Gary Jones came into view on his mountain bike. *Ugly damn bike.* Next to him was Sam Karpinski on horseback.

"Company's coming," I yelled into the house.

"Who is it?" Carol yelled back.

"Sam and Gary!"

The two men rode to the area just in front of the porch. Sam tied up his horse on the porch railing and Gary leaned his bike against the side of the cabin. We greeted each other, and I introduced them to everyone, and to Grady. They already knew Carol. The men gathered on the porch and the women started to go back inside.

"You ladies are a part of this, too," I said. "You need to stay."

They turned around and took chairs.

Craig and Brian sat on the steps with Mike, while Sam and Gary took the other chairs and I sat on the porch rail.

"Well, I'm glad you guys are here," I said. "We're waiting on Quint and Rick Stepanik. We need to talk about that looter band over by Stilwell's Pond Park. I figure they're the ones who burned down Carol's store and looted the Quik Mart."

"We going to attack them?" Gary asked.

"That's part of what we have to decide," I said. "Let's wait for the others to get here, and then we'll hash out how we're going to take care of them and help each other through this mess."

***

The small white frame house stood just off the road. The front porch, framed by a well-tended and soon to be blooming flower bed, presented a welcome mat to anyone approaching the front of the house. A porch swing, hanging from chains, sat perpendicular to the house. A cat rested lazily on the swing, oblivious and uncaring. Emmet and Katherine Mueller had lived in the house for almost all of their 55 years of marriage. Emmet had retired from the sawmill when it shut down almost fifteen years ago. Katherine had been a housewife and mother to their three children, all grown and living out of state. She was singing in the kitchen, while Emmet read an old western in the living room.

"Hello? Is anyone home?" a young woman called toward the open door on the porch.

Emmet got up from the chair he had been sitting in and walked toward the door. Before he reached it, Katherine joined him. They stopped in front of the screen door and looked outside, surprised to see a young woman almost crawling up the porch stairs.

The young woman, disheveled in appearance, her dirty jeans and t-shirt displaying her desperate state, staggered toward the porch door. The front door of the house, open to allow the fresh air of a warm May day inside, beckoned her forward.

Emmet pushed open the door, the familiar screech of an old door spring providing a soundtrack, and stepped outside. Katherine was right behind him, her hand over her mouth in shock.

"Oh, my Lord," Katherine gasped.

Emmet stooped down to help the woman.

"Are you all right, young lady?" he asked, concern evident in his voice.

"I'm hungry. I need help," she said in a tired, worn voice. "Help me, please."

Emmet and Katherine came to her side, each of them grasping her by an arm and helped her up the steps.

"Don't worry, dear. I'm Katherine, and this is Emmet. We'll help you," Katherine said, trying to comfort the girl.

Years of frugality, coupled with the common sense that comes from rural living, had prepared them better than most for the circumstances following the EMP event. Katherine had shelves full of jarred goods she had canned herself from their garden. A few years ago, she had begun canning a variety of meats from either Emmet's successful hunting or their chickens as they became good for little more than eating.

The couple put their arms around the woman and guided her toward the door. As Emmet reached for the door, the woman moved swiftly.

Reaching under her t-shirt, she grabbed a large hunting knife, plunging it into Emmet's stomach and ripping laterally across it, disemboweling him where he stood.

In a near fluid movement, the woman swung around, slashing the knife across Katherine's throat, the blood spurting across the woman's face and clothes.

Emmet and Katherine fell in a lump to the porch floor, their death throes mercifully short as their lifes' blood poured from their bodies. Neither had made a sound, so quick was the woman's attack.

The woman stepped back from them, bent over, and wiped the knife off on the flowered apron Katherine still wore.

Heavy, rapid footsteps sounded behind her as three men raced to the porch, one carrying a shotgun. Dressed much like her in scruffy, oily jeans and t-shirts, the one carrying the shotgun wore a long-sleeved t-shirt with a heavy metal rock band logo.

"That was easier than I thought," the woman said.

"Let's go inside," the man with the gun said. "I've been watching this house for two days and I'm hungry. We'll move them out of the way later."

***

Quint and Rick finally made it and we all got acquainted. Nancy, taking charge, announced that the food was ready and everyone should get something to eat and bring it back to the porch.

I thought it was a good idea; we could talk things over while we ate. The porch was better than my dining table because I only had eight chairs, and there were eleven of us. I did move a couple chairs out onto the porch, so no one would have to sit on the floor, although Craig and Brian did just that. I gave Craig a look as he shoveled chili into his mouth.

"What?" he mumbled as he ate a spoonful.

"Thought you'd sit in the chair," I said.

"Nope," he replied. "Too easy to spill. I'll sit here."

When everyone had their food and was situated comfortably, I started the conversation by explaining what we already knew about the situation. Then, I went into what I knew each person sitting around the group had in the way of skills and abilities to help make us a better team. As soon as I used the word "team," Quint spoke up.

"What do you mean by 'team,' John?" Quint asked.

"What I mean is all of us working together to survive, help each other out, lend talent and stuff to each other. None of us can do this alone."

"So, what are you suggesting?" Sam asked.

"Well, the first thing is, we all agree to band together, to become a *team*. We help each other, come to each others' defense when necessary…"

"We are kinda scattered, John," Quint said.

"Hmm," I said, "that does present a problem."

"So what are we going to do?" Carol asked.

She had been rather quiet during the meeting. I suspected she was still numb over her diner burning down and the reality of uprooting herself from her home to move out here to the cabin.

For the sake of survival, I needed to make sure my plan was clear to them. "What does everyone think about our grouping together?"

"You already said we were a team," Quint said. "Doesn't that mean we are already together?"

"Yes, it does," I answered. "But I'm talking about moving in together."

"I'm not moving, and these people can't fit here anyway. You don't have the space with all you have," Quint said, anger and frustration evident in his voice and face.

"That's true, we can't all fit here. But, Quint, you have a good-sized house, and Sam and Gary could move in with you…"

All three men spoke at once.

"Now, hold on just a minute," Quint said.

"What?" Gary said.

"John, what are you thinking?" Sam said.

"Hear me out," I interrupted them. "Scattered like we are, if any of us is attacked, we can't defend or help each other. The largest group, here at the cabin, has the best chance, but even that may not be enough."

"So, again, John, like Sam asked, what are you thinking? I'm not thrilled about moving anywhere," Gary said.

"I don't know that we have a realistic option. If Quint will allow it, if we move you and Sam lock, stock, and baggage into his place, then he has enough help to defend his property. We're all close enough to quickly get to each other and help."

"It could work," Sam said agreeably. "But I have horses."

"The boy's right," Quint replied. "I have a good size barn, and except for the two horses my grandson and I have, it's empty. You could put some of your horses in my barn. I can't take them all. I only have six stalls."

"I can take the rest here," I said. "We have eight empty stalls in the barn. We can use my field and your pasture to let them graze until we can figure out a feed plan or a way to gather some hay from one of the surrounding fields."

"It might work, but that's a lot to haul out here," Gary said.

"I've got all my ham radio stuff, plus horses, tack, and my own things I need. How will we haul it?"

"I have the truck and a trailer. There is plenty of fuel. I still have almost a thousand gallons stored, plus we can harvest more from abandoned cars along the road. It may take us a couple of days, but I think it's our best option."

"I'm in," Gary said.

"Me, too," added Sam.

"It's okay by me," Quint agreed, "but I hope you guys have plenty of food to bring. We're getting low at my place."

"I have plenty," Sam said.

"So do I," Gary added.

"Then, do we have a plan?" I asked.

"Mostly," Craig said. "What about the looter gang?"

I glanced at Craig, then at the others. "We aren't ready to take them on yet. Unfortunately, I think we need to watch them, not engage unless we have to; get as ready as we can for the time when they find us and come after our supplies."

"Sounds good, Pops," Brian finally spoke up. He'd been quiet the whole discussion, but I knew he'd be helpful with defensive strategies.

My eyes moved across each person in the group and when I met their eyes, each nodded their agreement.

I patted my thigh. "I think we have a plan. Just like eating the elephant, one bite at a time."

"Reminds me of Shakespeare," Quint said in an uncharacteristically timid tone.

"Shakespeare?" several of the group asked.

"Heathens, yes, Shakespeare. That Band of Brothers thing, 'we Band of Brothers,'" he answered.

"That's not right," Nancy said. "We have sisters here, too."

Carol and Donna agreed with smiles and high fives.

"No, you are all wrong," I said. "We aren't a band of anything. We *are* a family."

Chapter 11

"Do Good, Reap Good.
Do Evil, Reap Evil. "

—Chinese Proverb

I was where I usually was, just before the sun rises. Sitting on the porch, coffee in one hand, the other holding a cigar. The quiet of the early morning was the best. Everyone else went to bed after cleaning up from last evening's late meeting. I thought it went well. There were things we still needed to resolve, and of course I knew that a marine, a sailor, and a cranky old curmudgeon living in the same house was going to create other issues, but I believed we all had the conviction to do it.

King and Max were with me, as they usually were. Today, though, they were on either side of my chair instead of in their usual spot lying across the porch. Maybe they felt it, too. A coming together of all of us, a new family formed with everything that means. Amazing how events can create bonds, bonds that over time cannot be broken. Much like Brian and the first sergeant's bond because of Iraq and their shared experiences there.

The first hints of dawn were promising a new day, and I knew this day would be eventful. I had promised Carol the security of the cabin first, so she would be moved first. The looters had really scared her by burning down the diner and she didn't want to live alone.

Gary and Sam had a lot to do, too.

Sam had an old horse drawn wagon that he thought he had all the parts for that he could harness one of his horses to help balance the load for whichever one of his horses got the job of pulling. If it worked, that would help us a lot today. It wouldn't carry a load like my truck and trailer, but it would help now for the move and in the future, as we tried to conserve gas and be a bit quiet in how we did things. Engines, chainsaws, and other power tools made noise. Noise attracted attention, and right now, that was something we didn't need.

The park where the looters lived was maybe fifteen miles from us, and while not far in a modern era, given our new reality, it was far enough away. Yet, it was a different world now, and sound travelled.

***

"Boss," Kevin Schneider said. He stood outside of the pavilion where Tom Harvey had his shelter.

Tom stirred. He was under the leg of one of the young women he had taken as his, who was wedged up against him. Opening his eyes, he blinked a couple of times, grunted over being rudely awakened, and sat up. "What?"

"You need to come out here. We have visitors."

Pushing the leg off him and shoving the other woman

aside, he crawled out of the makeshift bed he had made from a large air mattress and a blanket, and stood up. Rubbing his face and beard with his hands, Tom looked toward the closed entrance.

"What?" he asked again, still disgusted at being awakened.

"We have visitors," Kevin said. "Caught them by our supplies."

Grabbing his pants from the picnic table inside his shelter, Tom pulled them on. Grabbing a t-shirt, he smelled it, wrinkled his nose, and put it on, too. Sitting, he put on dirty, stiff socks and then his grungy athletic shoes. Shuffling toward the entrance, he pushed the tarp open and stepped out into the early morning. The air was cool and slightly damp. Glaring at Kevin, he said, "Visitors? Where?"

"Sid and some of the guys have them over there." Kevin pointed off in the distance toward the back of the park. "They were caught taking our food."

"Show me," Tom muttered grumpily.

The two men walked toward the area where they kept their supplies under guard. As they got closer, and Tom had awakened a bit, he saw Sid standing with three men of their group. In front of them, kneeling on the ground, were a man, woman, and a teenage girl. They held their hands behind their heads.

The man's eye was swelling and blood ran from his nose and the corner of his mouth. The woman and girl were crying.

Tom stood in front of the man, glaring down at him. "You try to steal from me?"

The man began to shake. "We were hungry. We haven't had anything to eat in days."

Tom reached down and grabbed the front of the man's oxford shirt, its blue fabric stained by dirt, perspiration, and now blood. Pulling him up, the man began to whimper.

"Please, we just need something to eat."

"I don't like thieves," Tom said, his voice rising.

"Please don't hurt us," the woman cried. "Please, we're just hungry. We'll work for it. We'll do whatever we need to for it. Please…" She fell down, sobbing.

As the woman fell, the young girl beside her gave a low shriek. "Mom!"

Staring at the man he held at eye level, Tom mocked, "Oh, look, a family affair."

"Please, sir, we were just…"

Before the man could finish, Tom's fist smashed into the side of the man's face. Tom pulled him close again and *bam*. He hit him in the face again.

Tom continued to beat the man and accented each punch with "I, *bam,* don't, *bam,* like, *bam,* thieves, *bam*!"

With each strike, the woman and girl screamed louder and louder.

Tossing the man to the ground, Tom swung his arm and backhanded the woman on her head, causing her to crumble to the ground.

The girl, watching as her mother was struck down, curled up into a ball, whimpering.

"Shut the fuck up!" Tom shouted, pointing his finger at the now silent woman.

"Whattya want us to do, boss?" Kevin asked.

Looking at the now unconscious man, Tom said, "Take that piece of shit away. Tie him up, and we'll deal with him later."

"What about the women?" Sid asked. He had a sinister look in his eyes and licked his lips.

Tom shrugged. "Take the woman away and bring the girl to my shelter."

"What do we do with the woman?" Sid asked again.

"You can do anything you want. I don't care." Tom

walked to his shelter, his steps hard and exaggerated in his anger.

Sid laughed, then reached down, grabbing the woman by the arm as he started to drag her away. "One of you guys grab her other arm and help me," he ordered.

Kevin pointed at the two remaining men. "Take this pile of shit over to the detention area. Tie his ass up so he don't get away."

"Okay, Kevin. Can we go with Sid after we're done?" one of them asked.

"Yeah, go ahead," Kevin answered.

The woman screamed as they dragged her away. "Nooooo, you can't do this. Nooooo!"

Kevin lowered his weapon and poked it into the young girl's ribs. "Get up."

She coiled into an even tighter ball.

"I said, get up or I'll beat you til you get up," Kevin said.

The girl stopped her whimpering and slowly stood. Her entire body shook as she held her hands together in front of her.

Poking her again, Kevin directed her towards Tom's shelter.

"What's he going to do to me?" she cried, her voice accented with sobs.

"Shut up and walk," Kevin ordered. Poking her harder with his AR, she stumbled and walked toward the shelter.

Stopping outside the shelter, Kevin called, "Hey, boss, should I bring her in?"

"Yeah," Tom replied.

Kevin pushed her through the flaps of tarp.

As she entered, she looked around. A picnic table had been pushed to one side. In the back was a bundle of blankets and a couple of pillows. Two young women sat there, fear stark on their faces. A folding camp chair was on the other side, a table next to it, and a bottle of some kind stood on the table. Cigarette butts littered the concrete slab floor around the chair.

Kevin took the girl by the arm and made her stand straight.

Pointing to the two women on the bed, Tom said, "Take these two out of here. I'm through with them."

The two women scrambled off the bed and moved toward Kevin. He turned and pushed open the flap with his AR and they stumbled out. Kevin followed behind them.

"We're just hungry," the girl said, a small amount of courage building inside her. "What are you going to do to my parents?"

Tom stared at her, his cold blue eyes piercing into her. "I don't like thieves."

"We're hungry."

"I don't give a shit," he sneered. "You were stealing."

The girl began to sob again, her shoulders shaking with each breath. "What about my mother?" she asked, tears running down her face.

"That's up to Sid and the boys. They don't like thieves, either."

"What about me? What are you going to do to me?"

Reaching for her shirt and pulling it until the cloth tore, he said, "That's up to me."

Her screams, coupled with her mother's screams, sang throughout the camp.

Some of the men laughed at their predicament while the other women in the camp stayed silent, their fears kept hidden because eating was more important.

***

We got Carol moved quickly. Then, Sam got his wagon hitched and a load taken over to the Stepanik place. Tomorrow, we'd work on getting Gary moved, and then finish up with Sam's stuff.

I was planning to help Sam move his solar panels with the truck and get them hooked up onto Stepanik's property, as we feared the wagon might damage them. Wagons aren't necessarily known for a smooth ride.

Craig, Brian, and I were on the porch, our favorite gathering space while the weather was still nice. May was ending and June was approaching. Tomorrow, those not involved in the move would plant the garden, but I was concerned with how vulnerable we were with no one watching the road.

"Wish we had at least one more person," Brian said.

"We have to play cards with the hand we're dealt," I said. "So, you two and the others will have to take turns at the bunker Craig finished. We need to tweak it some, and then figure out a better way of communication other than using the radios."

"You think maybe we can get a couple of those TA-312s from the Guard?" Craig asked.

The TA-312 was a battery operated, two-wire, point to point telephone. If we could get a couple, we could string a wire from the bunker to the cabin. That would let us communicate better in case anything happened at either place.

I had several solar battery chargers and enough rechargeable batteries that we wouldn't be without. Someone could sit upstairs in one of the back bedrooms and watch the meadow behind the cabin, so we would only need the two. We'd have to rely on the radios between my place and Quint's.

"That would be nice," Brian said. "Once we get Sam set up, he can radio the armory and see if they can spare some. Probably best we ask the first sergeant instead of the captain. He doesn't seem too open to letting anything leave his control."

"So, we'll use radios until then?" Craig asked. It was more of a statement than a question.

"Yup," I said. "Eventually, we may have to set up some random patrols in the woods behind the cabin and around Quint's place. Until then, what we'll do is have you boys take turns. One travels with me and takes stuff over to Quint's. We can trade off until we get done. We'll have to let the ladies know, too. Everybody gets a turn. We'll start taking turns at night."

"Not Mike," Brian said, his voice firm.

"No shit, Sherlock. He's too young." I gave him a look, as if I'd put my grandson at risk. "However, if he wants and can sit still, he can be in the bunker with one of us. Remember, he was smart enough to let you know that someone was in the field recently, so he does understand."

"Understand what?" Donna said, as she came out on to the porch and joined us.

"We're talking about setting up guard shifts. Mike is too young, but he can be with one of us in the bunker. He'll learn early, and by the time he's old enough, he'll be an expert."

As soon as I said it, I realized Mike's world had changed. He wouldn't know the world we all grew up in, but if he was going to survive, he needed to learn everything. My teaching him woodcraft, stalking, and staying concealed in the woods now became his first lessons for surviving the future. We all had to learn or relearn. Times had changed.

"Just the one guard point?" Donna asked.

I was mildly impressed over how those of us who were veterans had suddenly reverted to a language common for us in the past and now common for all of us to learn.

"We'll actually have two," I confirmed. "One upstairs in one of the bedroom windows and the other at the bunker. Both are observing points of threat—we need the early warning they'll give us."

I then shared with her the idea of the field phones from the National Guard Armory and she agreed it would be a good idea. We chatted some more and were eventually joined by Nancy and Carol. I explained the plan and we set up a schedule for the night.

I sent Craig downstairs to get a couple of the Optiscope monocular night vision devices I had. There were four, so we'd be set. I knew that Gary had a couple they could use over at his new place, so all in all, we were in pretty good shape.

It had grown dark and almost time for us to get started. The rest of us would go to bed. Brian, Craig, and Carol would take shifts at the bunker while Nancy, Donna, and I took the watch from upstairs in the cabin. We'd all be tired come morning, but it had to be done.

Hopefully, nothing would happen tonight and we'd all get at least some sleep. Tomorrow, there was moving and garden planting to do. Our ancestors sure had it rougher than we gave them credit for.

I knew eventually we'd adapt, but until then, it was gonna be rough. I hoped we had the time to get to that point, and along the way, that the lack of sleep didn't put us at each others' throats.

***

We finished the moves in three days. The garden was planted, and the solar-powered pump from the well was our reassurance in case the rain wasn't enough. The garden had been tilled and planted in two patches, one hundred feet long and four feet wide. Donna said that this way, we could get at everything without worrying about trampling on anything growing.

We also created four 4 x 4 feet patches for herbs, mostly medicinal. Eventually, we'd add more for cooking and making herbal tea. We were homesteading in our new world. Everyone was working together, and we all took on tasks that we were both familiar with and needed to learn. We had quietly accepted that with our new existence, everyone knowing as much about how everything worked was just as important in case something bad happened. None of us was invincible, but we didn't mention that, either.

Today we were moving six of Sam's horses over my barn, along with riding tack, saddles, bridles, and blankets. Also, extra curry combs and hoof picks. I knew Sam could blacksmith some, but I didn't know how much he could help with putting shoes on the horses when their current shoes wore out.

Craig had offered to learn from Sam, which was very appreciated by Sam. My son had always had an interest in those things. He wanted to learn to make knives, and eventually, I'm sure he would. He already knew how to make chain mail and had the tools for it, but things hadn't gotten that bad where we were back to using swords and armor.

I was getting ready to head over to their place to start moving the horses when Nancy came out onto the porch, my new office. Handing me the radio, she said, "It's Gary. He says it's important."

Taking the radio from her, I said, "This is John."

"John, we need you and one of the ladies over here, probably Donna or Carol."

Nancy looked a bit miffed at that.

Ignoring her, I replied, "Why, what's up?"

"We have a visitor and she's hurt pretty bad," Gary said.

"A visitor?"

"Yeah, a young girl. Said she's from the looter camp. You need to come now."

"On my way," I replied and handed the radio to Nancy. "Where's Carol and Donna?"

"Inspecting the garden," she said. Her look had gone from getting mad to one of concern.

I ran to the garden, with Nancy close on my heels. "Donna, we need to get to Quint's place. Sounds like they need a nurse."

"What happened?" she and Carol asked at the same time.

"A young girl showed up. Said she was from the looter camp. Gary said she was hurt bad."

"I'll get my stuff," Donna said, and ran to the cabin.

Nancy and Carol looked at me. Immediately, Carol started asking questions I didn't have answers for.

"I'll let you know as soon as I know something," I told them.

Donna returned, and we went to the barn for the UTV, hopped in, and drove through the field on the path to Quint's farm.

The drive took about five minutes and we didn't speak a word on the trip. Pulling in front of his house, we ran inside, Donna grabbing her medical bag, which was a repurposed gym duffle. We hadn't even got a chance to knock when a voice shouted, "In here."

Inside, Gary, Sam, Quint, and Rick were standing around the couch in the living room. All of them looked as concerned as they did lost. Gary had done some basic first aid, his EMT things still in a pile around the room. A wash rag and a large bowl of bloody water were on the floor next to the couch.

Donna immediately began treating the young woman with Gary's help. The rest of us went out on the front porch, giving them privacy.

"What happened?" I asked.

"Not sure. I was riding my horse, checking out the pasture and scouting to make sure everything was okay," Rick said. "I saw her coming out of the woods. She saw me and ran back into the trees. After a bit of searching, I found her curled up and crying."

"Where did she come from?" I asked.

"After Rick got her here," Sam said, "she told us that she'd come from the looter camp. Said they killed her parents. Her father is hanging from one of the lamp posts, she didn't say how her mom died."

"Rick, tell John what she told you, what you told us," Quint said.

"She said her family was trying to steal some food," Rick said. "That they hadn't eaten in days. They were caught, and the leader beat her dad. Then, he made everyone watch while they hanged the man. They just pulled him up on a rope. She said they took her mom away and raped her. She could hear her screaming for a long time. Eventually, the screams stopped."

"Did they, um, did they…"

My question was interrupted as Donna came out of the house with Gary, the creaking screen door announcing them.

"Yes, she was assaulted," Donna said. "She told me the leader of the group did it. It went on for days."

"How did she get away?" I asked.

Donna shrugged. "She said everyone got drunk and passed out. While they were sleeping it off, she snuck away."

"Brave girl."

"John, she was raped and beaten," Donna said. "She saw her father hanged. We have to do something about them, and soon."

"We don't have the manpower, Donna. We don't have the ability to do anything except defend ourselves."

Donna shook her head. "God dammit, John, we *have* to do something."

I was surprised Quint didn't chastise her for blaspheming. One look at him told me why. He was beyond angry. I could see it in his eyes.

"We'll talk about it," I said, trying to defuse the situation. Maybe there was something we could do, but right now I didn't know what.

"What can we do for the young lady?" Quint asked.

"Her name is Addie, short for Addison," Donna said. "For now, she needs rest. John, I think I should stay here for a few days, help her out as much as possible. No offense, guys, but she needs a woman to help her through this."

Several heads nodded in agreement with "I understand" were the responses she got.

"John, can you let Carol know, and ask her if she can come over and help? Another female might be a good idea."

"Sure, I can do that."

"I'll follow you over," Sam said. "We need to talk about the solar panels, and this will leave you short-handed over there. I can help bring the horses in, too."

"Okay," I answered. "We should probably get started. I suspect Carol will want to come over as soon as she hears. Her horse is already there, so she can come back on it. You, Brian, and I need to talk anyway about the communication system."

Everyone went to work. Rick and Quint began hauling tack out of the barn and putting it in the bed of my UTV as Sam haltered up the horses and tied them up in a long string. Then, we began the ride to my place.

***

Tom walked toward the entrance of the park. Kevin and a few of the men had gone looking for the girl.

He saw Kevin coming back now, four people between him and his team of five. The people all had their hands on their heads—three men and a woman.

"Now what?" Tom asked himself aloud. He sat on the table outside of his shelter as Kevin came over.

"What's that?" Tom asked.

"We found them holing up in a farmhouse. Lots of food in it, so I'm sending some people back for it. An old couple were dead, laying on the porch. Found out the girl over there killed them. Seems they like to pretend she's hurt and running away from someone. When her new rescuers let their guard down, she kills them with this." Kevin pulled a chrome-colored Buck hunting knife out of his belt and handed it to Tom.

"I have to meet this chick," Tom said. "She sounds like my kind of girl."

Following Kevin, Tom went over to the four captives.

"Put your hands down," he ordered.

They complied, and their guards stepped back but kept their weapons at the ready.

Tom stood a few feet in front of the girl, and showing her the knife, said, "This yours?"

"Yeah, it's mine," she said.

The tone in her voice told Tom she wasn't afraid.

Turning his attention to the three men, he asked, "And you brave boys sent a woman to do your dirty work."

One of them started to step forward and then, catching himself, stopped. He was, like the other three men, scruffy-looking with a ragged beard and wearing stained, torn jeans. His long-sleeved shirt had a black heart with an A in the middle. The cross bar of the A touched both sides of the heart. Tall and thinner than the others, it was obvious he thought he was in charge of them.

"She volunteered and I agreed," the man said. "It seemed the best way to get them with their guard down." He stood defiantly, anger in his eyes.

He's nervous. Smart guy.

"Okay, tough guy," Tom grunted. "So, you sent a woman in because it was a good idea. I like creativity."

With that comment, the group noticeably relaxed.

"We can use some smart people who aren't afraid to act, to take some initiative. Where are you from?"

"Near Bonduel," the leader said.

"Big town," Tom quipped.

"We were up from Milwaukee. Wanted to get away and rest up after all the *activity* there."

"Activity?" Tom questioned. "What kind of 'activity'."

"Protesting, standing up to all the fascists and haters trying to control everything, starving the people."

Tom looked the group over. "What are you, some kinda communist or something?"

"We're none of that. We are Antifa," he snapped back.

"Antifa? Those punks wearing masks and shit?"

"We *ain't* punks, and we wear masks so that the fascists don't know who we are. We can't keep fighting them if they can identify and arrest us," the leader explained.

"You just might do, boy." Tom decided to push his authority. "I'm the head honcho, hear? And I give the orders. You got a problem with that?"

"Not yet," the man answered.

"What's your name, tough guy?" Tom asked.

"Brad. That's Sheri, and the other two are Carl and Frank."

"Well, get this straight, *Brad*. I'm in charge, and if

you challenge me, if you disrespect me, you'll end up like that." Tom pointed to the man hanging from the lamp post. "Are we clear?"

"Crystal," Brad replied.

"Kevin, take our new friends over to meet the others. Introduce them, and then get a group together. Brad here will be one of them, and go clean out that house. Bring anything you think we can use…food, weapons, whatever you can find."

"You got it boss," Kevin said.

"You, Sheri?"

"Yeah?" the woman asked.

"We'll talk more later," Tom said. "I like your style."

"Okay," she answered, somewhat warily.

"Don't get uppity. I'm not gonna try and jump your bones. Now go with Kevin and he'll take care of you. We'll talk later."

Exhaling with a huff, she walked off with the others.

Tom stood there alone. *This just keeps getting better and better.*

Chapter 12

"Beware of your neighbor!"

—Jeremiah 9:4

S am and I arrived at the cabin to a waiting gaggle
of questions. Everyone wanted to know what
happened, what the emergency was, and where Donna
was. With all of them talking at once, it was impossible
to give an answer.

"You gonna answer them?" Sam said softly out of
the corner of his mouth.

"In time," I said. "I want to get this done."

"Maybe you should tell them that."

I shrugged. "For now, we need to get your radio set
up. We have to contact the guard in Antigo."

"I won't get that done until tomorrow. So, you might
as well tell these people you'll talk to them after we get
unloaded and get the stuff I need for the solar panels."

"Fine." I blew out a breath. "Look, everybody. We'll
be done here shortly and talk on the porch."

Sam chuckled.

"How's that?" I asked.

"You are so lovable at times."

"Gee, thanks."

We finished putting the horses and tack up. Sam and I loaded some things into the wagon that would help him with power for his radio, and then we walked over to the porch.

No one looked pleased with me. While I expected that, it still was irritating. We had things to do and the situation over at Quint's wasn't going away.

I went to my chair on the porch and sat down. Before anyone could say a word, I jumped up, went inside, grabbed a cigar, and came back outside. The looks I was getting were barely tolerable, but I knew it was going to be a tough conversation.

I went through the brief ritual of cutting and lighting the cigar and then said, "Okay, here is the situation."

I told them about Addison and how Rick had found her. There was a lot of anger from the group at that point, and I deflected several questions. "Let me finish. Then, we'll get into the rest of this."

Nancy actually growled at me, causing Brian to laugh out loud. She gave him that infamous look of hers and he quieted right up.

I finished with telling them that Donna would be staying over at Quint's for a couple of days, both for Addie's physical and emotional healing.

Everybody seemed to agree that Addie needed a woman to help her through the turmoil. Nancy and Carol offered to take turns, if necessary.

I thanked them, but inside I didn't really know what they could do beyond emotional support. I had no experience with this, and beyond understanding that a woman being there was better than a man right now, I really didn't know what they could offer that Donna couldn't.

It took about thirty seconds of silence before anyone

began to react.

"So it was the looters, the ones over at Stilwell's Pond?" Carol asked.

"That's what she said," I confirmed.

Before I could finish, Craig interrupted. "So, what are we going to do? We can't leave them there."

"I don't think we should *do* anything yet, son."

"What do you mean?" he asked.

"He means we don't have enough people or weapons to do anything about it," Brian answered. "If we were to go over there guns a blazing, a lot of us probably wouldn't come back."

His words had a chilling effect on the conversation.

"So, what can we do?" Nancy asked. She had pulled Mike close to her, her concern clearly telegraphed in her actions.

"Once Sam gets his radio set up, we're going to contact the National Guard in Antigo," I said. "They're the only real law enforcement around here and we need to ask them for help."

"What if they won't?" Brian asked. "You were there, Dad. Captain Wolfe didn't seem too enthusiastic about doing anything to help, and Rahn pretty much said the same thing."

"You changing your mind about doing something?" I asked, the tone of my voice as much scolding as challenging.

"Not at all. All I'm saying is with a band of killers and rapists…"

"Brian!" Nancy said sharply, pointing her eyes quickly at Mike and then back at Brian.

Ignoring her chastisement, Brian continued, "We have to do something to protect ourselves. We have the bunker by the road, but if they come over here, they may not come that way. They may go through the woods. Then what?"

"Good point," I said. "The bunker alone, nor our lookouts from upstairs, is going to give us much warning if they come through the woods. What've you got in mind?"

A wicked grin crossed his face, a look I had not seen before. His eyes were dark and focused. "Perimeter security and early warning devices, Pops."

"Booby traps," I clarified.

"You betcha," Brian said. "We have everything we need. Wood, nails, shotgun shells, a couple of boxes of grenades, and a lot of other stuff. We can set up on the tree line and inside of it, before the edge of the field."

I heaved a sigh. "It's been a while."

Brian snorted. "Yeah, but it will come back. Besides, I saw your library."

"Library?"

"Yup, the *Anarchists Cookbook*." He grinned.

I had forgotten. I had so many books on just about everything we would need that I forgot I had that one. The book was filled with instructions on how to make a lot of things, most importantly for us, booby traps and explosives.

"That's a good idea. I have a lot of other information on primitive booby traps besides the book. Punji pits, swinging logs, and so forth. Between the book, the papers, and saved videos I have, we can put up one lethal protective perimeter."

"Isn't that dangerous?" Nancy asked.

"Duh!" Craig said.

"No, dammit," Nancy said, "I mean dangerous for us. What if we accidentally step on one or something?"

"We'll make sure everyone knows where they are. We can figure out some sort of way that only we know how to identify them in case we forget where they are," Brian answered, giving Craig a disapproving stare.

"We can start getting things together now," I said,

"and this evening, before it gets dark. In the morning, we can start putting the traps in place. We need to get back on guard duty at the bunker and upstairs, too. We're down one, so it's gonna be tiring for us."

"I can guard, Grampa," Mike piped in.

The look on Nancy's face was not supportive.

Before she could say anything, I replied, "Yes, you can, son, but only from upstairs. Right now, I think it's best you be here, close to us."

"The dogs should help," Carol added. "Max and King are German shepherds. They should be good guard dogs."

She wasn't even finished when, seeing the three dogs curled up asleep, I pointed toward them with my chin, "Yeah, they're good guard dogs, all right."

That seemed to lighten the mood as a few chuckles were heard from the group.

"You're being awfully quiet, Sam," I said.

"Just listening and thinking," Sam said. "We need to do the same thing at Quint's. Addie wasn't too far from Quint's place when Rick found her, and they might come looking for her. Seems logical that's the first place they'd look."

I nodded. "You're right."

"I'm a sailor, we're smarter than you guys," he said.

Brian let out a groan.

While Brian, Sam, Craig, and I began to gather some things, Nancy and Carol went inside and started dinner. It was funny how we'd all fallen into stereotypical roles. In this case, I wasn't objecting or criticizing. Neither of them knew what we were doing or how to do it. We had already begun to automatically do things based on our strengths. I'd eventually show the women how to create traps, even Mike would learn.

***

Over the course of the next several days we designed, built, and mapped many different booby traps, land mines, and other objects that we designed to either give us early warning of someone approaching or to help us defend our home. Our days were filled with constant running back and forth from the workshop in the garage to the UTV to transport parts or complete bombs. Nancy, Carol, and occasionally Craig went over to the Stepanik's farm to check on Addie. Craig had taken an interest suddenly, in ham radio operating so Sam was teaching him while they got the system up and running.

I wasn't sure if the traps we had made were a symbol of how cruel and depraved we had become or merely creative genius. We had made punji type traps that rolled when a foot went in them. The spikes, part of several large boxes of 40d nails I had, would then drive into the foot and ankle of anyone stepping into them.

I took some old leaf springs and turned them into traps that, when released, would sweep across a path about mid-calf high, breaking a leg. Other, more traditional, foot traps were simply nails driven through boards that, when placed at the bottom of a shallow pit, would impale the foot.

I had to laugh when Craig wanted to use a rope and tree to make a trap that would grab the victim by the ankle and hang them upside down. We didn't make that one. We had quite a few toe poppers made from shotgun shells, a board, and a nail as a firing pin. While all of these would only disable a single person, it was the incendiaries that we made that were true group killers. We'd filled glass jars with homemade napalm and a heat source that, when activated, would start a good-sized fire. We placed these inside brush piles. Anyone thinking they could watch us unobserved would find them very troublesome—and deadly.

I was in the garage cleaning up, while Brian was out at the bunker watching there. We had seen an increase in foot traffic. Small groups of people, mostly families, trudging by in the direction of town—we guessed either Antigo or east toward the communities there. I heard Craig's horse on the gravel before I saw him.

Putting the hammer I had in my hand on the bench, I turned to face him as he dismounted and walked into the barn, holding his AR. Seeing my boys go everywhere with a weapon in their hands was still something I didn't like, but the ways things had become and would continue, I knew it was necessary.

Some days, Craig would come back and bring me news of what Sam had learned from other operators around the US and overseas. I figured that was one of the reasons he'd returned.

"Hey, Craig," I said.

His shoulders drooped and I didn't know if he was tired or something was troubling him.

"Bad news, Dad."

The *once upon a time* way of storytelling had left Craig since all of this had started, and as had become his new way, he cut right to it.

"From what Sam is getting from the radio, the whole country has turned into a war zone."

"Oh?"

"Yeah," Craig explained. "Apparently, what they've started to call the shadow government is trying to fill the gap of the rest of the government officials that were killed in the DC blast. It seems some of the army leaders and a few government officials are inside Cheyenne Mountain…"

I immediately thought of Brian when he said that as Brian used to work there.

"…but overall, the military seems to have collapsed, with most of the personnel taking off to care for their families."

"Damn, I was afraid of that."

"Well, groups representing the shadow government are now using old FEMA stockpiles of everything—guns, ammo, vehicles, etcetera. They're driving people into what they call refugee centers, basically using them as slaves. Militia groups and hate groups are rising up everywhere, acting like bandits and killing each other in gunfights. It's not good."

"Any word from overseas?" I asked.

"Yeah, I'll get to that. Apparently, these so-called government groups are executing anyone who resists. Just driving them into small groups and machine gunning them down. Bands of motorcycle gangs, criminal gangs, and new gangs out for blood are terrorizing people everywhere."

I shook my head in sadness. "Didn't take us long to become savages again, did it?"

"No. What's left of the UN command is trying to get together a peace keeping rescue force to come over here, but what is left of the government in Colorado is objecting and so are some of the UN countries."

"Shit. It's bad then."

"Well, some of the countries seem to be untouched by all of this. Canada and Central America are out, just like us. Apparently, we really did nuke North Korea right after the EMP hit—and it's gone. China was pissed about that and threatened to retaliate. But the Russians saw an opportunity and moved into Manchuria, so while that got the Chinese off our backs, they're now fighting each other. The Middle East is still hostile and Israel is hanging on. Eventually, Sam says, they'll all run out of bullets, bombs, and fuel, so who knows what will happen then." Craig took a breath. "Europe is having food riots now and the Brits are doing okay, but not well enough to send anything to help here yet. Sam seems sure they will, and sure that the government will let them, but it isn't gonna come to Wisconsin anytime soon."

I rubbed my chin, thinking it over. "Sam got all of this from his ham buddies, huh?"

"Yeah, he's got quite a network. Seems the best groups are these prepper groups we all used to laugh at."

I gave him a look because while I didn't belong to a group, at least a formal one, I was a prepper.

"You know what I mean, Dad."

"Yeah, I do. I'll admit, I laughed at some of them, too. Pretending to be some kind of legitimate military force that was going to survive by will and firepower. Hell, most of them were overweight and out of shape. A lot had health conditions that wouldn't last the first month, and from what I remember, a lot of them were absolutely clueless but liked to collect gadgets. They'd last a minute against a better force—and there are plenty of those."

"Anyway, it doesn't look good," Craig said. "Being way up here in the middle of nowhere, we aren't going to see any relief anytime soon."

"Was Sam able to get hold of the guard in Antigo?"

"Yeah, your buddy the first sergeant said things are deteriorating there, too. Seems that the captain took off with a group to go down to Madison looking for orders. He doesn't know if they're coming back."

"So what's Rahn going to do? Did he say?"

Craig shrugged. "He said he was planning a trip out here to see you. Called it a reconnaissance in force, or something like that."

That made me curious. Was Rahn bugging out, or was he really coming for a visit?

"How's Addie doing?" I asked.

Craig glanced away, his voice soft when he spoke.

"She's still quiet. I've tried to talk to her a few times. Mom thought talking with someone her age might help."

"How'd that go?"

"Not well. I did most of the talking. She seems nice and all, but she's really hurting. I'll keep trying. Losing both her parents like that can't be easy."

I put my hand on his shoulder. "Don't be a pest. Listen to your mom."

"I will, Dad."

"I'm gonna finish here and then take the maps inside to share with everyone. I need to make copies for Quint and the guys over there. We don't need any accidents."

"We need to keep an eye on Mike, too," Craig said firmly. "He keeps trying to go out that way and…"

"Yeah, we do. I'll talk to him. He listens to me."

"Uh huh. I need to put the horse up and then relieve Brian. It's my turn out there."

He took the horse by the reins and headed toward the horse's stall. I didn't like his news, but I couldn't do anything about it. This was something I couldn't fix, and the news put everything we did into a different, more serious perspective. Not that it wasn't serious already.

***

A few days of quiet passed without incident. We tended the garden, made firewood, and placed early warning devices and booby traps around Quint's place. We saw more foot traffic on the road, making me glad I had asked Brian to cut the mailbox down, twice.

No one seemed to have seen the bunker or anyone sitting in it, which was good. I had given strict instructions that no one was to leave the bunker and talk to any refugee or anyone else travelling by. That didn't set well with a few of them, but I was adamant about it.

"So, we're going to sit here and watch everyone walk by to die?" Nancy asked. She was angry, her body in a ready-to-fight stance.

I knew how she felt, but my family's needs came first. "We can't take care of them all, Nancy."

"We couldn't even take water out to the side of the road for them?"

I didn't know what to say.

Sensing an opening, she pressed the issue. "Fil, I'm not saying we have to feed 'em, but they *are* human beings. We can't let them die of thirst. We have plenty of water."

She had me there. That well would most likely never go dry, and the added volume on the well from carrying water to the road for any refugees wasn't going to put a dent into it.

"Ok, water. Water only," I said sternly. "But no one comes back here from the road. They *stay* out there."

"Thanks, Fil," she said, a smile on her face.

Running off to tell the others, I suspected she was as happy about winning an argument with me as she was being able to put some humanity back into all of us. I knew Nancy was right. I wasn't going to say it out loud, though.

Watching her run toward the cabin, I was surprised by the roar of an engine behind me. Spinning around and raising my AR to my shoulder, I saw two Humvees pulling into the yard.

Behind one of them was a trailer with a canvas tarp over it. Keeping my AR at the ready, I saw a smiling face on the passenger side of the lead Humvee. Recognizing First Sergeant Rahn, I lowered my weapon. A smile hid my frustration. Whoever was in the bunker should've let me know they were coming down the drive.

Rahn jumped out as the Humvee came to a stop. "Hello, Mr. Henry," he shouted, a big shit-eating grin spread across his face.

"I told you it's John," I shouted back. "Mr. Henry is my son."

I walked toward the vehicles, and he met me halfway.

"Yeah, he let us in," Rahn said. "Nice bunker, by the way." He extended his hand.

I let my AR hang by the two-point sling I had it on. Never did like the single point. Taking his hand, I replied, "He should've let me know."

Rahn had the good sense not to feed the ass-chewing I was going to give Brian. "Got the message from your jarhead radio operator. Thought we'd bring you some toys to help out."

"What kind of toys?" I asked, curious.

He turned, waved his arm in a follow me gesture, and we headed toward the trailer. Untying the tarp, he pulled it back. Inside were several wooden crates.

I whistled.

"Your operator told me about your IED antics and Vietcong traps. Thought you could use something more modern." Pointing inside the trailer, I followed his arm. "We have a few cases of .22 caliber sentry alarms." Two large spools of OD trip wire were also in plain sight.

The two larger cases puzzled me. Then I saw the stenciling and suddenly, I had a big shit-eating grin of my own. *Mines*. "Holy shit," I said. "Claymores."

"Yep, I have exactly twenty-four for you."

"Geezus, Rahn, how…what…"

"You've got a lot of bad dudes around here, John. There are groups all over, from what I can tell, and that includes some roaming motorcycle gangs from The

Outlaws. You're gonna need this shit to stay safe."

"Captain Wolfe ain't gonna be happy about this, Rahn."

"He's gone, and I don't think he's ever coming back."

I stared at him. "You know something about that?"

"No, but he was getting real flaky before he decided to take three Hummers and head south to Madison. Took ten of my guys with him."

"How long has he been gone?" I asked, looking over the weapons in the trailer.

"Over a week."

"So now what?"

"Well, glad you asked," Rahn said. "We'll head back to the armory later and I'm gonna hang out there for about another week. I have eight guys there now."

I did a quick count. He had seven men with him, so that made sixteen.

"If he's not back in that time, I'm gonna give the guys a choice. I thought maybe we could come here, put ourselves under Mr. Henry's command. Those that don't want to come, I'd set them up with whatever they need and the rest would come here with me."

I gave him a sideways glance. "Cabin's kinda full, Rahn. Not that you aren't welcome."

"I figured. I have GP Larges and the liners and heaters to go with them. Or…" He paused, looked toward the barn. "Maybe we could set up housekeeping in there?"

I followed his gaze. My mind raced as I mulled it over. "That could work. You open to splitting your force up?"

"How so?" he asked.

"We have another location through the woods. That's where Sam, the jarhead, is. They could use some extra manpower, and it would get some of your guys into a better shelter. It'll be winter before you know it, and that barn's gonna get cold."

"Yeah, we can talk about that. I have some ideas."

Movement behind me caused a brief distraction from our conversation. I turned around to see Specialist Johnson, the young soldier I had first met at the armory.

"Hello, Mr. Henry," Johnson said.

"It's *John*," I said, probably a bit too firm.

"Sorry, John." He seemed genuinely contrite.

"Johnson," Rahn said, "get a couple of the guys and unload this trailer. Put it wherever John wants it."

"Okay, Top." Johnson nodded.

"Dammit, Johnson."

"Sorry, First Sergeant." He didn't seem all that contrite as he walked away as he grabbed the driver and a passenger from the other Hummer. "Where do you want these, John?" he shouted.

"Put 'em on the porch," I replied. Turning to Rahn, I said, "Want some coffee?"

"Is a pig's ass pork?"

I chuckled and we headed toward the cabin. As he walked alongside me, I noticed once again we were in step.

"We need to talk about those bad dudes you mentioned," I said as we walked. "We have a group not far from here that a girl escaped from. She was beaten and raped. They killed her parents, too."

"I've heard. That's part of why I'm here."

***

Rahn and his team hung around for about an hour before they left for the armory. Quint had come over while he was visiting and the two were introduced. Rahn blasphemed once; Quint put a quick stop to it.

Quint, Brian, and I sat on the porch sorting through our new toys, talking and planning a few things as we did so, not the least of which was navigating a path through the woods between our two places. We decided that we'd mostly use the road, especially now that Nancy and Craig were out front, along with Mike, giving water to the refugees as they came by.

"You soldier boys sure do like things that go boom," Quint said.

I glanced his way. "You were a soldier boy yourself, Quint. You never blew anything up?"

"No, I was a clerk. I had a typewriter. A manual typewriter, at that. Hated it, but I made the mistake of saying I took typing in high school."

I chuckled. I remembered my dad telling me stories like this about World War II. You didn't dare tell anyone you knew how to type or you'd spend the war as a clerk.

"So how do these Claymores work?" Quint asked. "Can't be too hard, they even tell you which way to point 'em."

Raised letters on the frontside of the Claymore said, "Front Toward Enemy," so it wasn't real hard to figure that part out.

"Here, let me show you," Brian replied, and spent about a minute showing Quint how to set them up.

"So, every one of them has to have one of these clicker things?" Quint asked.

"I'm sure we can wire them up somehow to a board so we only need one clicker or we can use a battery," I said.

"That could be good, Dad. Not bad for an old fart," Brian said, a grin on his face.

"Respect your father, son," Quint said quickly.

I liked the old man, especially now. He had a way about things.

"So, what're we going to do about them looters?" Quint asked. "We have all this new stuff, and if that first sergeant guy comes back with more soldiers…" He left the question hanging.

"I don't think we should outright attack them," I said. "From what I figure, they're a much bigger group than we are. We might have fire superiority, but they have the numbers."

Quint shook his head. "That don't sit well, John. You know it won't sit well with the others, either."

"Well, we can't do much of anything until Rahn joins us. *If* he joins us. Until then, all we can do is get our defenses set up better and keep an eye on things. The refugees on the road are increasing. Rahn tells me there are motorcycle gangs running around the area, too."

"What about our neighbors, John? Surely, they can get involved. It's their lives and safety, too," Quint asked.

"I plan on riding around to a few of them and telling them what's up. See if they want some kind of alliance with us. We have to work together out here. We can't do this alone."

"Mind if me and Rick ride along? Safety in numbers, and all that."

I shrugged. "Plus, you're probably nosy and want to see what's going on too, right?"

Quint cackled. "Well, there is that."

"Yes, there is," I said.

"We can't leave those people over in the park, John. We have to run them off at least."

"I'd settle for killin' 'em," Craig said.

I hadn't noticed him walk up. He had a bucket in one hand and his AR in the other.

"They're scum," Craig continued, "and after what they did to Addie and her parents, not to mention Carol's diner. Who the hell knows what else they'll do."

My son was mad. He got this way sometimes. When

he did, it was best to let him fume a bit.

"We can't do that, son. As much as I want them out of here, we don't have the manpower to drive them off or *kill* 'em," I said.

"Bro, Dad's right, now isn't the time," Brian interjected. "If Dad can get the neighbors to help, maybe then. If Rahn comes with more weapons and ammo, then maybe. But right now, we can't exact revenge."

"Maybe I can," he muttered. He walked off toward the water pump.

Brian, Quint, and I shared a look.

I had to make sure he didn't do anything rash. Craig had been spending time with Addie, and I thought his hormones and emotions were acting up. This was not going to be a good conversation, but I had to say my piece.

Chapter 13

"Who Dares Wins"

—Special Air Service (SAS) motto

O ver the next several days, Sam's horses got their exercise as Quint, Rick, Craig, and I rode all over the county to talk to as many survivors as we could. I made Craig ride along, as much to keep an eye on him as to give him time to cool off. My talk with him was clear, but it hadn't gone well. I felt he was giving me lip service on his agreement to not try and start anything with the looters. Brian had tried to talk to him, but it hadn't helped much. Craig remained angry. Understandably so, but there were other, more useful ways, to deal with it.

Most of the people we spoke to wanted no part of an alliance, or a mutual defense pact, as Quint called it. The fact that many of them were elderly probably had something to do with their decisions. Most were standoffish at best. One man even held a gun on us.

While I can't say that I blamed them, it was unsettling. Craig, in an unusual statement of humor on this journey, decided it was just unneighborly.

A scarce few thought it was a good idea. We left them one of the radios and told them to call if they needed help, and that soon we would call them to get together for a meeting and a chance to get better acquainted. It all was going fairly well—that is, until we met the Winstons.

Quint knew Old Man Winston, as he called him. He said he was crotchety and ornery to boot.

"Thought those were the same thing?" I said as we rode up the road to the Winstons' place.

"Let me do the talking here," Quint said. "They don't much like strangers, and I know the old man fairly well."

Quint explained to us that the family had come up from Kentucky back in the 70s. That wasn't uncommon around here, as we had many families who moved here from Kentucky since World War II. They mostly kept to themselves and lived in squalor. The term "Kentuck" became a somewhat derisive way of describing them.

I didn't see it as condemning someone of Kentucky as much as it was a put down on people who didn't have much to begin with, didn't want much, and who didn't want anything much to do with the rest of us. Over the years, some had gone to jail for everything from robbery and fighting to growing marijuana or making meth.

We rode up the drive, a dirt road leading to a rundown house. A mobile home sat on the property as well as what looked like a camping trailer. Each of them had rust stains on the sides. Everything was in need of paint and a cleaning.

BOOM!

A shot rang out. Dirt kicked up a few feet in front of us.

I heard the distinctive sound of a shotgun being

racked from inside the house. Immediately, I brought my horse to a halt. The racking noise made me want to run for cover, but instead I sat there on my horse. Other than a quick jump, it hadn't done much but nicker.

Quint was calm. "Just stand still, folks. It'll be alright."

"Stop right there!" a voice shouted from the house.

Who walked out on the porch could've come from any one of the recently popular shows on TV about hunters or mountain people. A man stood on the porch, heavily bearded and wearing what looked like a farm implement hat, green with stained yellow lettering. He wore tan overalls with a dingy looking long sleeved t-shirt underneath. He didn't look too friendly, but he wasn't looking unfriendly, either. His deer rifle— seemed everyone up here had one—was held across his chest.

"What do you want?" he demanded.

"Jesse, it's me, Quint. Quint Stepanik. The old man around?" Quint asked.

The man on the porch seemed to relax as he recognized Quint. He stepped down off the porch and stepped a few feet into the yard. "He's in the house. What do you want with him?"

Quint said, "I need to talk to him."

"Who's that with you?" Jesse said.

"I'm J…"

Quint put up a hand and stopped me from saying anything further. "My grandson, and this is my neighbor, John Henry, and his son, Craig. We need to talk to your dad."

"Stay here." He headed to the house, then he stopped and turned back toward us. "Ya'll can get down off the horses if you want."

"Thank you," Quint answered as Jesse went indoors. "Let's get off the horses and stretch a bit. Too much time in the saddle makes my behind hurt."

Quint's behind might've hurt, but my ass was sore and so was my back. I hadn't spent this much time in the saddle since my early days in the army when I had probably the coolest job ever and rode for a living. Of course, I was nineteen then and not in my fifties.

We all got down and stood by our horses, each of us making sure we were completely visible and that it was obvious that, while we were armed, our weapons were not out and threatening. Nowadays, it was plain smart to do this when meeting someone you didn't want to shoot. We'd already been shot at, but after Quint had been recognized I felt better about the possibility of not having to shoot our way out of here.

A few minutes later, Jesse came back out. He was followed by an older man that looked exactly like Jesse. Except for the grey hair and bald spot on top, the two could've been twins. They were even dressed alike.

As the two men walked down the steps of the porch, Quint and his horse headed toward them. The rest of us followed slowly a few feet behind.

The two older men stood in front of each other. Quint extended his hand to shake and the older Winston took it.

"What can I do for you, Quint? The boy here says you said you wanted to talk."

"Yes, Charlie," Quint confirmed, "we need to talk. I'm sure you know about everything that's happened with the electrical powers and government and such."

Old man Winston glanced at the rest of us, then looked at Quint. "I know the power is out and the TV don't work. Don't know or much care about the government." He pronounced it as gubmint.

"I understand. It's all gone. Somebody set off a nuclear bomb on Washington that pretty much killed everybody there. So, we're all on our own now."

"Can't say that's much of a bad thing, Quint. That's how it shoulda been all along. You know how I feel about the government."

"That's true, but now that we're all on our own, we have to help each other out more. That's how it should be, too."

"So, what do you want?" Charlie asked.

"There's trouble around here," Quint explained. "Real bad trouble. Seems there is a big gang of people over at Stilwell's Pond. They've been looting and burning, plus they killed a family, except for the daughter. They did bad things to her, Charlie."

Charlie harrumphed. "That's the sheriff's business, not mine. Sad about the girl and her family, though."

Craig started to step forward. I reached out and grabbed his arm to stop him. Charlie saw this, raised an eyebrow, and returned his attention to Quint.

"The sheriff needs to take care of that," Charlie said. "We can't do that. I ain't getting in the law's business and I don't want them in mine."

"There is no more law, Charlie. That's why we're here. No phones, just a few radios and such. No one has seen or heard from the sheriff at all. It's up to us."

"So, what are you asking, Quint?" Charlie asked.

"We need to band together and help each other out. I hear there are outlaw motorcycle gangs riding around, burning things down and killing people, among other things. You know what things, Charlie. You have a daughter."

A flash of anger spread across Charlie's face when Quint mentioned his daughter. I didn't see anyone else's face, although I could tell someone was watching us from inside the trailer and the house. The curtains had moved several times.

"No one better hurt my daughter," Charlie said, "and

you shouldn't even bring her up. She's safe here and don't go out nowhere."

"They're coming here. We don't have to go anywhere. They can come to us."

Charlie shook his head. "Me and the boys can handle that."

"Against a hundred men or more?" Quint asked. "They have machine guns and other stuff. You can't defend against that."

"I see your point. So, what are you and these other fellas asking? Y'all came here together, so what do y'all want?"

"We want you to band together with us, Charlie. We want you to help us and a few others stay safe. We'll do the same by you. That's all."

Charlie gave a thumbs up and gestured backwards. "I'll have to talk to the missus. She don't like us messin' with others too much. But if it's like you say it is, then we'll do our part."

"Thank you," Quint said, "that means a lot. This here is John Henry and that's his boy, Craig, there. He's my neighbor and he was a soldier. His other boy is a soldier and is back at John's place."

"Pleased to meet you, Mr. Winston. Thank you for agreeing to help." I extended my hand and we shook. He had a firm grip with skin like sandpaper, obviously still a hard-working man.

"I haven't said yes yet, young man," Charlie said, "but most likely I will."

I excused myself and went to my horse. I opened up a saddle bag, taking out one of my radios and a solar charger for it. I took them to Charlie.

"This here radio will help us all stay in touch. It has a solar charger, so the battery stays full. If you keep it on, you'll know when we call. You can call us, too." I extended it out toward Charlie, but Jesse took it.

"I know how to use these," Jesse remarked, and held onto the radio.

"In the next few days, we'll be calling everyone who has agreed to work together. Give us a chance to get to know one another better, and then, figure out how we will do that. With that gang of looters over at the pond, and them already burning down parts of Lake View, we need to be on guard," I said.

"That's what all that smoke was?" Charlie asked.

"Yeah, they burnt down the diner and the insurance office next to it," I confirmed. "Looted the Quik Mart."

"I get your point, young man. We'll do our part. Let me introduce you to the family." He turned and waved his arm. An older woman and a young woman, about Craig's age, came out of the house, followed by a man pretty close to the same age. From the trailer came another man, younger than Jesse but older than the others, then a woman and two kids, a boy and a girl.

The entire group joined us in the yard, each of them carrying a rifle or a shotgun.

"This is the family," Charlie said. "My wife Lucille, daughter Emma, that's Fred, my youngest son, and that's Billy, my middle son and his wife, Sarah. The kids are Emily and Clinton."

I shook hands with the boys and nodded politely to the ladies. This didn't seem like a family where the women shook hands.

I introduced Craig, and Quint introduced Rick. We spent the next thirty minutes getting acquainted as I explained who wasn't with us. I do believe they thought my having my ex-wife living with us was a bit odd. When we left, I felt that Charlie and his family would do their part to help; how much I wasn't certain, but they'd help. Just as I was getting ready to mount my horse, Jesse came up to me and stuck his hand out.

"Sorry for shooting at you, John. I didn't know who

you were," he said.

"I wasn't hit, so we're okay," I replied.

"Next time you come up, you might want to yell out who you are."

I nodded. "That won't be a problem, Jesse."

***

The trip home was uneventful. Besides keeping watch for anything or anyone lurking around intent on causing us harm, we had almost no excitement on the ride back. Rick and Craig had become a pair of chatterboxes, talking mostly about video games they would never play again.

We finally made it to the turn into the driveway. Mike and Nancy were in the bunker—well, Nancy was in the bunker. Mike was near the road with a bucket of well water looking for people.

"Hi, Grampa," he shouted.

"That boy sure does love his grampa," Quint said as Mike began to run toward us.

I got off my horse and gave the reins to Quint, then scooped him up as he jumped toward me. Spinning him around, I asked, "So, how's my boy?"

"I'm good, Grampa. Nobody came by today for water."

"That's probably good, Mike."

"Well," Mike said, "except for the two guys my dad has up at the cabin."

Nancy had walked over to us while Mike let me know that bit of news.

"We have visitors?" I asked her.

"Yeah, there's two boys up at the house. Brian has them under guard. They said they knew Craig."

"Who are they?" Craig asked.

Nancy shrugged. "Two boys from Appleton, said they knew you."

Craig glanced at me, a curious look on his face. Putting his horse into a canter, he shouted over his shoulder, "I'll find out, Dad." He turned down the drive and disappeared into the trees.

"I should check on this, too," I said and mounted my horse with a bit of a groan. A couple days in the saddle had made me sore at my old age.

Quint shouted, "We're going back to my place."

And with that our little gathering broke up.

I arrived in the yard to see Craig hugging two young men about his age. They were all embracing and laughing. I guess he *did* know them. Brian was up on the porch, sitting in my chair. He and I were going to have to have a talk about that.

Craig yelled to me, "Dad, this is Sajan and Allen, my friends from Appleton.

I got off my horse, curiosity overwhelming me as I made my way to them and we were all formally re-introduced.

Sajan looked Indian, and well-tanned at that. His dark hair and eyes emphasized an infectious smile. His rather filthy appearance—dirty jeans and a long sleeve shirt looked a bit crusty, along with athletic shoes, was all he had. Allen looked much the same, only his light brown hair was shorter but still over his ears.

Sajan said, "Hello, Mr. Henry, we've met before."

I thought a minute before I replied, "Your folks own that pizza place on Wisconsin Avenue, right?"

"Yes, sir. They're in Canada and I don't know when or if they'll ever come home. Allen and I went to Craig's place, but when we saw the gun fight you guys were having we thought we'd come back in the morning. When we went back, you guys were gone. So, Allen and I decided to come here."

"You saw the fight?" I asked.

"Yeah, we were across the street under a big blue spruce. Figured with all the excitement we might get shot, so we snuck off and hid."

"I'm sorry we missed you. Took you guys awhile. That was over a month ago," I said. "How'd you know to come here?"

"Craig's talked about this place a lot. Showed us on the map where it was, and he said he was going to ask you if we could come visit sometime."

"How was the trip?" I asked.

"Dangerous," Allen said. "People shooting and everything. We mostly travelled at night. I saw that in a movie once. We hid out during the day and either ate what we had or scavenged for some. People aren't very nice."

"Can't say as I blame them," Craig interjected.

"I'll put the horses up, Craig," I said, grabbing the reins for his horse. "You boys sit here and visit."

Brian joined me as I went to the barn. "Interesting story from those two," he said as we walked. "They only had a pellet rifle to protect themselves. Neither of them could shoot anything with it, but they figured it would scare away anyone trying to hurt them."

"I'm kinda surprised they made it. I remember Sajan. He never struck me as the outdoorsy type."

"He's smart, and Allen seems to know a bit about woodcraft and things. I'm glad they're here. We need the manpower."

"Yeah, there is that," I answered.

We spent the next hour putting up the horses, cleaning the tack, and filling each other in on all that had happened over the last few days. Finishing, we went to the cabin. It was dinner time."

***

Evening found all of us who weren't on guard duty conversing on the porch. The weather was still nice, and we'd be able to enjoy this pastime all summer and into the early fall.

I had my chair. I had once again explained the rules to Brian.

He'd smiled his mischievous smile and said, "Okay."

I figured we'd have to revisit the issue again.

Craig, Sajan, and Allen sat on the steps. Craig explained about our homestead, how we were defending it, and why. Over dinner, Craig had told them about Addie, and it sobered the mood at the table.

The conversation was more jovial now. Craig was showing them how to break down an AR, and the boys were seriously enraptured as they each took turns assembling and disassembling one.

Allen was having problems with one of the takedown pins and was using a large pocket knife to do that with. Craig teased him.

Allen said, "This is my knife. It does everything I want it to do or need it to do."

"It's a toothpick," Craig said, laughing at Allen's growing frustration both with the pin and his knife being picked on.

"Don't dis the knife, dude," Allen said.

Craig got up, walked into the house, and came out with his small duffle bag. Dropping it on the porch, he reached inside and took out a long belt knife. He pulled it out of the sheath, its wickedly long and slender fourteen-inch blade serrated at the top. In the front of the blade, on top, the edge was clearly present. Holding it by its dark brown handle, Craig grinned and said, "What you have isn't a knife. *This* is a knife."

"You did not just say that," Brian said, shaking his head in mock disgust.

"Yes, I did," Craig said, puffing his chest out a bit in

an exaggerated pose.

"That has to be the worst movie line ever, and you used it. Bro, that's just wrong."

The reference to the Australian guy in the movies wasn't lost on me. I let the boys banter for a bit, but then decided to break the mood and get serious again.

"Brian, you have the next watch. Why don't you take one or both of our new family members and show them how we do things? They can start their turns tomorrow."

"Okay, Pops." Standing up, Brian took his AR and went into the house. A few moments later, he came out with two more ARs and an ammo pouch for each, their bulge showing that he had several loaded magazines in them.

"All right, you two," Brian announced as he handed a weapon and pouch to both Sajan and Allen, "time to get serious."

They took the weapons, a bit awkwardly, but I could see the excitement in their eyes, even with the dim light of early evening.

"Make sure you keep the business end pointed away from people, unless you intend to shoot them," Brian said.

Both boys dutifully followed the instructions. He had them lock and load, and then started walking toward the bunker out front.

I couldn't help but think he was actually enjoying this. It seemed like he had a squad of new soldiers to train and was doing what he loved.

The next several days were going to prove interesting.

***

Craig, Sajan, and Allen left the breakfast table early.

Craig took them over to Quint's place to meet Addie, and to see if there might be a possibility that they could stay there. While the barn was comfortable for now, come fall and winter it would be *uncomfortable* on a good day. If we had a normal Wisconsin winter with below zero weather and long stretches of single digit temperatures, they'd want something warmer. Before we put any effort into making a bunkroom in the barn, it made sense they should at least check out the Stepanik place.

It was fun watching Craig show them how to saddle a horse. Both of the boys said they had ridden before, but Brian offered that the carousel horse at the grocery store didn't count.

Eventually, the boys mounted up and headed for the road. I didn't want anyone going through the woods until we had a couple of walk throughs with everyone learning where we had set all of our booby traps and warning devices.

***

Riding past the bunker, Craig left the drive and turned toward Quint's, with his friends following his path. There was no other traffic on the road, and things were quiet. The clip clop of the horseshoes as they stepped down the road were almost hypnotic, lulling them into a sense of peace and calm.

It took twenty minutes to walk the horses down the road and onto the drive to Quint's farm. The dirt road led back about twenty yards to the farmhouse, which faced the drive from the side. Its faded yellow wood siding and white trim welcomed them. As they arrived in front of the house, the screen door creaked its opening and Rick came out onto the porch.

Wearing his customary floppy boonie hat and digitals pants, he walked barefoot onto the porch, his rifle in hand.

"Hi, Craig," he shouted.

Craig, Sajan, and Allen dismounted their horses. Sajan and Allen, both a bit stiff after such a short ride, walked in a few small circles to loosen up the tightness from the ride.

"Hi, Rick, want you to meet some friends of mine." Craig took a few minutes making introductions. In these new times, it was important they all knew each other on sight.

"Is Addie around?" Craig asked. No one would tell him, but his voice changed a bit whenever he spoke of her.

"She's inside. I'll go get her." Rick went back inside the house, the door creaking in protest as it opened, then shutting itself with the spring attached to it, slapped the door frame twice before quieting.

The boys made themselves comfortable by sitting on the steps of the porch. A few minutes later, Rick came back outside with Addie. She was wearing jeans and a long sleeve denim shirt that was too big for her. She had knotted the tails in front of her to help it fit better, and the sleeves were rolled up about halfway to her elbows. She wore a pair of boots Carol had given her since she and Carol were the same size.

Craig stood up quickly when he saw her, pulling his hat from his head.

Sajan and Allen, glanced at each other and smiled.

"Hi, Addie," Craig said. He shuffled his feet nervously as he waited for her to respond.

"Hi, Craig," she replied nervously, her eyes cast down and her hair falling around her face. "Are these friends of yours?"

"Yes, they're came here from Appleton. Can you

believe they walked all the way here by themselves? This is Sajan and Allen. We've been friends forever."

Craig abruptly stopped himself. Sheepishly, he looked down at his feet, scuffing his shoes on the wooden porch step. Then, he spoke again. "Sorry, I got excited and I…"

He noticed Addie looked uncertain. "I'm sorry, Addie. I didn't mean to make you feel bad."

Nodding her head slowly, she replied, "It's okay. I know you didn't mean anything by it. These are your friends; you *should* be excited. I'm happy for you, Craig. It's just, it's just that…" She stopped and turned abruptly, then rushed back inside, almost running into Gary Jones as she passed him in the doorway.

Gary looked every bit the former marine. With a short, buzzed haircut and piercing, intense eyes, he came out onto the porch and stood in front of the boys. "She'll come around," he said. "It's got to be an adjustment, and you guys need to understand that."

"We do, Mr. Jones," Craig said. "I just feel bad for her."

"I told you to call me Gary, Craig."

"Yes, sir." Craig, seeing the grin rapidly creep across Gary's face at his use of the word sir, quickly corrected himself. "I mean Gary."

"That's better," Gary said. "So, what brings you here?"

"I wanted to introduce Sajan and Allen to Sam and let them see how the ham is set up," Craig explained.

Gary gave him a look. "Marines aren't good enough for you?"

"I, uh…" Grinning, Craig got the joke. "You know they are, Gary. It's just that, well…"

"Yeah, I know. Technology. The old tube head is upstairs, go on up." Gary waved them into the house.

Without wasting a second, the three boys trooped

quickly through the door and up the stairs. Rick stayed on guard duty.

As they walked inside, Craig saw Addie sitting on the couch, the "davenport" as Mr. Stepanik called it. Her chin rested on her hand.

She turned as the boys continued up the stairs, giving Craig a brief smile.

Returning the smile, Craig dashed up the stairway and caught up to Sajan and Allen.

In the room Sam had set up for his ham radio, they saw an older man wearing a headset furiously writing something on a note pad. Craig went over and lightly touched him on the shoulder.

Holding up his left hand, his index finger pointing upward in the *wait one-minute* signal, Sam continued to write. When he finished, he pushed the button on his microphone and said, "Thank you, K9wlf, this is K9SK signing off." Turning to face the three boys, he removed the headset. "Hello, Craig. Are these your friends from Appleton?"

"Yes, they are. This is Sajan and Allen, Sam. Guys, this is Sam and that's his radio, our most advanced technology. Well, except what the army gave us and the items Dad put in his Faraday cage."

"Hi, fellas, and welcome," Sam said.

"What were you writing so fast about?" Craig asked.

"Trouble, I think. It seems a convoy of FEMA trucks is heading up I-39 toward Stevens Point and Wausau. Most likely Wausau."

"Why is that trouble?" Allen asked.

"I've been getting a lot of reports of some very heavy-handed activity by FEMA troops in other parts of the country. We could be in for that here."

"What kind?" Sajan asked.

"Imprisonment and even summary execution on a large scale," Sam explained. "It appears that in some places, any resistance or objection to FEMA is considered a hostile act against the government."

"Mr. Henry told us there is no government anymore," Sajan replied.

"Best we can figure, there isn't. This is what appears to be what we used to call the shadow government, people who for the most part want to control everything from thought to education, and even what we eat and do. That's what is apparently driving FEMA now."

"What about the army?" Allen asked.

"For the most part, it has ceased to exist. There are pockets here and there, but most pretty much scattered to take care of themselves and their families. Any organized army appears to be in Colorado, and they aren't doing or saying much. After we nuked North Korea, there wasn't much for them to do, I guess."

"We nuked North Korea?" Allen asked, the astonishment and disbelief evident in his voice.

"Yeah, we did," Craig replied. "I'll tell you about that later."

"So how does this thing work?" Sajan asked.

"Well, let me show you. Come closer," Sam said, and he proceeded to show the boys how his ham set worked.

While they talked, Craig excused himself and left the room. He went downstairs in search of Addie.

***

"Company's arriving," Brian announced over the radio as he waved at the two Humvees driving past him on the driveway to the cabin. The dust cloud raised by the two vehicles wasn't heavy enough for him not to recognize the occupants, one of them being First

Sergeant Rahn. But Rahn didn't wave back.

Pulling up to the cabin, Rahn got out of the vehicle just as I walked onto the porch. He didn't look happy, but then first sergeants rarely do.

"Hello, First Sergeant," I said as he walked up the stairs. I extended my hand.

We shook as he replied, "John."

"To what do I owe this visit?" I asked.

"Trouble."

"What kind of trouble? You could have radioed. Sam would have got the message here."

Rahn shook his head. "The kind of trouble you don't talk about over the radio. The captain is returning."

"What's so bad about that?"

"He's bringing FEMA with him. They're going to set up a camp in Wausau. Based on what you told me earlier about what they're doing down south, I'm not at all comfortable about this. The captain, on the other hand, sounded like a high school boy peeking in the girls' locker room window."

I glanced at the Humvees. "Hmm, I suppose you want your toys back then?"

"No, I brought you more. Like I said, I'm not comfortable about this, and I'm hedging my bets."

I appreciated the new items but didn't want Rahn punished for it. "You won't get into trouble?"

"I keep the property books; everything is taken care of. You know how that works."

The fact was, I *did* know how that worked. During Desert Shield/Desert Storm, a lot of things fell off the books and never existed. I pretty much figured out what Rahn did. Eventually, with a deep audit, he might get caught, but without computers or access to a variety of databases that most likely didn't exist anymore, he'd probably get away with it.

Accepting what he said at face value, I asked, "So

what did you bring me?"

He grinned. "Another SAW, a shit-ton of ammo, more grenades and claymores and some flash bangs, first aid kits, sleeping bags, a GP Small tent, and a GP Large."

I laughed out loud. "Where am I putting up a GP large?"

"Nowhere, the canvas will come in handy. If I have to bug out, and I'd bring Johnson and a couple other guys with me, we ain't livin' in a tent come January, not up here. We can build a decent bunker or shelter, like my ancestors did. The tent can be used to waterproof the damn thing."

I eyed him, trying to gage his position. "You thinkin' of bugging out?"

"It seems likely, but that's a tough call. One I'm not ready to make yet. Johnson wants to go now, but I won't let him. He's a good soldier. He'll do what he's supposed to, but he doesn't like anything having to do with FEMA."

"Understood," I nodded. "Sam says the UN might be sending troops, too."

"Well, ain't that fuckin' dandy. Any more shitty news, John? Those blue helmet boys can go straight to hell. I was with them in Somalia. They are worthless, greedy, crooked bastards."

Changing the subject, I asked, "When's the good captain due back?"

"He said he'd be in Wausau tonight. He wants me and some of the rest of us to drive down and help them set up camp. I'm leaving Johnson and a small fire team at the armory to watch over things."

"So, you gonna go help?"

He looked at the Humvees. "Yep, and gather as much intel as I can. Know your enemy, if these stories are true."

"I have a group coming here today," I said, referring to the Winstons who were due in a little while. "You want to stick around for a meet and greet?"

"Bunch of people on horses? An old man who looks like he played in ZZ Top, plus two adults—a man and a woman?" he asked.

"Sounds like them, but they must not be bringing everyone. There's an older woman, another son, and some kids."

"Not a good idea traveling with all of that right now. We saw some shady looking types on the way here. They didn't do anything, a Ma-Deuce…" he said, pointing at the M2 fifty caliber mounted on the Hummer, "will keep anybody from acting stupid."

"Yeah, brings reach out and touch someone to a whole new level, doesn't it?" I chuckled.

"So, I'll pass on the social. If the time comes, and I fear it will, there will be plenty of time for that."

"The old man's name is Charlie Winston," I said.

"You gotta be shittin' me. Old rich guy, used to be a congressman in Texas?"

I laughed. "Not that one. This one isn't very trusting, and he's kinda anti-government."

"Sounds like someone you might need, John."

"Could be. Let's get your toys unloaded and in the barn. I suspect your captain will be calling soon and you shouldn't be too far from home when he does."

"Johnson," Rahn yelled.

"Yeah, Top!" Johnson answered.

"God dammit, Johnson, don't call me Top."

"Yes, *First* Sergeant!"

Rahn and I could clearly hear the sarcasm in his voice, but Rahn decided to let it go. Johnson was a good trooper. "Take the Hummers over to the barn."

He glanced at me to make sure that was okay and I nodded my agreement. "Take the Hummers over to the barn and unload that shit," Rahn said. "We have to get back to the armory pronto."

***

Craig came downstairs and saw Addie still sitting on the couch. "I'm sorry if I upset you," he said.

"You didn't, really," Addie replied. "I need time, that's all. I'll be okay. Your mom and Carol say so, too."

"Can I sit by you?" he asked. He had made his way over to the couch and stood next to her.

She nodded. "Sure, go ahead."

He sat down and put his AR down next to him, leaving space between them. "Addie, is there anything I can do to help? I feel like I should help somehow."

"No," she said, shaking her head. "I'm sorry, I didn't mean it that way. I appreciate you being my friend and trying to help me. I'm just gonna need a lot of time to get better."

Craig patted her hand. "I understand."

"Hello! Is anyone in the house?" a voice called.

The voice from outside, a woman's voice, surprised them both.

Addie jumped as Craig got up and walked over to the screen door. Looking out through it, he saw a woman standing in the yard. She was disheveled in appearance. Her dirty jeans and t-shirt showed a state of desperation, not unlike what Craig had seen in the stragglers and refugees along the road.

Seeing him, she said in a weak voice. "I'm hungry, can you spare any food?"

Craig started to open the door as Addie shouted, "Craig, no! I know that voice."

Stopping, Craig reached down and took his Glock from the holster on his leg. Standing inside the door,

Addie came up behind him.

"I know that voice," she said. "She's from the camp, the looter camp. Be careful."

Craig opened the door slowly and stepped out onto the porch, his weapon held alongside his hip. Inside, he could hear Addie running up the steps, shouting for Sam and the others.

"What do you want?" he asked the woman.

"I'm hungry, I just want something to eat," she replied.

Walking forward and down the steps, Craig approached her. She stood about six feet away, and he looked her in the eye. "You from the *looter* camp?"

"We are refugees, not looters. You don't have to say it with that tone."

"So why don't you get something from them?" Craig asked.

"They don't have enough. I'm hungry." She took a step forward.

Craig swiftly reacted, raising his weapon and pointing it at her. "Stop right there," he ordered.

He heard the creak of the screen door behind him, its slamming against the outer wall of the house, and the pounding of feet. It distracted him. He turned quickly to see what was behind him when a shriek drew his attention back around.

The woman, with her hand raised, held a large knife. She shrieked again. She was coming straight for him.

Craig didn't hesitate. He pulled the trigger, riddling her head and chest with bullets.

Her forward momentum carried her a few more steps, then she dropped like a stone, landing at his feet.

Another shot rang out and then another and another, kicking up dust at Craig's feet. Four men came out of the woods near the driveway. And they were shooting at him!

"You murdered Sheri, you fucker!" one of the men shouted.

Craig turned and ran back toward the house.

On the porch, Craig saw Sam's Remington 700 in his hand when the men started shooting.

Sam raised the rifle, aimed, and pulled the trigger, dropping a man where he stood. As he racked the bolt to chamber another round, the three remaining men ran off into the woods.

Stunned and holding ARs, Sajan and Allen stood there, paralyzed into inaction as Craig dove onto the porch and slid across it, coming to a stop as he collided with their legs, causing all of them to be one big tangle on the porch.

"They're gone, boys," Sam said quietly.

As the boys lay there, Craig yelled, "Get off of me, get off of me! I'm fucking shot!"

***

"What the hell do you mean she's dead?" Tom Harvey shouted. Three men stood in front of him.

"So," Tom continued, "you let her be the brave one again. Sheri went up to the house while you three pussies—" he pointed his finger at Brad, Frank, and Carl "—hid in the bushes."

"Bobby was with them, too, boss," Kevin Schneider said. He had brought the three men in to explain to Tom what happened.

"Who the fuck is Bobby?" Tom bellowed.

"He's Sid's cousin, two or three times removed," Kevin answered.

"So not only do you get my new girl killed, you get one of my people killed. How'd you three like to dance from one of my light poles?"

Brad, Frank, and Carl stood there silently. It was Brad who finally spoke.

"We found the other girl," Brad said.

"What?" Tom shouted at him.

Brad cringed. "Yeah, we found her, the runaway."

Tom stood nose to nose with him. "Where? Why isn't she here?"

"They outnumbered and outgunned us, boss. They'd already killed Sheri and Bobby. We couldn't do anymore," Brad explained.

Tom turned his attention away from the man. "Kevin, I want you to scout out that place. Make one of these, no, make all of these jackasses go with you. Get the lay of the land, then come back here and we'll make a plan. I want that girl, and I want those people dead."

"Yes, boss, I'm on it," Kevin said. He prodded the men out of the shelter with his weapon and moved them toward his raiding crew.

Tom knew Kevin had no intention of letting him down and feeling the effects of the punishment. They needed to abide by his orders. People were going to die, and most likely a few of Tom's as well, but that's how things were nowadays. Survival of the fittest. Or the baddest.

Chapter 14

"You will hear of wars and rumors of wars"

—Matthew 24:6

Charlie Winston, his son Billy, and wife Sarah arrived late afternoon at the cabin. They came on horseback, which was understandably becoming the preferred method of transportation due to gas shortages and a lack of availability of vehicles that worked. Having heard Rahn describe Charlie as looking like Billy Gibbons from ZZ Top, I couldn't help but laugh at the accuracy. They stopped in front of the cabin, exchanging greetings with us before dismounting. Following all the trouble over at Quint's place, we were a little unnerved, and Charlie picked up on it right away.

"This a bad time?" he asked.

"We had some trouble earlier, but that just shows how important this meeting is," I answered.

"What kind of trouble?"

I explained the incident that had occurred at Quint's.

"Your boy okay?" asked Charlie.

I nodded. "Yeah, he'll be fine. It was just a graze on his leg. He's angry about it, but other than worrying about an infection, he'll come around okay."

"That's good to hear."

I thanked him. "They hadn't put anyone out to watch for unexpected people showing up around the clock. They do now," I said. "Well, come on inside. Let's meet the rest of the family and we can get started."

With that invitation, everyone moved indoors.

I quickly realized my home wasn't as big as I thought it was. Besides the Winston three, there was Carol, Craig, Brian, Nancy, Donna, and Mike, plus three dogs who were immediately shooed back outside. Sajan and Allen were at the bunker. Quint, Sam, Gary, and Rick hadn't even shown up yet with Addie. I had not planned this well. Fortunately, it was a nice day. I had a long table in the house and a good-sized picnic table outside. We could move everything under the trees.

After everyone had arrived, we ate our dinner, and then sat around and talked. It didn't take Charlie long to get chatty, as he seemed to warm up to everyone.

"You knew this was going to happen?" Charlie said.

I chuckled, keeping the sarcasm from my tone. "What, the end of the world as we know it?"

"Something like that. You knew something was coming."

I shrugged. "If it wasn't this EMP thing, it would've been something else—a financial collapse, a civil war, something. It's been brewing for decades. We almost need it."

"What do you mean 'we almost need it'?" Nancy asked.

"It's simple," I explained. "Jefferson said, 'The tree of liberty must be refreshed from time to time with the

220

blood of patriots and tyrants.' And that's pretty much what is about to happen."

"So, all this violence that's been happening, the savagery, that's refreshing the tree of liberty?" she asked.

I shrugged. "Kind of. So many people have been *taking* and not giving. We created an entire dependent class. Then the political correctness thing, being offended at every little word and action. Shoot, somebody was even offended by a shoestring lying on the floor of some college dorm, for crying out loud. It's been coming."

Nancy shook her head. "I still don't get it."

"Those things started an attack on liberty, on freedom, those depending on the government for everything became slaves in a way."

"*Slaves?* You're saying that to me?" Nancy asked.

The ABW was starting to surface and I had to interrupt her. "I didn't mean slaves in the sense of slavery like it was back in the 1800s. I meant slavery in that if the government stopped supporting them, then they would all die. They kept the government leaders who provided for them in power."

"Exactly, John," Charlie confirmed. "That's the group, the politicians who bought votes by making people dependent on them, that the takers had no choice but to keep them in power. That's the same people who make up these looters that are causing you grief."

"They'll cause you grief, too, Charlie," Quint interjected. "It won't be long before they'll be at your door. After our run in with them this morning, they'll be heading our way again, and eventually your way if we don't do something to stop them."

"If I didn't believe that I wouldn't be here," Charlie said. "So, what are your plans, John? What do you think we should do?"

I leaned back and took a cigar from my pocket, then went through the ritual of clipping and lighting it. Blowing out a mouthful of smoke, I leaned forward and said calmly, "We kill them."

"Jesus, Dad," Brian said.

"Don't blaspheme," Quint and Charlie said simultaneously.

The laughter from everyone else at the table was met with stern looks from Quint and Charlie, which then caused another round of chuckles. Eventually, they grinned, although only slightly.

"We have to destroy them," I continued. "We can't leave them here in our backyard wreaking havoc."

"There will be more just like 'em," Charlie said.

"More?" Carol asked.

"All those people in the cities. Where exactly do you think they will go when they run out of food?" Charlie asked. "They're in there now killing each other over crumbs. They'll be here soon enough, too."

"Jes…I mean, damn," Brian said.

"You're learnin', young man," Quint said with a grin.

"This won't be over until the die off ends," Charlie explained. "People will do what we are doing. They'll fort up for protection and fight off anyone who tries to take what is theirs. There will still be gangs— marauding gangs, that we'll have to worry about. Then, there's that shadow government group that Sam told us about. The FEMA boys and anyone who supports them could be a problem."

"You make it seem like the Dark Ages, Charlie," Donna said.

He tipped his head at her. "Yes, ma'am, that's pretty much what life is going to be like for a while. The Dark Ages."

We spent the rest of the evening planning what we

would do to get ready for the inevitable—the next attack from the looters. Charlie and his family agreed to spend the night instead of trying to go back home in the dark.

I gave up my room and bunked on the couch in the living room until it was time for my guard shift. In the morning, we'd pack them up and send them home with some extra ammo and warning devices.

***

Nancy and I spent the day using the UTV to haul things back and forth between my place and Quint's. While we did that, Sam, Gary, Quint, and Rick, along with Sajan and Allen, spent their day building a bunker and placing a variety of warning devices, claymores, and booby traps around the perimeter of Quint's house. They had little doubt that the confrontation the other day was a signal that more was to come. While in their estimation it was more of a raiding party than anything else, the simple fact that shots were fired, people were killed, and Addie was most likely seen, gave us a strong warning that bad things were about to happen. Images of a beehive or ant hill, their flurry of activity, came to mind as one observed what was going on.

Carol and Donna prepared trauma kits for the Stepanik's farm. Even Mike helped, as he tried to roll bandages and placed items inside the gym bags that I had collected over the years. No one was left out of the preparations. Addie helped where she could, which was mostly loading magazines and unloading the trailer whenever it came back with supplies.

Brian had spent about an hour showing Quint, Rick, Sam, and Gary how to set up the mines, booby traps, and warning devices. Gary was a big help, as he had used some of them during his time in the

Marines, while Sam's military experience was almost exclusively on ships with little use for trip wires and anti-personnel mines. However, Sam did make another ignition board to allow for the claymores to be detonated from a single location instead of the standard clacker detonator that came with each one. There was a seriousness to their purpose, with none of the standard joking around or smart-ass comments. The time was fast approaching when we'd have to engage the looters, and we all knew deep inside that this meant killing. Perhaps, some of them would be killed as well.

"How much time do you think we have before something happens?" Sam asked.

"Not much," I answered. "I expect them to scout us out some. They could be doing that now."

Reflexively, we all paused in our activity and visually surveyed our surroundings. The unasked question was simple: who is looking and am I in someone's cross hairs right now?

***

Craig sat in the bunker watching the road. The bandage on his leg, where the bullet had fortunately only grazed him, was prominent even under his jeans.

It itches and I can feel the tightness of the bandage.

He hadn't even felt it until everyone fell on top of him on the porch. Yelling at them to get off of him was still fresh in his mind. *Dad always said you never forget being shot…or shot at, for that matter.*

Glancing up and down in both directions of the road in front of him, he saw nothing that would alarm or cause concern. The radio sat on a stump that had been placed inside the bunker to be used as a table of sorts or occasionally a seat when standing got tiresome. *Just because I'm supposedly wounded doesn't mean I have to be the only one sitting here, guarding.*

***

Brad snaked backward through the underbrush to where Kevin, Frank, Carl, and a few others were squatting or laying down, waiting.

"Looks like they're building fortifications and barriers," Brad said.

"What kind?" Kevin asked.

"Log walls, and it looks like booby traps of some kind. I saw them digging."

"We need more men," Frank said.

"We're only here to scout. That's what Tom told us to do. We aren't attacking, so we don't need more men," Kevin said with an authority that stunned Frank into silence. "Did you see the girl?"

"Yeah, I seen her," Brad confirmed. "She was on the porch loading clips for their guns. They have a lot of weapons, looks like mostly ARs and hunting rifles with scopes."

"How many people?"

"Looks like eight, counting the girl. Others are coming from back in the woods in a UTV, so there must be more. I don't know how many. I coulda shot that big muscled guy. He looks like he could be trouble."

"Okay, let's crawl out of here and tell Tom what we saw," Kevin said. "Then, we'll come back with more men and do what we have to do."

***

"I'm certain they've been watching us. They'd be

stupid not to be, especially now that they know Addie is here," Brian said to the group.

"We should probably drive them off," I said. "You think a patrol, a burst of rifle fire would work like the old mad minute?"

Quint, Nancy, and Rick looked at me like I was speaking in a foreign language.

"What's a 'mad minute,' Mr. Henry?" Rick asked.

I shook my head. *The only one with enough courage to ask the question none of them know the answer to.*

"Back in Vietnam," I began, then quickly glanced at Brian. I gave him a look that said *Don't even suggest I was in Vietnam, I'm not that old.* "Back in Vietnam," I said again, "soldiers would shoot every weapon they had toward the jungle around their perimeter for a minute every evening. It helped drive any enemy back who might be crawling up for a night-time attack or scouting their position."

"We don't have any automatic weapons," Quint said.

Brian started to speak, and I tapped him on the arm to shut up.

"No, we don't. I don't want to waste any of our grenades or claymores on them, either. Not yet, anyway. Let's take a break from this and grab your weapons. Sam, you take Rick and Quint that way," I pointed to an area between the barn and the house, "and swing south. Gary, Brian, and I will go this way." I pointed to my right and out toward one of the small corral areas on Quint's farm. "We'll head south and meet at the road. You see anybody, no questions, it's a free fire zone."

Everyone nodded their understanding.

"Nancy, would you be so kind as to let Addie know what we're doing? I don't want to scare her," I said. "Take your weapon with you, and another for Addie. She needs to be armed, too."

"Roger, Wilco, over and out, Fil," she replied with a snappy parade ground salute. She was pissed about something and I was sure I was going to hear about it later. Whatever it was, Nancy knew enough not to argue now.

"Sam, take your walkie talkie. Brian, you bring the other," I ordered. "If you stumble on someone or can't speak because you're outnumbered, break squelch three times, then sit tight. We'll come from your west. If you break squelch on us, then the free fire zone is closed and it's confirmed shots only."

Sam nodded his understanding.

"Anybody have any questions?" I made eye contact with everyone to make sure they understood. "Nancy, you have your walkie talkie?"

"Yes," she answered.

"Keep it on," I said, "and then maybe in forty-five minutes or so we can all take a break."

"Let's go, people. We're burning daylight," Brian said.

I simply hung my head and shook it from side to side. That boy was sometimes just not right.

We headed in our respective directions. I had a suspicion we'd most likely not cross paths with the looters on these patrols. However, the experience would do everyone some good. By putting Sam in charge of one group, it'd stop anyone from thinking this was a family affair with me or Brian always being in charge.

***

Craig sat on the stump, his leg stretched in front of him, when movement down the road grabbed his attention. Picking up his binoculars, he peered into them and focused down the road.

As he watched, seven armed men went across the road about a quarter mile away. They ran as if they were coming from the Stepanik's place.

Craig watched them cross the road, run up the embankment, and disappear into the trees. Setting the binoculars down, he reached over and grabbed the canvas carrier the field phone was in. Picking up the handset, he set the TA-312 in his lap and turned the handle on the side several times.

"What's up, Craig? Is everything okay?" Donna asked as she answered the phone from the bag sitting on the table near her.

"I'm okay, Mom," he answered. "Can you get Dad on the radio? I just saw some men cross the road leaving Quint's place."

"How many, and when do you expect them to get there?"

"No, Mom, they were *leaving* his place. Looks like there was seven of them. They all had long guns."

"Okay, I'll call him. Stand by."

"I'm not going anywhere, Mom."

***

Donna shook her head in exasperation. Craig was still her only child and her baby, but he'd grown up so fast since the EMP. He'd changed, and at times she didn't recognize him anymore. He had become hard and distant, like his dad.

Picking up the walkie talkie from the solar charger, she keyed it and said, "John, can you hear me?"

The hiss of the radio told her no one was responding. Bringing it toward her mouth to speak again she heard someone speak.

"Donna? Is anything wrong?"

"Craig saw seven men crossing the road near Quint's place with long guns," she explained.

"Which way are they going?"

"Oh, sorry. He said they were leaving from his direction and had crossed the road about halfway to his place. They went into the woods heading south."

"You said seven, armed with long guns?"

"Yes, that's what he said," she said.

"Okay, thanks. Thank him for me. Tell him his job is important, even if he is whining about it right now."

"I will, John. Thank you."

***

"Brian, I guess you heard that," I said. "Let's keep an eye out. They may be gone, but could've left someone behind."

"You gonna call Sam?" Brian asked.

"Doin' it now." I spoke into the walkie talkie. "Sam, this is John."

A few seconds later Sam answered. "Nice radio procedure there, Henry, what's up?"

"Uh huh. Listen, Craig just saw seven men crossing the road going away from our location. All were armed with long guns. Be cautious. They're probably gone, but may have left a scout behind."

"Roger that. See you in the middle."

I set the radio back in my tactical vest pocket, and putting my weapon at port arms, led the way into the bushes. Everyone followed me, and I reminded them to watch their sides and our back.

After a while, we made our way to the road where we saw Sam, Rick, and Quint sitting under a large maple tree, waiting for us.

"You see anything?" I asked.

"A spot back there where it looked like they had been observing us. A cigarette butt and trampled bushes," Sam explained.

"You and Brian should go booby trap the location later," I said. "They'll probably try and use it again when they come back."

"They really coming back, Mr. Henry?" Rick asked.

I nodded grimly. "You betcha, son. They'll be back."

"Good," Rick said. "They need to pay for what they did to Addie and her family. And for shooting Craig, too."

"They will, son. They will," said Quint. "We should head back and finish getting ready for them. I doubt they'll be back today anymore, but maybe tonight. We should be prepared."

"That's what I think, too," I said. "Brian, why don't you and Sam go get some booby traps and maybe a claymore or two? Set up a welcome for them back at that site Sam found."

"Can I go, too, Mr. Henry? Grampa?" Rick asked.

Quint and I nodded our heads.

"Sure," Quint said.

"Brian, put them where you think they'll do the most good."

"I'm thinking in the trees, Dad. They won't be looking up, and the tree placement will spread maximum destruction."

"Good idea. Let's get back to work, everyone. Break's over," I said.

We headed the short distance to the farmhouse where Nancy and Addie were on the porch loading magazines and talking.

***

Kevin led the group with Frank and Carl back to

Stilwell's Pond Park. As they walked into the park itself, he saw Tom standing by his pavilion, arms across his chest, straining toward them.

"Frank, you take these guys down there and get something to eat and some sleep," Kevin said. "I suspect we'll be going back out shortly."

"I wanna talk to Tom," Frank said.

Kevin moved toward Frank and stopped inches in front of him, their noses almost touching, each feeling the breath of the other. Without warning, Kevin pushed the butt of his weapon into Frank's stomach, stepping back as Frank doubled over with a *woof*.

Frank wrapped his arms around his abdomen and let out a groan.

Lifting his rifle, Kevin brought it crashing across the back of Frank's head, driving him into the ground. As Frank rolled around, Kevin kicked him in the ribs. "When I tell you to do something, Antifa Boy, you do it." He turned, spitting on Frank as he did so, and walked toward Tom.

"What was that about?" Tom asked.

"He was hard of hearing," Kevin answered. "I think he'll listen better from now on."

"So, what did you find out?"

"I think they're ready for us. We saw at least eight at the farm. The girl is among them."

Tom eyed him. "At least eight, huh?"

"Three of them don't live there. They live close, though. They came over with a UTV bringing stuff. Looked like weapons and booby traps."

"Where's the other place?"

Kevin half-shrugged. "I don't know. They came through the woods behind the farm. Could be anywhere back there."

"You said eight, including the girl?"

"Yeah, eight."

"How well armed are they, Kevin?"

"Well, it looked like some were carrying ARs, some hunting rifles, maybe a shotgun or two, and pistols."

Tom nodded. "So, no better than we are. Okay, get Sid and your little bitch Frank and come back here. It's time to go to war."

Chapter 15

*"The spot where we intend to fight must not be made
known; for then the enemy will have to prepare
against a possible attack at several different points;"*

—Sun Tzu

Nancy had gone back to the cabin early, taking the
UTV through the woods. Brian and I, walking
back the same way, discussed our plans for early
tomorrow. It was going to be a long night, and neither
of us was going to get any sleep. We had little doubt
that the looters would come our way tomorrow or the
next day. We needed to be ready. There wasn't any
more time to waste.

"How'd you set up your greeting?" I asked.

"I have two in the trees, spread wide enough apart
that it will sweep the area we expect them to be in, and
then some," Brian explained. "It should drive them
toward the driveway. I have three set up there for when
they get into the open. If they retreat, we set up two
more near the entrance of the driveway. If they move

toward the farmhouse, the people there can take care of them with rifle fire."

"Sounds wonderful," I replied.

"It gets better, Dad. Sam's bump stock will provide a heavy rate of fire on them when they go that way. It'll be a slaughter."

"That's what we need. We need to *end* them. There are other gangs running around and we'll probably have to deal with them eventually, too."

"Why didn't you want me to tell them about the SAWs?" Brian asked, his tone curious.

"That's our little surprise. I think it best we not let anyone know we have them. I don't want any chance of word getting out."

"You planning on using them for this fight?"

"If need be. I figure we'll hold Craig back with one of the SAWs and the UTV. Maybe use one the boys, either Sajan or Allen, with him. Worse case, they can be the cavalry coming to our rescue."

"Through the woods?" Brian asked.

"Nope. Straight up the damn road and they can poke 'em in the ass."

Brian gave me a serious look. "We need to scout out the looters. We need to know when they move."

"So, what's your plan?"

"I'm taking Allen with me tonight. We'll leave at dark and that will get us set up before midnight. We can scope them out, try to learn when they're leaving."

"You taking a radio?" I asked.

"Well, I wasn't gonna holler, Dad. I'm not as loud as you."

***

"Two groups. Sid, you take one, Kevin, you the other," Tom said.

"How many in each group, boss?" Sid asked.

"You said there were eight there, including the girl, right, Kevin?"

"Yeah, eight," Kevin confirmed.

"Then I want each of you to take ten with you."

"You comin', too, boss?" Sid asked.

The room grew silent. Frank, Kevin, and two others seemed to step back and away from Sid, expecting to see Tom wail the hell out of him.

To Tom, the challenge was obvious, and he didn't like it. The angry look on his face and the ice-cold stare in his eyes sent a strong message to Sid. He knew he had a choice, make a big deal out of the challenge or ignore it.

"Well, Sid, if you'd let me finish, I'll take ten of my own. Sid, you'll be on my right and Kevin, on my left."

Both men nodded. Sid, looking nervous, visibly swallowed.

"I'm going up the middle," Tom explained, "right down their driveway. I want you guys to quietly go through the woods and get close enough that when the shooting starts, and oh it will start, you can surprise them. They won't know what hit 'em."

"Boss, remember, there are those other people we don't know nuthin' about," Kevin said.

"That's why we're taking thirty with us, Kevin. They can't have more than three or four more."

"When do we head out?" Kevin asked.

"You two need to move out first. I want you to sneak in through the woods, and that means quietly. No smoking or grab assing. I find out anyone does that, or gets high before going out, I'll deal with you." Tom let his eyes travel across the room at the few gathered in front of him. "You make sure everyone you take understands that. Leave at about two. Should take you about two hours to get there, and maybe another hour to sneak in and get set up. Kevin, you said that place you spied on them from was close but had plenty of cover to hide in?"

"Yeah, boss, a slight dip in the ground behind some dirt mounds and brush. It's maybe fifty or sixty feet away from the edge of their yard."

"Okay. You guys be set up before five AM. If they have anybody guarding, they'll be tired about the time you show up. Be fucking quiet. You got me?"

"Yeah, boss, we got you," Sid replied.

Kevin quickly nodded his head.

"I'll arrive at sun up. I want them to think we showed up for a little parley between neighbors."

***

Brian and Allen were finishing their preparations in the yard. Brian grabbed Allen by the shirt. "Come with me," he said, and took him over to the fire pit. Scooping up a handful of ash, he spread it all over Allen's face and then did the same to himself, making sure he covered his almost shaved head while Allen sputtered and spit.

"What the hell did you do that for?" Allen shouted.

"Camouflage. Keeps the light from reflecting off of our faces. Don't you ever watch movies, kid?"

"Yeah, but I thought they used burnt cork."

"You see any burnt cork?" Brian quipped as he walked toward the front of the cabin. He put his Glock inside his tactical vest holster. Then, he added two magazines for it, and four for the AR. Putting the Optiscope monocular night vision device in another pouch, he reached down and picked up his AR. "You ready, Allen?"

Picking up his own weapon, Allen nodded that he

was ready.

Brian went over and hugged Nancy, ruffling the top of Mike's head. He stepped back and let his eyes wander around the cabin and the rest of us gathered on the porch. Then, slowly but with a purpose, he walked away.

"Brian," I called. "Be careful out there."

He waved a hand. "We got this, Pops, no problem."

"I mean it. We need you two safe back here. No engaging, just observing. We need to know when they head out."

"We'll be okay, Dad." He glanced at Allen, who wide-eyed nodded his head, and they headed across the yard and down the drive.

I was pretty certain they'd stop briefly and talk to Sajan, who was on guard in the bunker. I went and sat in my chair on the porch. It was going to be a long night.

***

Quint, Rick, Sam, and Gary were busy. While Addie sat on the floor in the living room sliding cartridges into magazines for the ARs, they checked the lines for the claymores near the edge of the driveway and the woods. One on each side was angled to sweep down the drive, clearing anything that came up it that wasn't welcome. They had earlier put ammo and water inside the bunker that was to their right of the drive, positioned so that it could see to the road, some hundred yards away, all the way down.

"I still think we need an LP/OP down close to the road," Gary said.

"You wanna speak English there, Gary?" Sam commented, trying to good naturedly antagonize his friend.

"A listening post, observation post. It will give us early warning that they're coming."

"We don't have time to build anything like that right now," Quint said.

"Sure we do. It can be as simple as a little hidey hole under some brush, just enough that you can't be seen. That's all we need."

"So, who is the brave soul that will sit out there all night and do that?" Quint asked.

The words had no sooner left Quint's mouth when Rick blurted, "I will. I can do that."

"Oh, no, you won't," Quint quickly answered.

"He's right, Rick," Gary said, trying to keep things calm. "It's much too dangerous. If they see you, then you're either dead or a prisoner. Neither is a good thing, and if I had to choose between the two after what Addie shared, I think I'd rather be dead."

"I know the risks, Gary, but I can do it," Rick said. "I'm just as good as a shot as the rest of you. And I'm in better shape, too."

"He's got you there, Gary," Sam chuckled as he poked Gary in his expanding waistline. "So, who's going to do it?"

"It's either you or me, Sam," Gary replied.

The two men stood there staring at one another and then almost simultaneously grinned. Extending their hands in a fist, they shook their fists up and down three times vigorously, then stopped.

Sam held out two fingers and Gary had his hand flat. Rock, Paper, Scissors was an old game and Sam had just won. Scissors cuts paper. Sam was the LP/OP for tonight.

"I win, buddy," Sam said needlessly. "If necessary, you can go tomorrow night."

"Okay," Gary agreed. "Hopefully, it rains tonight."

"Thanks, buddy," Sam croaked, his voice both

communicating the discomfort as much as the value of the words.

"The rain will keep them in if it comes."

"Well, whatever happens, I need to get going. I have to find a good spot and camouflage it. I need my AR and the radio with the ear buds."

"One squelch break answered by two for a comm check. You break squelch three times if they're coming. I'll answer with two, and then you break squelch once for each person you see," Gary instructed.

"Sounds simple enough," Sam said.

"Why don't you talk?" Rick asked.

"They might hear us talking. This way, we can communicate a simple message without them hearing us," Gary answered.

"Well, I'm off," Sam said as he grabbed his AR and the radio. "Mine is not to reason why…"

"Let's not finish that one, okay, bud."
Sam nodded. "Yeah, poor choice of words on my part."

***

Brian and Allen were about half a mile from the park. The woods were thick, and a quarter moon gave them some light. Grabbing Allen's arm, Brian stopped him.

"We're going in low and slow from here. When you see me stop, you stop. When I drop on the ground, you drop. Do everything I do. No talking. If we have to communicate, it will either be by hand signals or I'll get close and whisper in your ear. Any questions?"

"No," Allen said, but his voice quavered.

"It's okay to be nervous. Just don't let your fear get the better of you."

"You aren't scared?" he asked.

"Yeah, I'm scared. Only an idiot wouldn't be. Just do what I do, and you'll be fine."

Allen nodded his head as Brian took out the radio.

"Covey leader, this is Raven," he said.

"You there, Rambo?" John's voice asked through the radio.

"We're close, just wanted to check to make sure you could hear me. We can see the objective."

"Be careful. I'm on radio watch. If you need to, bug out and head back home. We'll be waiting."

"Roger."

Brian dropped into a crouch and headed toward the park. The trees and brush, along with the limited light, kept them concealed. He could see a big glow ahead from what appeared to be a bonfire. Shouting and other noises told him they were definitely heading in the right direction.

Holding his hand up as a stop signal, he turned, went back to Allen, and whispered, "Keep your eyes moving around the camp. Don't look in the same spot for more than a few seconds. Whatever you do, don't look at the fire. It will ruin your night vision. Stay behind me about five or six feet, okay?"

"Okay," Allen whispered back. He was breathing fast.

"Relax. Try and control your breathing. They don't know we're here and probably never will."

"Okay," Allen replied again.

Brian led them to about ten feet from the edge of the trees where it opened into the park. Dropping to his hands and knees, he started to crawl toward the edge and then, dropping onto his stomach, he began a traditional low crawl toward the end of the trees.

Allen copied his every move and stopped when Brian did. Brian turned and motioned for Allen to come up alongside him. They laid there, watching the park and all that was going on. It looked like a party.

"What are they doing?" Allen whispered.

"Looks like they're getting ready. Psyching themselves up."

***

Screams of joy and laughter poured out from the park. Tom stood and watched, a look of disgust on his face.

"Kevin, Sid," he shouted. "Get your asses over here."

The two men quickly moved to stand in front of Tom. Before they could speak, he shouted at them. "I told you I didn't want *any* of this. Why are you letting this happen?" He pointed his arm toward a group that was drinking and grappling with each other.

"Sorry, boss. We'll stop it," Kevin said.

"It should've never started," he bellowed.

Sid and Kevin ran toward the group and started grabbing the men. Taking bottles of liquor from them, they threw the bottles to the ground and ordered the men to stop. One of the men, objecting to being pushed and punched, raised a bottle in his hand, preparing to hit Kevin.

A shot rang out.

The man dropped immediately to the ground, a wet stain spreading across his chest. A few people screamed or shouted, then there was silence.

"Knock this shit off!" Tom yelled, an AR held in his hands.

Everyone started to mill around. No one said a word.

"We have work to do tonight. You can party after. I want you sober, ready. We're going to take down a threat. Sid and Kevin will explain to the groups they are taking, the rest of you will stay here. But no more of this bullshit, do you hear me?" Tom said.

***

Brian tapped Allen on the shoulder and motioned for him to follow him. They crept silently on their stomachs back into the woods until Brian felt they were far enough back that they wouldn't be seen. Reaching into the pouch of his tactical vest, Brian took out the walkie talkie.

"Home Base, this is Scout," he said.

After a moment, he heard a reply. "This is Home Base."

"It's on for tonight, Home Base."

"How many?"

"A lot," Brian said.

"Roger, Scout. Return at your discretion."

"Shortly," Brian said into the walkie talkie. Turning toward Allen, he whispered, "Very shortly."

Allen stared back, wide-eyed. "Good," he whispered.

Brian and Allen crawled back to the edge of the park and kept watch on the looters.

***

I put the radio down and started to wake people up. Craig, Nancy, and I would move to where Brian had left the wires for the claymore detonator. He had placed them by a stump near the spot where we expected the looters to gather. When ready, we would detonate the claymores and drive them into a kill position in the driveway toward Quint's house. Between our weapon fire and the claymores, we expected a high kill rate. Then, the rest could be cleaned out by the other claymores he had set up in the woods on the other side of the driveway. Quint, Rick, Sam, and Gary would be able to fire down the drive and take care of the rest. I hoped to wipe them all out but didn't really expect to.

Carol would move to a position in the woods behind

the house and have an aid station set up in case we had casualties. Sajan would stay in the bunker, while Donna and Mike would remain in the cabin with the dogs.

When Brian and Allen got back, Allen would stay in the cabin and Brian would link up with Carol. All I could think of was the old saying, "No plan survives first contact." Regardless, that was our plan and I was sticking to it.

***

Sam had placed himself in a depression and covered himself with brush and leaves. Taking his walkie talkie, he called to Gary. "LP/OP to Base."

"Go, OP," Gary answered.

"I'm in position. I'll message you as we planned if anything happens."

"Roger that. Stay frosty, my friend."

"Wilco."

Sam settled in for what he hoped was a quiet night.

***

"I wish Craig was here," Addie whispered while sitting on the dark porch. She began to wring her hands in circles.

"I'm here," Rick answered, a little more loudly than necessary. "I can protect you."

"I know you can, but Craig… Craig makes me feel safe. I like him."

"Oh."

"I'm sorry, Rick. I like you, too," She quickly interjected. "I just feel special with Craig, that's all. I know you can protect us, too."

"Of course I can," he said. His head bowed as he sat next to her in the dark. Picking up a small stick from on the floor next to him, he traced a line over the top of his boots in a nonsensical pattern. "You'll be safe here, Addie, you'll see. Besides, you have a shotgun, and you're good with it, too."

A Remington Model 11 twelve-gauge shotgun rested against the wall next to her. Its semi-automatic feature made it easier for her to use, and its six shot capacity gave her plenty of fire power.

"I only want to use it against Tom. I hope he shows up, 'cuz he's dead if he does," she said, an angry tone infused in her words. "You hear me, Rick? I swear he's dead if he shows up."

"I hear ya'."

The squeak of the screen door opening made the two young people look toward it. Gary stood there, adjusting his tactical vest. It had his Glock and four spare magazines, as well as another five 30-round magazines for his AR. A Marine Ka-Bar, compliments of Sam's collection, was attached upside down on the vest. The back of the vest held a ballistic plate that would stop, or at least slow down, most ammunition.

"I hate this thing," he said aloud as he let the door slam shut behind him. The spring pull on it made the door bounce twice before it came to rest against the jamb.

"I wish I had one," Rick announced from the darkness.

"I didn't see you there," Gary said, a slight nervousness in his voice. "You startled me."

"Sorry," Rick said.

"That's okay. I should be more observant. We all need to be observant."

"I guess I should go down by Gramps at the bunker,"

Rick announced as he stood up and grabbed his deer rifle.

"I'll be there directly, Rick. We should alternate keeping watch and listening for Sam on the radio."

"Yes, sir," Rick replied as he trooped down the steps.

"You okay, Addie?" Gary asked.

"I'm good," she said. "Where do you want me?"

"I'd tell you in the house, but that would probably make you mad. How about right here, but keep in the shadows so no one can see you, okay?"

"How about in the bunker?" Addie asked.

Gary shook his head. "This is an important spot. If for some reason, they sneak around the house and try to come up from behind us, you're here."

"Sounds like a crock, Mr. Jones. Like something you tell little kids to keep 'em out of the way."

"I hear ya', but that's not true. We aren't very many here and we know this is where they'll come, not *if* but when. What we don't know is if they're dumb enough to sneak up from the front or smarter than that and sneak around behind us. We need someone here for that. That would be you."

"If you put it that way, Mr. Jones, it makes sense," she said.

"Addie?"

"Yes, sir."

"Please call me Gary. Mr. Jones makes me feel old."

She giggled. "Well, you are old, Mr. Jones."

Gary couldn't see her grin in the dark, but the tone in her voice clearly showed she was kidding.

"I got yer old, Addie. You stay awake up here now."

"I will, Gary."

***

Brian and Allen lay in the bushes watching the

preparations in the looter camp. It was obvious to Brian that there were going to be three groups, and as he counted, he figured each group would have about ten people in it. What he couldn't figure out and didn't quite know how to learn it was how they would approach the Stepanik farm.

Reaching in the dark, he grabbed Allen by the shoulder. He could feel the boy tense up as Brian grabbed him. Pulling him close, Brian whispered, "Stay here and keep an eye on them. No one knows we're here, so you're safe. I need to call my dad."

Allen nodded his head, indicating he understood, and taking the night vision monocle from Brian, proceeded to do as he was told.

Snaking his way through the brush about twenty yards, Brian keyed the radio and whispered, "Home Base, this is Scout."

After a moment, the reply came, "Go ahead, Scout."

"Looks like three groups, maybe thirty people total. They look like they're heading out soon."

"As soon as they move, you return to base."

"You betcha."

He hates when I talk to him that way. All I needed was a dontchya know hey and he'd have hit the roof.

Brian grinned and put the radio back in the holster on his tactical vest and returned to Allen.

"Everything okay?" Allen whispered.

Leaning toward him, Brian replied, "Yes. As soon as they start heading out, we're going back to the base. We have to clear out and make it home before they get to the Stepanik's place."

***

As soon as my call ended with Brian, I radioed over to Gary. Keying the mike, I said, "Farm 2, this is Cabin."

246

Gary was on top of things, as I knew he would be.

"Go, Cabin," Gary replied.

"Looks like the party is a go. Plan on a big attendance."

"How big?"

"Around thirty," I said.

"Roger."

I went and gathered up Craig and Nancy. It was time for us to move into position.

As we walked across the yard in the dark, I explained again what we would do.

"Craig, I want you on my left about fifteen feet away. Nancy, you'll be on my right the same distance. Get yourself comfortable and well concealed. I have the charger for the claymores, and nobody shoots until I fire those off."

"Okay," they responded in quavering voices.

"It's okay to be scared, you two. Just don't let it control you."

"You don't look scared, Fil," Nancy remarked.

"Dad don't get scared," Craig quipped.

"Like hell I don't. I wouldn't give two cents for a man who doesn't get scared. Those are the ones that get you killed," I said.

I let those words sink in, then I continued. "I'm scared, too. Any sane person would be. Now listen up. Get yourself into position, comfortable, and concealed. No talking, whispering, anything. If our plan works, they'll walk right in front of us and hunker down right where we want them to."

I almost called it the kill zone, but I didn't want to make Nancy any more nervous. Craig was doing okay, but Nancy was untested.

"If they get too close to you, put your face in the dirt. Look down, don't let them see your eyes. Plus, if you aren't looking at them, there's less chance they'll see you or you'll give your position away."

"Got it, Dad," Craig said.

"They gonna be that close, Fil?" Nancy asked.

"Not sure. They could be, we don't know. Better to know what to do and not have to then to not know and have to. Any more questions?"

Neither responded, so I said, "Okay, single file after me. When we get to the stump, I'll point to my right and then my left, you guys take up positions and I'll hook up the charger for a test and then live. No more talking."

I looked them both in the eyes to make certain they understood, fearing that it could be the last time I looked at them alive. This was my youngest son and my daughter-in-law. Yeah, I was scared, too. I was scared for them, and for the others.

I put the earbud for the radio in my ear, and waving my hand, led them into the woods.

***

"Let's go," Brian said as he tapped Allen on the shoulder. The two crawled back deeper into the woods along the edge of the park. After about twenty yards of crawling, Brian stopped them and raised himself up on his knees.

Allen, mimicking everything Brian did, was less than an arm's length away. "I'm getting up and heading that way," Brian whispered, his arm pointing into the woods. "We have to move fast, so don't lose me. We gotta beat them back so that you and I can get into the positions Dad set up for us."

"Got it," Allen said.

"If we get separated, don't call out for me. Just keep heading north by northwest. When you get to the road, head north until Sajan sees you or you see the road."

"Okay."

"Let's move now."

They hadn't taken two steps before Allen tripped and fell flat on his face, discharging his weapon.

Brian reached down, grabbed him by the back of his vest and lifted him up. *"Run!"*

The two of them took off, dashing through the woods.

***

"What the hell was that?" Tom shouted.

"Sounds like a gunshot over in the woods," Kevin answered, pointing west.

"Well, get someone over there and find out."

Kevin grabbed two men standing nearby and said, "Come with me."

They ran toward where the sound had come from and stopped at the edge of the woods.

Kevin shouted, "Stop!"

He lined up the men and they walked slowly forward, their weapons held against their chests as they moved. Each step they took brought them deeper into the darkness, making it almost impossible to see anything.

After about ten minutes of searching, Kevin stopped them and had them turn around, walking back to the park and the rest of the looter gang.

"We didn't find anything, Tom," he reported.

"Well, it sure as hell wasn't hunters," Tom said. "Somebody shot something."

"We didn't see anything. It's too dark. Somebody shot a gun, sure, but it was only once. I didn't hear anything else, and neither did the other guys."

"Okay, get everybody together. It's time for you to move out. Keep 'em quiet, Kevin, I don't want any smokin' or jokin' out there."

"No problem, boss," Kevin said.

"I'll follow in about an hour. I want you there, in place and ready. Keep 'em quiet, or I'll have your ass. Sid!"

"Yeah, boss?" Sid said.

"You hear what I told Kevin. No grab assin' out there. I want these people, and I want that girl."

Sid nodded. "You betcha, boss. I'm on it."

***

Tom watched as the two groups marched down the road, out of the park and toward the house where the girl was seen. It was time for him to take control of this place and end this little bit of rebellion against his rule.

As they walked out, he saw Brad and Frank in the groups. He was pleased they weren't together.

Still don't trust those two. Then, they disappeared into the darkness.

***

Sam lay under the brush and leaves. He was awake, but uncomfortable. The ground was wet and had soaked through his clothes.

I'll have to remember to tell Gary to bring a poncho or something to lay on.

The thought no sooner left his mind when he saw movement across the road. Then, he heard trampling feet on the road surface.

Reaching for the radio, he keyed it, breaking squelch three times.

A few seconds later, he heard the squelch break twice.

Sam pressed the button once, twice, three times as he counted the men crossing the road and walking by just feet away from where he lay. Eleven times he broke squelch.

He was perspiring now. As cold and wet as he was, the sweat broke out on his forehead and ran down his face. He thought they were all through when he noticed, up the road a bit, another group crossing.

He quickly pressed the key on the mike three more times in rapid succession. The two responses came back to him, and again he began to count off. Eleven more times he broke squelch.

Son of a bitch. Shit's about to get real.

***

Gary counted the number of squelch breaks. When eleven signals came through, he got nervous. Whispering to Quint, he said, "Looks like eleven just entered the area."

"We can handle them," Quint whispered back.

Then Gary heard three quick breaks and counted again. Eleven more signals came through. "Shit, we got eleven more coming. That makes twenty-two."

"Not good," Quint said.

"I hope John was able to get in position. Rick, you got the charger for those claymores to the right?" Gary asked.

"Yeah, yes sir," Rick replied. He was obviously nervous, licking his lips and beginning to shake.

Quint reached over to his grandson, putting his hand around his arm. "You'll be okay, son. Just remember who you are and what you're fighting for."

Rick nodded his head, then glanced toward the house. While he couldn't see her, he knew Addie was there on the porch. He felt like going back to help protect her but knew he couldn't. He had to man-up, as his dad had said before he went off to war.

Now was his time.

Chapter 16

"The true soldier fights not because he hates what is in front of him, but because he loves what is behind him."

—G.K. Chesterton

A rustling in the trees in front of John caught his attention. *No noise discipline.* He picked up the charger for the claymores and waited. He could hear the men in front of him as they made their way into the small depression that they had been using before.

He smiled. Brian had set up the mines perfectly. This was going to be a blood bath.

***

Brian and Allen made their way across the road, stopping at the bunker long enough to scare Sajan half to death and let him know it was *game on.*

Quickly, they ran toward the cabin. Allen stayed to help Donna and Mike.

Brian made his way across the meadow behind the cabin to meet up with Carol near the rear entrance of the Stepanik farm. It didn't take him long to find her, but he was almost greeted with a 5.56 round for his efforts.

"I damn near shot you," Carol said as he dropped to the ground next to her. "I take it they're coming."

"Oh yeah, about thirty of them," Brian answered as he took out his canteen, then drank about half of its contents. "Looks like three groups."

"This isn't good," she stated flatly, the emotion in her voice gone.

"Not good for them, you mean. We'll take out most of them before they ever do much damage, then Dad and the others can clean up."

"You think we'll win?" she asked.

"Yes, yes I do. We have no choice but to win. I don't think we'll come out of this unscathed, though."

"I was afraid you'd say that."

A noticeable lightness started to appear as Carol spoke those words. Daylight was approaching.

***

Sajan, secure in the bunker, watched the road, when in the distance, he saw a group of people cross.

Oh shit, it's starting.

Picking up the field phone, he cranked it, causing the phone on the other end to start clacking loudly.

Donna picked it up. "Cabin," she said into the headset.

"I just saw a group crossing the road down toward the Stepanik's. I think it's the last group."

"Stay in the bunker, Sajan. Do not leave the bunker, no matter what you hear, understand?"

"Yes, ma'am."

***

Donna set down the handset and turned toward Allen. "It's starting."

Allen sat there feeling sick. Last night was one thing with his epic screw up of keeping his finger on the trigger and causing his weapon to discharge was bad enough. The tightening in his stomach warned him now he was about to puke; he couldn't do that now.

Donna sat down at the kitchen table, the dogs laying on the floor around her, having all been brought inside to keep them from following John or Brian.

Bowing her head, she prayed. She was once a very religious person and now it seemed proper. She remembered a Psalm from when she first went into the army, a portion of it anyway, a part of Psalm 91, the soldier's Psalm.

> *"You will not fear the terror of night,*
> *nor the arrow that flies by day,*
> *nor the pestilence that stalks in the darkness,*
> *nor the plague that destroys at midday.*
> *A thousand may fall at your side,*
> *ten thousand at your right hand,*
> *but it will not come near you."*

It was all she could remember, and it would have to do. She and John had been Episcopalian, so in that tradition she made the sign of the cross and said, "Amen." Now all she could do was wait, painfully and nervously wait. Everyone she cared about was out there in danger.

***

Tom led his men across the road and straight toward the drive to the Stepanik farm. They were clustered behind him, bunched up and walking arrogantly, as they entered the drive.

"That's far enough! You can turn around and go back where you came from," a voice shouted.

Tom stood in the drive, a smirk on his face, as the voice of an old man in front of him echoed through the trees. His men stopped behind him.

"You sound real brave, old man," he replied loudly. "Real brave and real *stupid*."

"I said *leave*," the man yelled, his weapon pointed down the drive. "You'll leave now, or you'll die where you stand."

"Shut up, old man, and put down your gun and we'll let you die fast. Every one of my men is pointing a gun at you right now. You make a wrong move and you're dead."

Movement to Tom's right briefly caught his attention. Sid waved at him to let him know he was in position.

He couldn't see Kevin's group, but if Sid was in position, so was Kevin. He turned his attention back toward the old man when a loud roar and explosion to his left broke the silence. Screams and rifle fire erupted in the woods as a crashing of movement came toward him.

The men in the driveway ran, a few shooting toward the old man.

A couple of men, some bloody and staggering, came out of the woods from where the explosion had occurred.

Then another loud boom sounded, then another, came from his right. Tom dropped to the ground as people in a bunker began to shoot at him and the few men remaining around him. Those men in the woods to his right also began to shoot. The staccato of gunfire erupted everywhere.

Two more loud explosions erupted. Tom could hear something ripping through the trees and his men screaming. The gunfire from his men was barely noticeable as the fire from the bunker and his right continued.

He heard a voice shout from the trees, "Let's get the hell out of here!"

He tried to stand, then realized he'd been shot in both legs, the pain beginning to take hold as the gunfire waned and then grew silent.

A crunching on the gravel caused him to look up, and he saw a man coming toward him, an AR pointed at him. An older man, decked out like a soldier, was doing the pointing. Tom realized he'd been outgunned and outmatched.

***

"Don't even think about moving," I said to the man as I walked up to who I guessed was the leader of the looter band. Around him, a few men were writhing on the ground. I saw Craig and Sam—*where the hell did Sam come from?*—going around and picking up weapons, taking them away from the dead and wounded in the driveway. Running footsteps behind me caused me to turn, and had I not recognized Gary I may well have shot him.

"John, we have a problem," Gary said.

Looking behind him, I saw Rick kneeling over a body, sobbing.

"Oh, shit," I said. "Quint?"

"Yeah, he's dead," Gary confirmed. "Shot several times, one in the head. I told him to stay in the bunker, but that stubborn old man doesn't listen."

I stood there for a moment, not really sure what to do next. Behind them, I saw Brian and Carol coming up in the UTV.

Addie headed toward Rick, then stopped to hug him as she knelt beside him.

I turned back around and looked down at the so-called leader.

"You caused a lot of pain, asshole," I remarked as he laid there, a grimace of pain crossing his face.

"I did what I had to do to survive. You're doing the same."

"We don't rape and kill innocent people."

I barely had time to turn around when a scream of rage and anger burst out next to me. *Boom, boom, boom, boom.*

The noise from the shotgun almost blew out what hearing I had left. Four twelve-gauge double ought buck shredded the man before me, turning him into red mist and hamburger.

"You bastard!" Addie yelled as she fired two more shells, and then continued to pull the trigger several more times before Gary reached from behind her and put his hand on the gun.

"It's over, Addie," he said. "You've had your justice."

Addie let go of the weapon and fell to the ground, sobbing.

Gary stooped down to hold her.

"That's okay, Gary. I'll take care of her."

I turned to see Craig, covered in dirt, sweat, and some blood that I quickly saw was not his, sit down next to Addie and put his arms around her. Pulling her close, he rocked her while she sobbed. He looked up at me briefly.

I saw tears in his eyes. My youngest son was truly hurt, but doing what he always did—helping others with their pain.

As Craig held Addie, I walked toward Rick and Quint. Carol and Brian were already there, and Carol was stooped down next to Rick, rubbing his back and talking softly to him.

"Looks like we kicked their ass, Dad," Brian said, but there was no joy in his voice. He liked the old man and I knew that he, too, mourned his loss.

"Yeah, but some got away," I replied. "I don't know how many."

"We going after them?" Brian asked.

"I think we've had enough killing for one day. I don't think they'll be a problem anymore. Give it a few days and we'll check the park."

"Where's Nancy?" he asked.

"She should be…" I started to say as I pointed down the drive. But Nancy wasn't there.

"Oh, shit," Brian said.

He ran toward where he knew the first ambush site had been set. His large frame crashed through the brush as he hollered her name.

A few seconds later, I heard another shout.

"She's been shot!"

I raced into the brush and shouted for Carol. I didn't have to go far before I saw Brian bent over, holding a bandage against Nancy's head, trying to open another to cover a chest wound.

"Help me, she's still alive!" he cried.

I raced over toward them, ripping the Israeli bandage out of my vest. I slid down next to them and pressed it over the wound on her chest.

"It's all the way through, Dad," he said as I put pressure on the wound. I searched for the wrappers for the bandages to help make a seal on both sides as I was pretty certain it had collapsed her lung. It was then I felt a nudge against me.

"Get out of the way, I've got this."

Carol.

She immediately took my hands away and began instructing Brian with what to do. I stood up, blood covered my hands, feeling helpless now.

After a few minutes, I saw Carol sigh. My heart raced as I prepared myself for the inevitable.

She put her hand on Brian's shoulder and said, "We've got her stable now. We have to get her back to the cabin. Donna is there, and she's better at this than I am."

"I'll get the UTV," I said and took off through the woods to get it.

As I ran past Gary and Sam, Gary shouted, "Everything all right?"

"Nancy's been shot, but Carol got her stabilized. We got to get her back to the cabin."

"What about them?" Gary asked as he pointed to the several wounded looters still laying in the drive.

"Fuck them. I have family to take care of first," I shouted and jumped into the UTV. I drove it as close to Nancy as I could. We carefully laid her inside, then Brian and Carol took off down the driveway and onto the road, racing back to the cabin.

I stood there, feeling helpless again as I watched them drive away. A hand on my arm caused me to jump. It was Craig.

"Carol's good, Dad. So is Mom. She'll be okay," he assured me.

"I hope so." I stood there a moment, my mind racing all kinds of ways. My family had just gone to war. We killed people, a lot of people. A friend had died, his grandson now an orphan, and my daughter-in-law could die, too. Craig had been wounded days earlier. Things had changed, and I was supposed to be the pillar of stability to guide them. And I felt lost.

***

Brian slid to a stop in front of the cabin and shouted, "Donna!"

He didn't wait long for an answer as she and Allen burst through the door and ran into the yard.

"Your dad called me," Donna said. "We have a bed set up."

Lifting Nancy, they moved her as gently and quickly as possible into the cabin and the bed that was in John's office.

"Everybody out but Carol," she commanded.

Allen moved quickly, his nervousness evident. Obviously, he did not want to be there.

Brian held back, not wanting to move.

"I said *out*, Brian," she said, a bit more softly this time. "You don't need to be here for this."

"But she's my wife…"

"You can help her by letting me and Carol do what we do best. Now get out," Donna asserted.

Brian headed toward the door. Mike was standing there, tears running down his face. Grady, Max, and King crowded behind him, trying to get into the room.

"Why is Mom bleeding?" he asked between sobs.

"She was hurt, son," Brian said, choking on his own words. "Donna and Carol are going to help her." He reached down and picked Mike up, hugging him tightly and heading for the kitchen.

Carol closed the door behind him.

Entering the kitchen, Brian headed toward the windows facing out toward the field behind the cabin. *I have to be strong now.*

He held Mike until the boy began to squirm and then, setting him down, stared out the window, looking at nothing in particular. Mike's movement caught his attention, and he turned, seeing Mike head back toward the room where Nancy was. "Stay here, son."

"I want my mom," Mike replied. His tears were a gusher now, streaming down his face.

"We have to stay here so they can help her," Brian insisted.

"I want my mom," Mike said loudly. He started to run toward the room.

Jumping up, Brian grabbed him, picked him up, and went out onto the porch.

The porch had taken on the role of a sanctuary, someplace safe. He went over to the steps and set Mike down. Grady, having followed him, nudged Brian out of the way and put his massive head against Mike's.

King and Max went to their usual place and laid down, not understanding what was going on, but knowing enough to stay out of the way.

Brian stood there, shock taking over as he watched Mike and Grady. He couldn't stop the tears anymore and they rolled down his face.

***

Walking back to where Gary, Sam, and Rick were, I saw Quint, my friend and neighbor, lying dead on the ground. Rick, sitting cross-legged beside him, was no longer crying. Addie sat next to him, her hand rubbing his back as she whispered something to him.

Gary came to me and said, "How's Nancy?"

"It's bad. Carol took her back to the cabin so Donna can help her."

"What about those bodies? There are still wounded over there."

Hearing that, Rick jumped up, grabbed his rifle, and

ran toward the mess of men still lying in the road. He started shooting at the bodies on the ground, some not moving and others stopping as he emptied what was left in his rifle into them.

Sam was quicker than I in getting to him and wrapped his arms around Rick.

"They need to die, all of them!" Rick shouted. Anger had replaced his grief.

"We've had enough killing for one day, son," Sam replied softly. Gently taking the rifle away from Rick, he reached back and handed it to me.

"They killed my grampa," he said, the bitterness in his voice projecting what he was thinking.

"They paid for it," I said.

"Not all of them," he replied, and he turned and walked back toward where his grandfather lay.

"We have graves to dig," Sam said, scanning over the bodies we could see and knowing that more were in the woods. "And we have to do something about the wounded."

"We'll get to the wounded later," I responded tersely. "We have our own to care for first."

Sam started to say something, but then stopped. I guess he figured there was no sense arguing the point. With Carol and Donna busy with Nancy, there was little we could do right now anyway.

"Let's get Quint into the house and clean him up. We'll bury him later," I said. We walked back toward our friend to do what we had to do to honor him.

Chapter 17

"The whole world can become the enemy when you lose what you love."

—Kristina McMorris

Stumbling through the woods, Brad led what was left of the looter band that had attacked the farm toward the park. Counting quickly, there were only six of them—six out of the thirty men that had headed out that morning. Two were wounded, but their wounds didn't look too bad. Only he and another man still had weapons. The others had dropped or thrown away their guns in the mad rush to escape the heavy fire they had faced.

A small crowd of people waited for them. Standing anxiously, some looked behind the small group of survivors as they emerged on the road into the park. But what they looked for wasn't there—Tom and the rest of the men who were left behind.

Brad was numb, but he was also enraged. "God dammit!" he shouted. "You people need to get what guns you have and prepare to defend us. Get off your asses and move *now!*"

I'm in charge now. This is my band.

"We need to get out of here," Sid said as he staggered toward Brad. "We need to go now before they come and finish us off."

"We're not going anywhere," Brad said as he wheeled around and stared angrily at Sid. "I'm in charge now, and we go when I say we go."

Sid was in no shape to challenge him. A cut on his head still bled, causing him to squint and use his shirtsleeve to wipe the blood from his eyes. A bullet had grazed his arm and it, too, was still bleeding.

"So, what do we do…boss?" Sid asked, accepting his new reality.

"We get ready to defend ourselves if they come, is what we do."

"What about Tom and the others?"

"Fuck them, they're dead," Brad said. "We can't do anything for them. Let those assholes take care of burying 'em. We have other things to do."

"Okay, boss," Sid replied, and then walked over to where a small group of women were bandaging the other wounded man.

***

After we got Quint onto his bed, Sam and Gary began to clean him up and prepare him for the funeral we all knew we'd have.

I went into the living room where Addie was sitting with Rick on the couch. Both were silent as I walked toward them.

"Your grampa was a brave man, Rick," I said.

"They murdered him," was all he said.

I didn't know what to say, so I sat down next to him.

The room was silent as the three of us sat there, each reflecting in our own way over what had happened and trying, at least I was, to not think about what would happen next. After a while, I stood up and said, "I need to go home and check on Nancy."

Walking out the door, I saw Craig, sitting on the bunker wall, watching the bodies in the drive, his AR cradled across his lap. The look in his eyes was a combination of what I could only describe as anger, disgust, and sadness all rolled in together.

"How you doin', son?" I asked.

"I feel dirty, is how I'm doing," he answered, a sharp, bitter tone to his voice. "I have no idea how many we killed, no idea at all. This isn't right, Dad, but it doesn't feel wrong, either."

"I know, son. The last few months have been bad. I never thought any of this would happen."

"So now what? We going after the survivors? Are we going to clean out that camp and kill some more? Who's going to die on our side next?"

As soon as he said that, I immediately had visions of Nancy lying in the woods, bleeding, her dark skin turning gray as we put her in the UTV. *Was she still alive?* "I'm going to the cabin. Are you staying here, or do you want to come along?"

"Nobody here is in any shape to keep watch, Dad. I'll stay here. I can't do anything back at the cabin anyway."

I touched his shoulder. "You gonna be all right?"

"I'll be fine. I just need to process all of this. It's a bit much."

Smiling at him, and trying to lighten the mood, I quipped, "Ya think?"

It had the desired effect as he returned the smile. I embraced him and we hugged, then I headed off to the cabin.

***

The next several days happened in a fog. We buried Quint in the yard across from his house. Rick felt that this was where his grampa would want to be, close by where he could still keep an eye on things. Charlie Winston, his wife Lucille, Emma, Fred, Billy, and his wife Sarah, and Jesse all showed up for the funeral. Charlie took Quint's death especially hard as they had mostly grown up together.

"He was my friend," Charlie said as we stood by Quint's grave.

"I really liked him. He was a good man, took care of Rick," Lucille said.

"You want me to take the boy with me to my place?" Charlie asked me.

I half-shrugged, not knowing the answer. "I'm not sure he would go. He has revenge in his heart and he won't leave til he's had it."

Charlie shook his head in sadness. "That's not a good way to live. I'd do the same if one of mine were in the ground because of them, but still, it's no way to live."

"We'll keep an eye on him. I think his being here will turn out for the best, anyway.

Charlie patted my shoulder. "You're right, John, and I trust you to do that."

Cleaning the bodies out of the woods, picking up a variety of weapons, and using the frontend loader that Quint had in the barn to dig a pit and bury the looters took us two days. I had to keep an eye on Rick as Addie had told me he was dead set on going to Stilwell's Park and killing everyone he could find. Sam and Gary were keeping a close eye on him, too, when I wasn't around.

I was sitting on the cabin's porch when I heard the roar of engines and then the clatter of a TA-312. Craig was at the bunker out front and called in to let me know Rahn and two Humvees were here. I stood up as they entered the yard, and Rahn hopped out as they coasted to a stop.

"Heard you had some trouble," he said as we shook hands.

"Word travels fast in the Northwoods," I answered.

"Sam told us on the radio this morning. Wish we could have been here."

"I appreciate that," I said. "We lost Quint, and my daughter-in-law is in a coma, shot in the chest and head."

"Well, I have more bad news for you then, John," Rahn said. "We've been ordered to the FEMA camp in Wausau. I'm supposed to take the people I have, load everything I can into our only 5-Ton and the Hummers, then drive everything there."

"When's that supposed to happen?" I asked.

"A-S-A-P. The good captain was none too subtle about it. Seems he is the military leader for all of the northern third of the state now. Calls himself the Northern Zone of Recovery Commander."

I shook my head with a chuckle. Sometimes people get real hung up on power and titles. Elias Wolfe seemed to be one of those types.

"Why are you here then?" I asked.

"Well, I wasn't actually *going* to come. I figured that you had enough of my stuff and that if I needed to come here it would be fast, most likely with the captain and whatever troops he can muster chasing after me."

I looked at him, trying to gage his reaction. "You think that's going to happen?"

"You hear the same chatter over the radio that we do. FEMA isn't being kind about rounding people up and forcing them into the camps. A lot of people all over the country are resisting, at least those that are left."

"That bad, huh?"

"Yeah, planes lost power and crashed into cities, starting fires. People are starving; there's no medication. Then the criminals and gangs are taking control. Speaking of gangs, you may have taken care of one, but you have another in the area."

"Yeah, the Outlaws, heard about them," I replied. "My looter gang isn't all wiped out, either. They're still over at the park."

"I've got time. Wanna go pay 'em a visit and encourage them to leave?" Rahn asked.

Both Humvees had pedestal mounted SAWs on them. I glanced at them, then at Rahn, and said, "Sure, let's do it."

"Right now?" he said, a wicked grin spreading across his face.

"Well you asked, Top," I said, grinning at him.

"Don't call me Top. Specialist Johnson, get those two SAWs ready. We're going hunting."

"Roger, First Sergeant," came the shouted response.

"He's been properly trained," Rahn said with a wink.

I knew all too well what that most likely meant. I called and told Brian that he, Allen, and Sajan were coming along. I asked Carol to call over to Sam and let him know what we were going to do.

We piled into the Humvees and Rahn, waving his hand out the window, motioned for everyone to move out.

I waved at Craig as we drove by and shouted, "We're cleaning out the park."

He responded with a thumbs up.

The ride didn't take very long. We drove slowly up the park drive and into the park itself. What greeted us was surprising.

The looters had cleared out, nothing but garbage was left. It had only been about a week since the fight and I believed they were still there. Somewhere. I wanted them all dead, but for now gone was good.

Rahn and I exited the vehicles and walked toward each other.

Specialist Johnson stood outside the driver's door of Rahn's Humvee, a gunner standing up swinging the SAW slowly back and forth across the park.

My driver remained in the vehicle while the gunner mimicked what the other was doing.

Rahn and I walked the grounds. In front of us was a pavilion with a single picnic table under its roof. As we approached, I saw something sticking up from the tabletop.

We walked closer. It was an old-fashioned ice pick stabbed into a piece of brown paper. The crude lettering on it I suspected was meant for me.

WE WILL BE BACK

PREPARE TO DIE

The message was unmistakably clear.

"I don't think they like you very much," Rahn said.

"They'll like me even less when we meet again."

"Think they're watching us?" he asked, his eyes roaming over the park and the edge of the woods surrounding it.

"Of that I have no doubt. I almost bet we're in somebody's crosshairs right now."

"Not a very comforting thought, Henry."

I glanced toward the Humvees. "I doubt they'll try anything with two SAWs present," I replied. "I don't think they're that stupid or desperate."

"We should get out of here. I have a trip to make."

"Roger that, Rahn."

We walked back and climbed into our vehicles. Rahn led the way as we drove out of the park and back to my cabin.

***

"I should've shot that son of a bitch," Brad said, holding the deer rifle loosely in his hand.

"You woulda got him, too, boss," Sid answered, an AR clutched in his left hand while his other hand rested on the handle of a large Bowie style knife in a sheath on his belt.

They stood together, looking at the park road, both quiet for a moment.

Slinging his rifle over his shoulder, Brad said, "Let's go. It's a long walk to that state fishing area. We need to get everyone there and start planning our next attack."

"It's good you knew about that place, boss," Sid said matter-of-factly, the emotion absent from his voice.

"My old man used to take me fishing there when I was a kid. The only thing he ever did with me that was worth a damn. There's some old DNR buildings there that we can set up in, keep everyone out of the weather."

"Then what?" Sid asked.

"Then we rebuild. We scavenge for whatever we need around there, take control." Brad looked back toward where the two Humvees had disappeared from view. Pointing in that direction, he said, "And come back to take *care* of those people."

***

It didn't take us long to get back to the cabin. Carol and Donna were on the porch watching Mike play with the dogs.

"Hi, Grampa!" he shouted as the Humvees stopped. Then he went back to playing. Kids.

Both women stood up and walked down the steps. After greeting Rahn and his men, Donna offered them fresh cookies she had baked in the wood fired oven. The three soldiers walked off with her, stomping their boots clean on the steps before being admonished by Donna for the noise because Nancy was resting.

"Problem solved, John?" Carol asked.

"Yes and no," I answered. "They were gone, which solves one problem. They were gone who knows where, which creates another."

"Damn," she said.

"Rahn's leaving for Wausau, too." I nodded at him where he stood munching on a cookie.

"Oh?"

"Yes, ma'am," Rahn said. "My captain has ordered me and the men I have left to convoy to the FEMA camp there."

"When will we see you again, First Sergeant?" she asked.

"If my gut is correct, I suspect soon. The captain's mission is to round up everyone he can and put them in the camp. If what we hear on the radio from other places is true, and I think it is, then most won't go kindly."

"You're going to force them to go?" Carol asked.

"Well, force is a strong word, ma'am. I'll obey my lawful orders, you know that. I'm not shooting Americans unless they shoot at me. So, the word force is relative in my mind."

"So, when you choose to interpret your orders that way, then what?" I asked, curious.

Rahn stared at me, his face serious. "Remember when I said I hedged my bets?"

I stood there, thinking of all the equipment he had brought us and realized exactly what he meant. "They'll come looking for you next."

"Are you going to the camp?"

"Nope." I shook my head.

"Then you'll need help," Rahn said. "I figure my boys will come with me, and a few more that aren't here now. So, let them come."

"You're putting us at risk."

"John, you're at risk now. It just hasn't arrived yet."

I glanced toward the Humvees, and sighed. "I know."

We stood there, silent, Carol between us, looking at us both, accepting what we were saying but not objecting. Rahn and I were sealing an alliance that was already there. It would come to that. I always knew it from the first I had heard of the FEMA camps. I just thought we'd have more time.

"Well, we need to head out," Rahn said.

We shook hands as he walked toward his Humvee, shouting for his men to follow. They trampled down the steps, mouths full of cookies and hands filled as well. He stood by the Humvee and shouted, "You should get your people together, as many as you can. They'll be back."

"I will," I replied.

He mounted his vehicle, and with a wave of his hand, they drove out the drive.

"Will they come for us, John?" Carol asked.

"I'm afraid so. We need to get the others together and prepare. Prepare for the looters, the Outlaws, and any other groups out there."

She crossed her arms over her chest and shivered. "I hate this. I hate what we've become."

"So do I, Carol. So do I."

Chapter 18

"Prepare for the unknown by studying how others in the past have coped with the unforeseeable and the unpredictable."

—George S. Patton

We spent the next week getting the word out to everyone we knew that was in the area. I had spoken to Sam and we decided to use his place for the meeting. It was in town, he wasn't using it, and it was pretty much empty except for a few things he'd left behind. The weather had been nice and if it didn't rain, we could meet in his yard using a picnic table and some benches he had there. The good news was that no one said they wouldn't show up. Some were in pretty bad shape and I wasn't sure if they'd actually be able to make it, much less participate in our working together to defend what we had.

A few others were apprehensive—gotta love the north woods' spirit of independence and self-reliance. I also had to laugh at it, because it was completely unrealistic. We would have never survived the looters

274

without the help of others. Even with the weapons and equipment Rahn had given us, we simply didn't have enough people to stand off a group of their size.

With the threat of the Outlaw motorcycle gang and this expected demand to move into a FEMA camp, there was no way an individual or a small family could stand up to those challenges.

I told them so in no uncertain terms, too.

They listened.

After I explained what happened to Emmet and Katherine Mueller who had been killed by looters, they listened better. Now all I had to hope for was everyone showing up.

The night before the meeting I went out into the field behind the cabin. There were some logs left there from when we had been gathering firewood. It had become a quiet place for me to sit and reflect. I took one of my few remaining cigars with me, parked my behind on one of the logs, and used a few of the others next to it to rest against. I called it my Lincoln Log recliner. Max and King had followed me, and being the good dogs they were, sat alongside the logs. After a moment, they laid down and promptly went to sleep.

I cut my cigar, pulled out a match from my shirt pocket, and lighting the cigar, leaned back against the logs to ponder our predicament.

A light breeze carried away both my cigar smoke and any mosquitos that would be out here. Biting flies were another thing, but those had been mild this year. Crickets and frogs were chirping everywhere, and the clear night made for a great backdrop to this little nature symphony that was entertaining me.

A lot had happened since the lights went out. I was glad that Brian and his family were here, even if Nancy was still in what Donna described as a coma. Craig and she were a very welcome addition, and I was happy that two of my three sons were with me.

I was worried about John and had been mulling over how to make the long trek to try and find him. I knew that a strong objection would be raised by everyone, family and friend alike. What was I thinking…friend, we had all become family, just a different kind.

I knew they would try to discourage me from going, and in a way, I couldn't blame them. It was hard for me to accept that John and his kids, my remaining two grandkids aside from Mike, had not survived this. I had to believe they had, but they lived so close to Indianapolis that I couldn't be certain. So, an argument to not go could be made.

Still, I wanted my whole family safe and together.

"Dad."

Brian's voice in the dark robbed me of my ruminations. Sitting up, I glanced in the direction of his voice and saw both him and Craig standing there.

"Hello, you two," I replied. "What brings you out this way?"

"Just some father and sons' time," Brian answered.

He was always quick like that with some snappy reply.

"Yeah, we needed some time with you," Craig added.

"Pull up a log," I said.

They made their way over and plopped down alongside me.

"I'd offer you a cigar, Brian," I said with a bit of sarcasm in my tone, "but I only have a few left—so I hid them."

"I know," he laughed. "I looked before coming out here."

"Good thing I don't smoke, 'cuz I don't want in the middle of this when you run out, Dad," Craig quipped.

"So, what's on your mind, boys?" I asked.

"Everything, nothing, the weight of the world,"

Brian replied.

"It's all hard to process," Craig said. "So much has happened. I can't get any of it straight in my head. Jesus, Dad, do you know how many people I've shot and killed? I'm not even in the army like you and Brian, and I've been to war already."

I leaned forward, resting my arms on my knees. "I know, son." Looking at them, I let my gaze drift back down to the ground in front of me. "Twenty plus years in the army and I never shot anyone," I said quietly. "Never, not once."

"But I thought…" Craig said incredulously. "You were in the infantry, a paratrooper, you went to Ranger School, Dad. I thought you were some kind of Rambo super soldier."

"Did I ever say I was?"

"He never did, Craig," Brian interjected. "Dad did all of those things, but he never once said he'd been to war or any of that stuff."

"Wow." Craig exhaled as he leaned back. "You deal with it like it's nothing, like you did it all the time."

"That's what you see." I shook my head. "What you don't see is how much it bothers me. If you saw that, if any of you saw that, we'd probably all be dead. You needed me to be that super warrior. Before all of this, Brian had more combat experience in his little finger than I had in my entire body."

"Coulda fooled me on that one, Dad," Brian said. "Craig's right, you masked it well."

"That's why I'm out here. I have to process all of this, too. I hate every bit of this just as much as you two do, and I know this is just the beginning. We haven't seen the worst of it yet."

"Waddya mean?" Craig asked.

"I mean the dying times are just starting. People are dying of hunger, illness, and by killing each other for a moldy piece of bread. Some are settling old arguments, some are just sick human beings and enjoy it."

"That's what I'm worried about," Craig said, his head lolling forward as he sat there. "I killed those people and it was like nothing while I did it. I even went to sleep after the first time, back at the house."

"Everybody handles it in their own way, bro. Some guys can put it aside and not worry. Other guys let it eat at them forever. I heard you talking to Addie, so I know it bothered you somewhat. I think you're handling it just fine."

"I hope so. Sometimes, I see that guy back at the house in my dreams, the one begging for food for his family."

"We'll see more of that, too," I said. "People will find their way out here because the Nicolet Forest is here. They'll think it's safe, that food is everywhere. They'll be hungry and they'll beg."

"We can't say no to everyone, Dad," Brian said.

"I know. That bothers me, because while we need to help each other, we also need to look out for ourselves."

"So what do we do?" Craig asked.

"Unfortunately, we have to do what we've been doing. We share with people we know when we know it won't hurt us. We can help neighbors plant and harvest, just like in the olden days."

"Olden days? I haven't heard you say that in a long time," Brian quipped. "Grampa used to say that."

I remembered my dad well. He loved the north woods, and family was more important to him than almost anything. As much as I missed him, I was glad he wasn't here now, to see what had happened and what was going to happen.

"I'm serious, boys. We only share what we can when we can and not any other time. We'll probably start seeing refugees again in a few weeks, and as word gets out about the camps, that will drive others through here. We can't feed them all and we aren't going to try."

"What about water?" Craig asked.

"We can still do that. We have plenty, and as long as we keep them on the road and not let them back here by the cabin, we'll be fine, I guess."

"What about…" Craig asked again.

I put up a hand and stopped him. "I'm not going to sit here and discuss every *what about* possible situation, dammit. Water, nothing more, and I mean it."

"Yes, sir," he answered.

Brian looked like he was going to make a smartass remark but stopped himself. I knew what it was going to be, too. We shared a knowing glance and kept on with our conversation.

"Are we going to be okay tomorrow?" Brian asked.

Tomorrow was our meeting at Sam's old place with whoever from the area chose to show up.

"I hope so," I said. "Depends on who shows up, how much we can all trust each other, and who doesn't run away scared to Wausau and the camps."

"What are you going to say?"

I shrugged. "I have no idea."

***

I took almost everyone with me. Donna stayed at the cabin to watch Mike and Nancy, while Sajan watched the road from the bunker. Sam and Addie stayed at the Stepanik's farm. Sam didn't want to go to his old place and preferred to monitor the ham radio. Addie said he needed a guard, but I suspect she really wasn't ready to go out much in public, so I let her stay. I figured she could handle herself just fine if there was trouble. They had walkie talkies if they needed us, and while we were a couple miles away, the truck still had gas so we could get there quickly.

When we arrived, a few people were already there milling about. A couple stood on the front porch, but as I expected, no one had gone inside Sam's place. That wasn't done here without an invitation, and customs die hard.

I could see others heading toward us on ATVs, foot, and horseback. I even saw a horse drawn wagon, so people were beginning to get creative. In the distance, I could see a group on the road and guessed it was the Winstons. From what I could tell, it looked like we were going to have around fifty or sixty people, which was a much better turnout than I thought.

Carol and Allen unloaded the bed of my truck. I had brought along a couple of very large stew pots, fixin's for a decent venison chili, plus bowls, cups, and whatever I had to serve it in. I figured the day would be long and we'd need to keep everyone there. Food, I knew, would do it, and at the risk of everyone thinking I was the local grocery store and had more than enough, I decided we'd keep them there by feeding them.

Once everyone arrived, I had Brian and Craig usher everyone toward the backyard. As the people moved, there were a lot of hugs and handshakes as we greeted each other and took heart in knowing that after a few months so many friends were still with us. Once we got situated under the trees in Sam's backyard, I began the meeting.

I made it very clear I had called the meeting, but that I wasn't placing myself in charge of anything. Gary took care of that real quick and nominated me to be the leader.

I said I didn't want it, at which point he and Charlie

Winston said, "Tough."

I pushed back. "I'm not from here, folks. Gary is the better choice. He's lived here his whole life, except for when he was in the Marines. And there is that as well—Gary was a Marine. Nobody is tougher than a Marine."

The look Gary gave me would have melted snow. He knew I had him with that. A voiced vote made it official. Gary was now the leader of the band in Lake View, Wisconsin, population, less than 100.

Probably going to be even less than that by spring next year.

"I'll get even with you for this, John," he whispered as he walked past me and stood in front of the group.

"Okay, everyone, now that I am your fearless leader…" He was interrupted by several guffaws and a smattering of applause. Gary gave me that look again.

"Folks, I don't need to tell you how bad things are," he said.

For the next twenty minutes or so, maybe longer, he explained to them everything that we knew. Gary told them about the looter band and exactly what had happened. He told them about the Outlaws Motorcycle gang. As he was explaining that, a younger woman in the crowd interrupted him.

"I saw some people the other day out on the road. They were riding motorcycles. Could that be them?"

"It's possible," Gary replied, "but I don't think we need to fear everyone on a motorcycle. Be cautious, yes, but afraid, not so much."

"They didn't see me, though," she added and then, sensing everyone was looking at her, quickly sat back down.

Gary continued to explain about the National Guard and how they had helped us. He didn't mention any of the weapons or some of the other supplies they gave us. I was grateful for that. He did mention some of the supplies, though, and I supposed that eventually word would have gotten out anyway. He shared with them that the Guard was going to Wausau and a FEMA camp was there. That took off as an issue of debate, as several wanted to go to the camp.

Gary squelched that idea quickly when he began to describe what Sam had learned from his ham radio friends from around the US. A near panic set in after that.

"What will we do?" several people shouted.

A few brought up the camps and said that at least in the camps they'd be alive. It was then that I realized that my old Marine friend was a master. He had them right where they needed to be.

"That," he said firmly, "is exactly why we need to band together and help each other. We need to work together, just like in the 1800s, to farm, hunt, gather wood, defend, everything… We need to band together to do all of that."

"You want us all to move in together?" a man asked.

"I'm not livin' in the same house with Fred," another person said. "He never bathes."

"No," Gary soothed. "For now, we can all stay in our homes, but it might come to that. Everyone needs to understand that might happen."

"For how long?" someone shouted.

"Could be a year, could be several years, could be a very long time." Gary went on to explain. "We don't know, but this much I do know. It will be at least a year, and folks, like that TV show said, Winter is Coming, and everyone knows what that means."

Gary had them now and they were eating out of his hand. He spent the rest of the morning outlining his ideas, and it was obvious he had borrowed liberally from the early settler days of fur trappers and frontiersmen here in Wisconsin and east.

We broke for lunch and he let everyone go about their own private conversations. After lunch, he would get questions, objections, and I suspect some hostility that would mostly be fear talking.

We finished the meeting after lunch. The consensus was most of us would do as our ancestors had. We would work together like an early American settlement by helping one another on our homesteads and banding together for defense. It wasn't perfect, but it was a start. The biggest issues were how we would alert each other and where, if necessary, we would fort up. Many agreed that my cabin was a good place, but like everyone else's, we had no fortification. It was agreed that we would get back together and discuss how that would work. Some even suggested a traditional log fort with blockhouses. In theory a good idea, but with high powered weapons still available, it needed a lot of work.

Some of the locals had walkie talkies they had used for hunting. Gary said he'd have Sam connect with everyone to get us all on the same emergency frequency. The rest would have to depend on neighbors to let them know.

Inwardly, I was chuckling a bit because I thought I was living in the movie *Unconquered* with Gary Cooper, or *Drums Along the Mohawk* with Henry Fonda. Settlers living in the woods, waiting for bands of marauding Indians and French to attack. *History repeating itself, again.*

The ride back home was quiet. I dropped everyone off at my cabin and then took Gary back to the Stepanik's where we met with Sam and filled him in on his new duties.

I wanted to know if he'd picked up any chatter on the radio. He told me there was still fighting down south. Milwaukee, Madison, and now over in Appleton were ablaze with looting, killing, and any other kind of mayhem I could imagine. It sounded so bad I didn't want to imagine any of it, but I was glad I had gone and picked up Craig and Donna in the first days after the EMP.

"Anything else?" I asked.

"Message from Rahn. One if by land," he said.

"What's that mean?" I asked.

"Rahn radioed, and that's what the message was."

"I don't get it," Gary said.

"Paul Revere," I answered. It had just popped into my head.

"What?" Gary asked.

"Paul Revere, the redcoats are coming. One if by land and two if by sea."

"So does that mean he's coming, or that his captain is coming?" Sam asked.

"Good question," I said. "Let's hope it's Rahn."

The next morning Rahn showed up. He and his ever-present driver Specialist Johnson blew past the bunker and were in the yard before Allen could call it in. I'd have to talk to him about his alertness later.

I was in the barn feeding the horses while Craig and Sajan mucked the stalls. Brian, Mike, and Carol were tending the garden. Donna was on duty in the cabin while she tended to Nancy. We had all fallen into a variety of roles rather easily. Mike had taken a liking to the garden, but I suspect it was because I also had strawberries in it. I couldn't help but notice the red ring around his mouth on some days.

Rahn's Hummer slid to a stop in the yard. Before it had even completely stopped, he had hopped out.

The sound of his vehicle had brought me out of the barn, along with Craig and Sajan, each of us armed.

"Hello, John Henry!" Rahn shouted as he walked

across the yard.

I waved at him, but for some reason I felt suspicious. I didn't speak until I was in front of him.

"First Sergeant," I said, smiling to show I welcomed him, "what brings you out here, and what's the mystery of one if by land?"

"I'm supposed to be in Antigo with two platoons rounding people up. I couldn't very well say I was coming here."

"Oh," I said, and then paused. "The captain with you?"

"Are you kidding? He's got a cushy desk job giving orders. He and his FEMA buddies are running roughshod over all the detainees."

"Detainees?"

"Well, they sure as hell aren't refugees the way they're being treated."

"Come again?" I asked.

"They're being forced into heavy labor, locked up in GP Large tents at night, given only two meals a day, and when they get sick they're trucked off so as to not infect the others."

"How do you lock up a tent, First Sergeant?" Craig asked.

I could see the mischief in his eyes and figured I'd let him dig this hole with Rahn.

Rahn stood there, putting his hands behind his back and then slowly rocked back and forth on his heels. I was pretty sure I was witnessing a classic build up your energy before you explode on the unsuspecting victim move perfected by sergeants throughout history. It wasn't to be.

Shaking his head slowly from side to side, Rahn answered, "You don't, son. You just put 'em inside and tell 'em if they get out, they might get shot."

"So, they *are* shooting the refugees?" I asked.

"Two so far, trying to escape."

I whistled low. "How in the hell do you get shot for trying to leave a refugee camp?"

"FEMA's orders. Nobody leaves or violators will be shot. Nobody comes in without being brought in by an escort, or they will be shot."

"Jesus…" Craig said.

I needed more details. "And Wolfe goes along with that?"

"He's in charge of enforcing it. He's all buddy buddy with the top FEMA people there and they call the shots. They state they are the lawful Constitutional government now."

"Are they?" I asked.

"I don't know," Rahn said. "There are rumors of the Army, Marines, and Air Force fighting each other over who's in charge, who's legal, and who isn't."

"Who's side you on, Rahn?" I guess my voice was a little too firm because he took a step back and looked mad.

"You have to ask me that after everything I've done for you, John? I could be shot for what I've done for you."

"Sorry, Rahn, I was pissed. I shouldn't have…"

"It's okay," he interrupted. "I get it. For the record, I'm an American and I don't like these camps, and there are a lot more like us. We're outnumbered by the FEMA security forces, though, so we've got to be careful."

Curious, I asked, "Speaking of careful, how long can you be gone before you're missed?"

"Not much longer, I imagine. We've got to get back and escort the trucks to Wausau."

"You be careful, First Sergeant."

"Oh, I will. You guys be careful, too. There's a war coming. A civil war. Nobody is going to win it, either.

UN troops will be coming in soon, the Navy's trying to stop the Chinese on the West Coast, and we're all in the middle of one big shit sandwich."

"When will you be back?" I asked.

"I don't know. We're clearing out the larger communities first and then we'll get to unincorporated places like here. I'll let you know."

"One if by land?" I asked.

"Nah, I'll come up with something more original. Good thing you know your history, John. How are your music references?"

I chuckled. "They suck. I'm sure somebody here will know them, though."

"Well, regardless, it will be from me. If I use a baseball term, then you know it's some kind of early warning. Best I can do."

"Thanks, Rahn," I replied as I held out my hand.

We shook and he jumped in the Hummer. "Onward and upward, Johnson," he said. The vehicle made a wide circle and headed back out the drive.

"We're in the shit, aren't we, Dad?" Craig asked.

"Looks that way, but we have time to prepare."

"What are we going to do?"

"I don't know, son. We'll have to all get together and figure that out."

"I guess that's all we can do."

"No, we can get back to work and take care of these horses, then we have to start making hay for the winter. I've got an idea for forting up that I want to think over. We have to look around the field a bit first."

"So, we're gonna be farmers?" Craig said.

"Farmers and settlers, warriors, and inventors, son. We're going back in time to come back into the present."

I walked back to the barn. I had a lot to think over, and it wasn't just what Rahn said. I'd come to Lake

View alone and sought out peace and quiet, and I'd found a family I could depend on. Carol, Gary, Sam, Addie, and Rick had all been added to that family, too. I still needed to figure out what to do about John Jr., Will, and Darla. They were in Indianapolis, and I didn't know if they were alive or dead. I couldn't do anything about that now, but I had to do something. And soon.

First, I had to finish taking care of things here at my place. Then, I'd think on what to do regarding my oldest son.

Work cleared my mind and allowed me to look more closely at things. I had a lot of thinking to do. And I was determined to help my new family survive and be successful in this new reality of what we called life.

Epilogue

The sky to the east was starting to glow as the sun began to slowly rise. The young girl sat still, enraptured by the story as it unfolded. As sleepy as she was, she sat silently, hanging on every word as the two men unraveled the story for her. Realizing that it was now false dawn, that time before the sun actually rises, they stopped their story.

"We shouldn't have talked so long," one of the men said.

"I wanna hear more," the girl demanded. "What happened next?"

"Sweetie, we've been up all night and now we got chores to do. So do you."

"I'm too tired. Ma won't mind."

"You willing to test her?" the man asked.

"No." She stood and stretched. Sitting on the ground, leaning against the long log they sometimes used as a bench by the fire pit, had made her stiff. Arching her back as she bent backward, her long hair fell straight behind her. A few muffled cracking sounds came from her as she popped the stiffness out of her body.

"So, what happened next?" she asked, clearly trying to avoid the chores that awaited her.

"That's for another time, sweetie, another time."

"Ohhhh," she uttered, huffing as she walked away.

"Farmers and settlers, warriors and inventors, you remember that?" One of the men asked the other once she was out of ear shot.

"It's what was said," the other replied.

"It was a long time ago."

"Yeah; yeah it was. But not that long ago."

"You gonna tell her more of the story?" the man asked.

"You really think she'll go away and not demand I do?"

"I don't imagine so. She can be persistent, ya know."

He laughed. "She's a Henry, of course she's persistent."

"I need to go to bed, but that isn't going to happen in the cabin. Let's get the horses and wagon hitched, sneak off to the creek, and do some fishin' and nappin'."

"Seriously?"

"Yeah, I'm serious."

"Sounds like a plan. Let's make it happen."

Rising from their seats, the men walked toward the barn. A new day was beginning.

Acknowledgements

I became interested in EMP when reading about the Carrington Event, a solar storm in 1859. This resulted in what is called a Coronal Mass Ejection, or CME, that reached the earth. This CME or Solar EMP struck the earth between September 1 and 2, 1859. Without getting into too much science, a CME is a large mass of electro magnetitic energy that disrupts the magnetic field of the earth. When this happened in 1859 telegraph wires, burst into flames. Scientists estimate that were this to happen today a catastrophic failure of most of the planet's technology would occur. It would take decades to recover from this.

I want to thank those who helped or inspired me in the writing of this book. Out of fear of offending some by either forgetting them or in a few cases mentioning them, I will offer this broad thank you. Writers need ideas, and sometimes those can come from the most amazing places when they come from friendly firepit chats, the stories take on an incredible depth and in the instance of this book resulted in the epilogue and prologue. So, for those of who I chatted with, literally at the fire pit or virtually, thank you for your input, support, and feedback.

Those who read the book before publishing and

offering feedback, ideas, support, and opinion. Thank you. LH, MF, JC, CD, and LJ—THANK YOU. Your input was helpful, supportive, and inspiring.

This also includes a wonderful Post-Apocalyptic Readers group I belong to, The Dirty Dozen Post Apoc Army of Readers, or DD12. A collection of some of the finest salt of the earth people, with a few oddballs because real good groups have oddballs in them. The conversations I have lurked and read or participated in helped me immensely.

For the skeptics or critics, for those who see a book like this and wonder where the tinfoil hats of the Authors and Readers are stored, I offer this. In March 1989, a geomagnetic storm knocked out power across large sections of Quebec. In July 2012, a "Carrington-class" solar was observed; it narrowly missed the earth. Scientists state it isn't a question of if, but of when. If mother nature and science isn't enough, we also have man. Nuclear weapons blasts at high altitudes will have the same effect as a CME. A single high-altitude nuclear blast, depending on the size of the nuclear weapon and the distance above the earth's surface, could have the same effect as the Carrington Event.

—D.M. Herrmann

About the Author

D.M. Herrmann is a retired soldier, having spent twenty years in the US Army. He has authored three fiction novels under the pseudonym Evan Michael Martin. He lives in Wisconsin.